12/17

PETER ACKROYD

Peter Ackroyd is an award-winning historian, biographer, novelist, poet and broadcaster. He is the author of the acclaimed non-fiction best-sellers *London: The Biography*, *Thames: Sacred River* and *London Under*; biographies of figures including Charles Dickens, William Blake, Charlie Chaplin and Alfred Hitchcock; and a multi-volume history of England. He has won the Whitbread Biography Award, the Royal Society of Literature's William Heinemann Award, the James Tait Black Memorial Prize, the Guardian Fiction Prize, the Somerset Maugham Award and the South Bank Prize for Literature. He holds a CBE for services to literature.

ALSO BY PETER ACKROYD

Non-fiction

London: The Biography
Albion: The Origins of the English Imagination
The Collection: Journalism, Reviews, Essays, Short
Stories, Lectures (edited by Thomas Wright)
Thames: Sacred River
Venice: Pure City
The English Ghost
London Under
Queer City

Fiction

The Great Fire of London
The Last Testament of Oscar Wilde
Hawksmoor
Chatterton
First Light
English Music
The House of Doctor Dee
Milton in America
The Plato Papers
The Clerkenwell Tales
The Lambs of London
The Fall of Troy
The Casebook of Victor Frankenstein
Three Brothers

Biography

Ezra Pound and his World
T. S. Eliot
Dickens
Blake
The Life of Thomas More
Shakespeare: The Biography

Brief Lives

Chaucer
J. M. W. Turner
Newton
Poe: A Life Cut Short
Wilkie Collins
Charlie Chaplin
Alfred Hitchcock

PETER ACKROYD

The Limehouse Golem

VINTAGE

2 4 6 8 10 9 7 5 3 1

Vintage
20 Vauxhall Bridge Road,
London SW1V 2SA

Vintage is part of the Penguin Random House group of companies
whose addresses can be found at global.penguinrandomhouse.com

Copyright © Peter Ackroyd 1994

Peter Ackroyd has asserted his right to be identified as the author of this
Work in accordance with the Copyright, Designs and Patents Act 1988

This edition published in Vintage in 2017
First published in Vintage in 1994 with the title
Dan Leno and the Limehouse Golem
First published in hardback by Sinclair-Stevenson in 1994
with the title *Dan Leno and the Limehouse Golem*

penguin.co.uk/vintage

A CIP catalogue record for this book is available from the British Library

ISBN 9781784708207

Typeset in 11.5/14 pt Adobe Garamond by Jouve (UK), Milton Keynes

Printed and bound by Clays Ltd, St Ives plc

Penguin Random House is committed to a sustainable future
for our business, our readers and our planet. This book is made
from Forest Stewardship Council® certified paper.

One

On the 6th April, 1881, a woman was hanged within the walls of Camberwell Prison. The ceremony was to be performed at eight o'clock, according to custom, and just after dawn the other prisoners began their ritual howling. The death bell of the prison chapel tolled as she was led from the condemned cell and joined a procession which included the governor, the prison chaplain, the prison doctor, the Roman Catholic priest, who had heard her confession the night before, her solicitor, and two witnesses appointed by the Home Office. The public executioner was waiting for them in a wooden shed across the yard where a gallows had been erected – only a few years before the woman could have been hanged beside the walls of Newgate Prison, to the delight of the vast crowd assembled there throughout the night, but the chance of such a great performance had been denied her by the progressive legislation of 1868. So she had to die in mid-Victorian privacy, in a wooden shed that smelled of the sweat of the workmen who had erected it two days earlier. The only tribute to sensationalism was her coffin, which had been strategically placed in the prison yard so that she might pass it on the way to her death.

The Burial Office was read, and it was noticed that she participated in this with great fervour. The condemned are supposed to remain quite silent at this solemn time but she lifted her head

1

and, staring through the little roof of glass at the foggy air beyond, begged loudly for the safety of her own soul. The customary incantation came to an end, and the hangman stood behind her as she climbed the wooden block; he was about to place the coarsely woven cloth over her, but she brushed it away with the motion of her head. Her hands had already been bound behind her back with leathern thongs, but there was no difficulty in interpreting the gesture. While she stared down at the official witnesses, the rope was placed around her neck (the executioner, knowing her precise size and weight, had measured the hemp exactly). She spoke only once before he pulled the lever and the wooden trapdoor opened beneath her. She said, 'Here we are again!' Her eyes were still upon them as she fell. Her name was Elizabeth Cree. She was thirty-one years old.

She had been wearing a white smock, or gown, at the moment of her deliverance. It had been the custom, during the days of public execution, for the dress of the dead to be torn apart and sold in pieces to the assembled crowd as mementoes or magical talismans. But this had become an age of private possessiveness, and the white gown was taken from the body of the hanged woman with great reverence. Later that day it was handed to the governor of the prison, Mr Stephens, who accepted it without a word from the female warder who carried it to his office. He did not need to enquire about the body itself; he had already agreed that it should be despatched to the medical surgeon of Limehouse Division, who specialised in examining the brains of murderers for any signs of abnormality. As soon as the warder had closed the door behind her, Mr Stephens folded the white gown very neatly and placed it in the Gladstone bag which he kept behind his desk. That night, in his small house on Hornsey Rise, he took it carefully from the bag; he lifted it above his head, and put it on. He was wearing nothing else and, with a sigh, he lay down upon the carpet in the gown of the hanged woman.

Two

Who now remembers the story of the Limehouse Golem, or cares to be reminded of the history of that mythical creature? 'Golem' is the medieval Jewish word for an artificial being, created by the magician or the rabbi; it literally means 'thing without form', and perhaps sprang from the same fears which surrounded the fifteenth-century concept of the 'homunculus' which was supposed to have been given material shape in the laboratories of Hamburg and Moscow. It was an object of horror, sometimes said to be made of red clay or sand, and in the mid-eighteenth century it was associated with spectres and succubi who have a taste for blood. The secret of how it came to be revived in the last decades of the nineteenth century, and how it aroused the same anxieties and horrors as its medieval counterpart, is to be found within the annals of London's past.

The first killing occurred on the 10th September, 1880, along Limehouse Reach: this, as its name implies, was an ancient lane which led from a small thoroughfare of mean houses to a flight of stone steps just above the bank of the Thames. It had been used by porters over many centuries for convenient if somewhat cramped access to the cargo of smaller boats which anchored here, but the dock redevelopments of the 1830s had left it marooned on the edge of the mud banks. It reeked of dampness and old stone, but it also possessed a stranger and more fugitive odour which was aptly described by one of the residents of the neighbourhood as that of 'dead feet'. It was here, at first light on a September morning, that the body of Jane Quig was discovered. She had been left upon the old steps in three separate parts; her head was upon the upper step, with her torso arranged beneath it in some parody of the human form, while certain of her internal organs had been impaled upon a wooden post by the riverside. She had been a prostitute who had found her custom among the sailors of the area and, although she was only in her early twenties, had been known to her neighbours as 'Old Salty'. Of course the popular opinion, inflamed by gruesome reports in the *Daily News* and *Morning Advertiser*, declared that a 'fiend in human form' was at work – a supposition which was strengthened when, six nights later, another killing took place in the same area.

The Jewish quarter of Limehouse comprised three streets beyond the Highway; it was known as 'Old Jerusalem' both by those who inhabited it and those who lived beside it. There was a lodging house here, in Scofield Street, where an old scholar by the name of Solomon Weil resided; he had two rooms upon the top floor, filled with old volumes and manuscripts of Hasidic lore, from which he journeyed every weekday morning to the Reading Room of the British Museum; he always travelled there on foot, leaving his house at eight in the morning, and arriving at Great Russell Street by nine. On the morning of September the 17th, however, he did not leave his rooms. His downstairs neighbour, a clerk with the Commission on Sanitation and Metropolitan Improvements, was sufficiently alarmed to knock gently upon his door. There was no reply and, believing that Solomon Weil might have been taken ill, he boldly entered the room. 'Well, this is a pretty business!' he exclaimed when he came upon a scene of indescribable confusion. But, as he soon discovered, it was not pretty at all. The old scholar had been mutilated in a most strange manner; his nose had been cut off and placed upon a small pewter plate, while his penis and testicles had been left upon the open page of a book which he must have been reading when he was so savagely disturbed. Or had the volume been left by the killer as some clue to his appetites? The severed penis was decorating a long entry on the golem, as the police detectives from 'H' Division duly noted, and within a few hours this was the word being whispered throughout Old Jerusalem and its environs.

The reality of this malevolent spirit was enhanced by the circumstances surrounding the murder in Limehouse two days later. Another female prostitute, Alice Stanton, was found lying against the small white pyramid in front of the church of St Anne's. Her neck had been broken, and her head unnaturally turned so that she seemed to be staring just beyond the church itself; her tongue had been cut out and placed within her vagina, while her body itself was mutilated in a manner reminiscent of the killing of Jane Quig nine days before. Upon the pyramid itself the word 'golem' had been traced in the blood of the dead woman.

By now the inhabitants of the entire East End of London were thoroughly alarmed and inflamed by the sequence of strange deaths. The daily newspapers reported every practice in which 'The Golem' or 'The Golem of Limehouse' engaged, while certain details were embellished, or on occasions invented, in order to ensure more notoriety for what were already gruesome accounts. Could it have been the journalist on the *Morning Advertiser*, for example, who decided that the 'Golem' had been chased by an 'irate crowd' only to be seen 'fading away' into the wall of a bakery by Hayley Street? But perhaps that was not an instance of editorial licence since, as soon as the report was published, several residents of Limehouse confirmed that they had been among the mob which had pursued the creature and watched it disappear. An old woman who lived by Limehouse Breach swore that she had seen a 'transparent gentleman' moving swiftly by the waterside, while an unemployed tallow chandler told the world through the pages of the *Gazette* that he had seen a figure soaring into the air above Limehouse Basin. So the legend of the Golem was born, even before the final and most shocking act of murder. Four days after the killing of Alice Stanton by St Anne's, an entire family was found slaughtered in their house beside the Ratcliffe Highway.

And what of the police throughout this affair? They had followed their customary procedures. They had set bloodhounds on the scent of the putative murderer; they had made detailed enquiries from door to door throughout Limehouse; the divisional surgeon was called on each occasion and minutely inspected the remains of the victims, while the post-mortem examinations at the police station itself were conducted with exemplary thoroughness. A number of suspects were closely questioned although, since the Golem had never really been glimpsed in human form, the evidence against them was at best circumstantial. No one was charged, therefore, and 'H' Division became the target of much injurious newspaper criticism. There was even a limerick published in the *Illustrated Sun* which attacked the senior officer in the case:

> Chief Inspector Kildare
> Couldn't catch a tame bear,
> He told 'em
> He would find the Golem
> But he's ended up with thin air.

Three

All extracts from the trial of Elizabeth Cree, for the murder of her husband, are taken from the full reports in the Illustrated Police News Law Courts and Weekly Record *from the 4th to the 12th of February, 1881.*

MR GREATOREX: Did you purchase arsenic powder from Hanways in Great Titchfield Street on the morning of October the 23rd of last year?

ELIZABETH CREE: Yes, sir. I did.

MR GREATOREX: Why did you do so, Mrs Cree?

ELIZABETH CREE: There was a rat in the basement.

MR GREATOREX: There was a rat in the basement?

ELIZABETH CREE: Yes, sir. A rat.

MR GREATOREX: Surely there were establishments in the New Cross area where arsenic powder could be procured. Why did you travel to Great Titchfield Street?

ELIZABETH CREE: I had a mind to visit a friend who lived in that neighbourhood.

MR GREATOREX: And did you?

ELIZABETH CREE: She was not at home, sir.

MR GREATOREX: So you came back to New Cross with your

arsenic powder, but without having visited your friend. Is that not so?

ELIZABETH CREE: It is, sir.

MR GREATOREX: And what happened to the rat?

ELIZABETH CREE: Oh, he's dead, sir. (*Laughter.*)

MR GREATOREX: You killed it?

ELIZABETH CREE: Yes, sir.

MR GREATOREX: So now let us return to that other and more serious fatality. Your husband became ill soon after your visit to Great Titchfield Street, I believe.

ELIZABETH CREE: He has always suffered with his stomach, sir. Ever since we first met.

MR GREATOREX: And when was that, precisely?

ELIZABETH CREE: We met when I was very young.

MR GREATOREX: Am I correct in supposing that you were then known as 'Lambeth Marsh Lizzie'?

ELIZABETH CREE: That was once my name, sir.

Four

I was my mother's only child, and always an unloved one. Perhaps she had wanted a son to provide for her, but I cannot be sure of that. No, she wanted no one. God forgive her, I think she would have destroyed me if she had possessed the strength. I was the bitter fruit of her womb, the outward sign of her inward corruption, the token of her lust and the symbol of her fall. My father was dead, she used to tell me, having been terribly maimed in the Kentish mines; she performed his last moments for me, pretending to cradle his head in her arms. But he was not dead. I discovered, from a letter she kept hidden beneath the mattress of the bed we shared, that he had left her. He was not her husband but some masher, some fancy man who had got her in the family way. I was the family, and I was the one forced to bear her shame. Sometimes she knelt through the night, calling upon Jesus and all the saints to preserve her from hell: she will be frying there tonight, if there is any justice beyond the grave. Well, let her burn.

Our lodgings were in Peter Street, Lambeth Marsh, and we earned our keep by sewing the sailing cloths for the fishermen by the horse ferry; it was exceedingly difficult work, and even my leather gloves could not keep the cloth and the needle from chafing my hands. Look at them now, so worn and so raw.

9

When I put them against my face, I can feel the ridges upon them like cart-tracks. Big hands, my mother used to say. No female should have big hands. And none, I thought, should have so big a mouth as yours. How she prayed and moaned while we worked, repeating all the bunkum she had learned from the Reverend Style who kept a chapel on the Lambeth High Road. One moment it was 'God pardon me for my sins!' and then it was 'How I am exalted!' She used to take me with her to that chapel; all I can remember is the tapping of the rain on its roof as we sang from the Wesley Hymnal. And then it was back to the sewing. When we had finished mending one of the sailcloths we would take it down to the horse ferry. Once I tried to carry it upon my head, but she slapped me and said that it was common. Of course she knew what it was to be common; a reformed whore is a whore still. And who but a whore would have a child without husband? The fishermen knew me as 'Little Lizzie' and meant me no harm, but there were gentlemen who whispered things to me by the waterside and made me smile. I knew such words as the worst teachers in the world had imparted to me, and at night I would speak them into my pillow.

Our two rooms were bare enough, except for the pages of the Bible which she had pasted to the walls. There was hardly an inch of paper to be made out between them, and from my earliest childhood I could see nothing but words. I even taught myself to read from them, and I still have by heart the passages which I learned in those days: 'And he took all the fat that was upon the inwards, and the caul above the liver, and the two kidneys, and their fat, and Moses burned it upon the altar.' There was another I recall: 'He that is wounded in the stones, or hath his privy member cut off, shall not enter into the congregation of the Lord.' I recited them in the morning and in the night; I saw them as soon as I rose from my bed, and gazed at them before I closed my eyes in sleep.

There is a place between my legs which my mother loathed and cursed – when I was very little she would pinch it fiercely, or prick it with her needle, in order to teach me that it was the home of pain and punishment. But later, at the sight of my first menstrual issue, she truly became a demon. She tried to stuff some old rags within me, and I pushed her away. I had been afraid of her before but, when she spat at me and hit me across the face, I was filled with horror; so I took one of our needles and stabbed her in the wrist. Then, when she saw the blood flow, she put her hand up to her face and laughed. 'Blood for blood,' she said. 'New blood for old.' She began to sicken after that. I bought some purging pills and palliative mixtures from the dispensary in Orchard Street, but nothing seemed to give her any benefit. She became as pale as the cloths we stitched, and so weak that she could hardly manage the work; you can imagine, with her frequent vomitings throughout the day and night, how much now rested upon my own shoulders.

There was a young doctor who sometimes came among us, from the charity hospital in the Borough Road, and I prevailed upon him to visit our lodgings; he felt my mother's pulse, looked at her tongue and then smelled her breath before step-ping back quickly. He said that it was some slow putrefaction of the kidneys, and at that she set up yet another wailing to her god. Then he took my hands, told me to be a good girl, and gave me a bottle of medical water from his bag.

'Be quiet, Mother,' I said as soon as he had left us. 'Do you think your god is moved by your screeching? I wonder at you for being such a fool.' Of course she was too weak to raise her hand against me now, so I saw no need to comfort her further. 'He must be a very strange demon indeed, if he has left you to perish so miserably. To be pitched from Lambeth Marsh into hell – is that the answer to all your prayers?'

'Oh God my help in ages past. Be now the water to comfort

me in my affliction.' These were no more than the words she had learned by rote from the hymnal, and I laughed as she passed her tongue across her lips. I could see the sores upon it.

'I shall bring you some comfort, Mother. I will bring you real water.' I poured out a little of the doctor's cordial upon a spoon, and made her drink it. I glanced up and saw a passage she had pasted on to the ceiling. 'Look here, Mother,' I said. 'Here is another sign for you. Can you not read it now, you naughty girl? "Father Abraham have mercy on me and send Lazarus" – you know Lazarus, Mother? – "that he may dip the tip of his finger in water, and cool my tongue. For I am tormented in this flame." Is that your torment, Mother? Or will it become so?'

She could scarcely speak, so I bent over her and listened to her foul-smelling whisper. 'Only God can make the judgement.'

'But look at you now. He has already made his judgement.' At that she set up another such wailing that I could no longer endure the sound of it. So I went down into the street and walked towards the riverside. The females of Lambeth Marsh are considered easy prey but, when a foreign-looking gentleman glanced at me in that way, I gave him no joy but laughed and went down to the water. I could see that the ferry was about to move off, so I lifted up my skirt, jumped over the ditch, and ran towards it; my mother said that it was common for a young woman to run, but how was she ever going to catch me now? The ferryman knew me well enough, and would not take my penny from me – so I came over to the Mill Bank with more coin than I expected!

I had only one wish in my life, and that was to see the music-hall. Curry's Variety was by the obelisk, close to our lodgings, but Mother told me it was the abode of the devil which I was never to enter. I had seen the bills announcing the comedians and duettists, but I knew no more of them than I did of the cherubim and seraphim to whom my mother cried aloud. To me these patterers and sand-dancers were also fabulous beings, wonderfully exalted and worthy of worship.

I took off from the Mill Bank as fast as ever I could, and walked down towards the new bridge; I did not know London so well in those days, and it still seemed to me so vast and so wild that, for a moment, I looked back at my old patch in Lambeth. But she lay putrefying there, and with a lighter heart I continued my course beside the shops and houses; I was alive with curiosity, and never once did it occur to me that a young girl was in any danger among these streets. I came out upon the Strand and turned down Craven Street, just by the water pump, when I saw a penny gaff with some people loitering outside it. It seemed to be a penny gaff, at least, but, when I walked a little closer, I realised that it was a proper saloon of varieties with its coloured glass and painted figures making such a contrast to the plain old houses to either side of it. It had an odour all of its own, too, with its mixture of spices and oranges and beer; it was a little like the smell of the wharves down Southwark way, but so much richer and more potent. There was a poster in bright green letters plastered at an angle on the front of the theatre: the manager must have just put it there, because the crowd had gathered to read it. I looked at it in wonder, because up till that time I had never heard of 'Dan Leno, the Whipper-Snapper, Contortionist and Posturer'.

Five

Elizabeth walked through the streets until it became quite dark but she did not want to stray too far from the little theatre, so she lingered among the congeries of byways and alleys that lead into the Strand. Once or twice she heard a soft, low whistle and believed that she was being followed. By the corner of Villiers Street a man beckoned to her – but she swore at him fiercely and, when she put up her large raw hands marked by the thick fibres of the sail-cloth, quietly he backed away. Only once did she think of her mother, when she passed the old churchyard in Mitre Court, but it was close to the time of Dan Leno's performance and she hurried back to Craven Street. It was twopence for the gods and fourpence for the pit, but she chose the pit.

The customers sat at several old wooden tables with their food and drink in front of them, while three waiters in black-and-white check aprons were being harassed by continual calls for more pickled salmon, or cheese, or beer. An ancient and very red-faced woman, with extraordinary ringlets of artificial hair cascading across her forehead and cheeks, sat down beside her. 'Just the rakings here, dear,' she said as soon as she had sat down. 'I don't know why I bother.' Elizabeth could hardly hear her, through all the noise and uproar. The woman

14

reached out and purchased an orange from a small child, who could barely carry his basket of fruit, and then stuffed it between her breasts. 'That's for later.' Then she made a grimace and fanned her face with one of the plates discarded on the table. 'Aren't they rank?'

But Elizabeth was accustomed to the human smell – or, rather, she was hardly aware of the sharp odour of flesh – and her attention was entirely concentrated upon the threadbare stage-curtain ahead of her. A very large man in the most extraordinary striped top-coat was being helped onto the raised wooden boards, and although he seemed the worse for drink he managed to stand upright and raise his arms in the air. He called, 'Silence, if you please!' in a very stern voice and Elizabeth noticed, with some surprise, that a whole bouquet of geraniums was pinned to his buttonhole. Finally, to much cheering and laughter, he began to speak. 'A keen east wind has spoiled my voice,' he bellowed out, and then had to wait for the cheers and catcalls to subside. 'I am overwhelmed by your generosity. I have never know so many dear boys with such perfect manners. I feel as if I am at a tea-party.' There was so much noise now that Elizabeth had to put her hands to her ears; the red-faced old woman turned and winked at her, then raised the little finger of her right hand in some kind of salute. 'It is not in the power of mortals to command success,' he went on, 'but I will do more. I will endeavour to deserve it. Please to note that the oxtail in jelly is only threepence tonight.'

There was much more in this vein, which seemed very tedious to Elizabeth, but eventually the curtain was pulled aside by a young girl in a large old-fashioned bonnet; it revealed a London street scene which, in the flickering gaslight, seemed to Elizabeth the most wonderful sight in the world. The only paintings she had ever seen had been the crude images daubed upon the boats by the riverside, and here was a picture of the

15

Strand along which she had just walked – but how much more glorious and iridescent it now seemed, with its red and blue shop-fronts, its tall lamp-posts, and its stalls and their goods piled high. This was better than any memory.

A boy came out from the wings, and at once the spectators began to whistle and stamp their feet in anticipation. He had the strangest face she had ever seen; it was so slim that his mouth seemed to stretch from one side to the other, and she was sure that it must have continued around his neck; he was so pale that his large dark eyes seemed to shine out, and to be gazing at something beyond the world itself. He was wearing a stove-pipe hat which was almost as tall as he was, with the strangest medley of patched cloths turned into a coat. Elizabeth realised at once that he was acting the part of an Italian hurdy-gurdy boy, and the entire audience stayed silent as, in a slow, sweet voice, he began to sing 'Pity the Poor Italian'. She was ready to cry at the sorrow of it, as he depicted his life of poverty and misery, but then after a few verses he sauntered off the stage with his hands in his pockets. A few moments later an old woman emerged – except that, as far as Elizabeth could tell, she was not really old at all. She was of no age, and any age, dressed in a plain gown with an apron tied around her front. 'I was in a terrible state last night,' she told the audience who, much to Elizabeth's surprise, were already laughing. 'A very terrible state. My daughter came back to me, you see.' Suddenly Elizabeth was reminded of her mother, lying with her putrefying kidney, and she began to laugh as well. Even as she laughed she realised that this was the same boy, dressed in female clothes: there was no more pain now, and no more suffering. 'Oh she's a mean woman, that daughter of mine. She's so mean that she'll buy half-a-dozen oysters and eat them in front of a mirror to make them look like a dozen. Oh you *must* know my daughter. Good life-a-mighty. Don't look so simple.

Everybody knows my daughter.' The boy in the clothes of the old woman now lifted up his skirt and began to perform a clog dance, while the little theatre seemed to glow with the force of his personality. Elizabeth understood now that this must be the Dan Leno she had seen on the bills. She did not know how long his act continued but, afterwards, she was scarcely aware of the singing duets, the acrobats and the coloured minstrels. She was conscious only of the strange comedy with which Leno had assuaged the misery of her life.

It was over. When she shuffled out with the others into the street, it was as if she had been banished from some world of light. She walked down Craven Street and then crept over Hungerford Bridge – she knew her way to Lambeth Marsh well enough, even in the darkness, and she walked slowly past the river bank where the rats and the 'mud-larks' went about their work. There were three small boys dragging something out of the water, but even this spectacle could not satisfy her after the enchantment of the Craven Street theatre. By the time she arrived back at her lodgings in Peter Street, she was quite worn down by the excitements of the evening, and paid only cursory attention to her mother lying upon the bed; there was some white and green spittle coming from the side of her mouth, and her body trembled in a fit or delirium. Eventually Elizabeth brought her a cordial which she had prepared with her own hands, and forced her to drink it. 'Don't look so simple, Mother,' she whispered. 'You're very nicely, thank you.' Then she began to rip down the pages of the Bible which had been pasted to the walls.

Her mother was given a pauper's funeral two days later, and the night after the burial Elizabeth returned to the theatre in Craven Street where she heard Dan Leno sing one of those ditties which led to his being known as 'The Funniest Man On Earth':

I really think Jim's very partial to me,
Though never a word has he said.
But this moment I passed where he's building a house,
And he threw half a brick at my head.

Six

Dan Leno was widely believed to be the funniest man of that, or any, age but the best description of him is probably Max Beerbohm's in the *Saturday Review*: 'I defy anyone not to have loved Dan Leno at first sight. The moment he capered on, with that air of wild determination, squirming in every limb with some deep grievance that must be out-poured, all hearts were his ... that poor little battered personage, so put upon, yet so plucky, with his squeaky voice and his sweeping gestures, bent but not broken, faint but pursuing, incarnate of the will to live in a world not at all worth living in ...'

He was born at Number 4, Eve Court, in a neighbourhood beside the old church of St Pancras before the Midland Railway Company erected its station there – the day of his birth, the 20th December, 1850, was also, curiously enough, that of Elizabeth Cree. His parents were already 'theatricals' and toured the music-halls and variety saloons as 'Mr and Mrs Johnny Wilde, the Singing and Acting Duettists' (Dan Leno's real name was actually George Galvin but he quickly discarded it, just as Elizabeth Cree was never known to use her mother's surname). Their son first appeared on the stage at the age of four, at the Cosmotheka Music Hall in Paddington, wearing an outfit which his mother had manufactured from the silk of an old carriage umbrella. He was billed as a 'contortionist and posturer' at this early point in his career – he did indeed perform some very neat turns and tricks, perhaps the most remarkable being his impression of a corkscrew opening a wine bottle. At the age of eight he was billed as 'The Great Little Leno' (all his life he remained of very small stature) and then a year later he became known as 'Great Little Leno, the Quintessence of Cockney Comedians' or, on occasions, 'Descriptive and Cockney Character Vocalist'. By the autumn of 1864, when Elizabeth first saw him, he had already developed that humour for which he was to become truly famous. Yet how was it that, less than twenty years later, Dan Leno was suspected by the police officers of the Limehouse Division of being the murderous Limehouse Golem?

Seven

These extracts are taken from the diary of Mr John Cree of New Cross Villas, South London, now preserved in the Manuscript Department of the British Museum, with the call-mark Add. Ms. 1624/566.

September 6, 1880: It was a fine bright morning, and I could feel a murder coming on. I had to put out that fire, so I took a cab to Aldgate and then walked down Whitechapel way. I may say that I was eager to begin, because I had in mind a novelty for the first time: to suck out the breath of a dying child, and see if all its youthful spirit mingled with mine. Oh, in that case, I might go on for ever! But why do I say child, when I mean any life? Look, I am trembling again.

I had thought to see more people around Gammon Square, but in these poor lodging houses they are glad to sleep all day and take off the hunger. In earlier years they would have been put out in the streets at dawn, but these days standards are crumbling altogether – what have we come to, when the labouring poor no longer need to labour? I turned down into Hanbury Street, and a pretty stench they all made. There was the filthy aroma of a pie-stall, where no doubt cat meat and dog meat were as plentiful as ever, and all manner of Jew merchants with their 'Why hurry past?' and 'How are you on a fine day such as this?' I can bear the smell of the Jew but the smell of the Irish, as thick and heavy as old cheese, is not to be endured. There were two of them lying dead drunk outside a free-and-easy, and I crossed the street to get them out of my nostrils. I entered a crumbling confectionery shop on that side, and purchased a pennyworth of liquorice to make my tongue black. Who knows where I would have to place it that night?

Then another fine thought occurred to me. I had an hour or two before the night came on and I knew well enough that, a little way down towards the river, stood the house which had witnessed the immortal Ratcliffe Highway murders of 1812. On a spot as sacred to the memory as Tyburn or Golgotha, an entire family had been mysteriously and silently despatched into eternity by an artist whose exploits will be preserved for ever in the pages of Thomas De Quincey. John Williams had come upon the household of the Marrs and wiped them from the world as you would wipe a dish. So what more pleasant excursion than a stroll down the Highway itself?

In truth it was a mean dwelling for such a glorious crime – no more than a narrow shop-front with some rooms above it. The man Marr, whose blood had been shed for the sake of greatness, had been a hosier by trade. Now, in his place, was a second-hand clothes seller. Thus, as the Bible tells us, are the sacred temples defiled. I walked in at once, and asked him how he did. 'Pretty poor, sir,' he said. 'Pretty poor.' I looked upon the place, just behind the counter, where Williams had split open the skull of one child.

'This is a good spot for trade, is it not?'

'It is said to be, sir. But all times are hard times along the Highway.' He watched me, as I stooped over and touched the ground with my forefinger. 'A gentleman like yourself has no call for custom here, sir. Am I right?'

'My wife has a maid, who needs no finery. Do you have something like an old-fashioned dress?'

'Oh, there are many dresses and gowns, sir. Feel the quality in these ones.' He brushed his hand against a row of fusty objects, and I hovered close so that I might smell them. What dirty flesh had been pressed against this cloth? In this same room – perhaps upon these very boards – the artist had craved for more blood and hunted out the mistress of the house.

'Do you have a wife and daughter?'

He looked at me for a moment, and then laughed. 'Oh, I know what you mean, sir. No. They never wear the articles. We are not of the poorest sort.'

John Williams had climbed those stairs, and clubbed her down even as she bent over the grate. 'And do you wonder, then, that these are not for me or my maid? Good day to you. I have a little business waiting for me elsewhere.' I walked out into Ratcliffe Highway, but I could not resist looking up at the rooms above the shop. What wonders had been performed in that narrow confined space? And what if they might come again? That would be a consummation never before seen in this city.

But I had other fish to fry – some little sprat to catch and cook. It was growing dark now, and the gas was being lit by the time I came into Limehouse. It was the hour to show my hand but, as yet, I was a mere tyro, a beginner, an understudy who could not appear on the great stage without rehearsal. I had first to perfect my work in a secret hour, stolen from the tumult of the city: if only I could find some secluded grove and, like some pastoral being, shed London blood within a green shade. But that was not to be. I was still in my own particular private theatre, this garish spot beneath the gas lamps, and here I must perform. But, at first, let it be behind the curtain . . .

There was a pert little thing lingering outside the alley by the Laburnum Playhouse; she could have been no more than eighteen or nineteen, but in the ways of the street she was already old. She knew the bible of the world, for she had learned it by heart. And what a heart it might prove to be, if it were removed with love and care. I shadowed her as she walked towards the lodging house for seamen at the corner of Globe Lane. You see how I had studied the streets? I had purchased Murray's *New Plan of London*, and had plotted all my exits and entrances. There she stood and a few moments later some labouring man, still with the brick dust upon his clothes, came up and whispered to her. She said something in return, and it was all quick motion after that: she led him down Globe Lane towards a ruined house. She had his dust on her when they came out into the light again.

I waited until he had left her, and then made my approach. 'Why, little chicken, you must have performed a nice bit of business to become so dusty.'

She laughed, and I could smell the gin upon her breath. Even now her organs were being pickled, as if they were in a surgeon's jar. 'It's all one to me,' she said. 'Have you any money?'

'Look.' I brought out a shining coin. 'But consider me. Am I a gentleman? Can you expect me to lie upon the street? I need a good bed and four walls.'

She laughed again. 'Well then, gentleman, you must stop at the Bladebone.'

'Where is your bladebone?'

'We need gin, sir. More gin, if you want to be pleased with me.'

It was a public saloon off Wick Street, and looked to be a den of the vilest sort filled with the refuse of London. I would have enjoyed the reek of it, as a plain man – I would have raised my arms, and joined the general uproar against heaven – but, as an artist, I demurred. I could not be seen before my first great work. She noticed that I hesitated, and seemed to smile.

'I can tell you are a gentleman, and there is no need to accompany me. I was born here. I know my way well enough.' She took some coins from me and returned a few minutes later with a chamber-pot filled with gin. 'It is clean,' she said, 'quite clean. We never use it for that. We have the streets, don't we?' She led me into a nearby court, no bigger than a pocket handkerchief; she staggered as she began to climb the wormeaten stairs, and some of the gin spilled over the side of the pot. Someone was singing in one of the rooms which we passed, and I knew the words of the old music-hall ditty as well as if I had written them myself:

> When nobody was looking,
> I took my virgin mild,
> It must have been her cooking,
> Because I got rather wild.

Then all was silence as we climbed up to the topmost storey, and entered a room which seemed to be no more than a den or hut. There was a soiled mattress upon the floor, while on the walls she had pasted photographs of Walter Butt, George Byron and other idols of the stage. Everything smelled of stale drink, and a torn sheet had been carelessly draped across a tiny window. So this was to be my green room or, rather, my red room. This was to mark my entrance upon the stage of the world. She had taken a dirty cup and dipped it into the chamber-pot, swallowing the gin all at once. I was concerned that she might miss the fun but I knew well enough that she wished to be free of this sad world, in one way or another. Who was I to forestall her, or persuade her otherwise? I made no move but watched her take another cup of gin. Then, as she lay down upon the bed, I leaned over her and began to brush the dirt and brick dust from her dress. She had almost passed out with the drink, but she managed to clutch my arm as I touched her. 'What do you intend to do with me now, sir?' She still lay upon the bed quite dazed, and it occurred to me that she suspected my game and offered herself willingly to my knife. There are those poor souls who, on hearing of an outbreak of cholera, have hastened to the district in the hope of being infected with the disease. Was that her way? Then it would be a crime to leave her in suspense, would it not?

I did not want a drop of her blood upon my clothes and so I took off my ulster, jacket, waistcoat and trousers; hanging upon the back of her door was a faded coat, bordered with thin fur, and I wrapped it around myself before taking out my knife. That knife is a lovely object with a carved ivory handle; I purchased it at Gibbon's in the Haymarket for fifteen shillings and the pity of it was that, after I had entered her, its shine would be lost for ever. I remember in my schooldays how I mourned when my first line of ink spotted the purity of a new book of exercises – now I was about to write my name again, but with a different instrument. She only began to stir after I had taken out a piece of intestine and blown softly upon it; there was a moan or sigh coming from her although, on looking back and surveying the scene in my mind's eye, I believe that it might have been her spirit leaving the earth. Her eyes had opened, and I had to take them out with my knife for fear that my image had been seared upon them. I dipped my hands into the chamber-pot and washed off her blood with her gin; then, out of sheer delight, I shat into it. It was over. She had been evacuated from the world, and I had evacuated. We were both now empty vessels, waiting for the presence of God.

September 7, 1880: May I quote Thomas De Quincey? In the pages of his essay 'On Murder Considered As One of the Fine Arts' I first learned of the Ratcliffe Highway deaths, and ever since that time his work has been a source of perpetual delight and astonishment to me. Who could fail to be moved by his description of the murderer, John Williams, who committed his acts out of 'pure voluptuousness, entirely disinterested' and who provoked an exterminating tragedy worthy of Middleton or Tourneur? The destroyer of the Marr family was 'a solitary artist, who rested in the centre of London, self-supported by his own conscious grandeur', an artist who used London as the 'studio' to display his works. And what a marvellous touch by De Quincey, to suggest that Williams' bright yellow hair, 'something between an orange and a lemon colour', had been dyed to create a deliberate contrast to the 'bloodless ghostly pallor' of his face. I hugged myself in delight when I first read how he had dressed for each murder as if he were going upon the stage: 'when he went out for a grand compound massacre he always assumed black silk stockings and pumps; nor would he on any account have degraded his position as an artist by wearing a morning gown. In his second great performance, it was particularly noticed and recorded by the one sole trembling man, who under killing agonies of fear was compelled (as the reader will find) from a secret stand to become the solitary spectator of his atrocities, that Mr Williams wore a long blue frock, of the very finest cloth, and richly lined with silk.' But no more now: I can heartily recommend this work. Is that not what they say?

September 8, 1880: Rain all day. Read some Tennyson to my dear wife, Elizabeth, before we retired.

Eight

ELIZABETH CREE: I believed that my husband had come down with a gastric fever. So I recommended that he send for a doctor.

MR GREATOREX: Was his health good usually?

ELIZABETH CREE: He always had a bad stomach, which we took to be the gases.

MR GREATOREX: And did he have any medical attention that night?

ELIZABETH CREE: No. He declined it.

MR GREATOREX: He declined it? Why?

ELIZABETH CREE: He told me that it was not necessary, and asked me instead for a lime cordial.

MR GREATOREX: That was a very extraordinary request, was it not, for a man in such severe pain?

ELIZABETH CREE: I believe that he wished to bathe his forehead and temples with it.

MR GREATOREX: Can you tell the court what happened next?

ELIZABETH CREE: I had gone downstairs to prepare the cordial, when I heard a sudden noise from his room. I returned to him at once, and saw that he had fallen from his bed and was lying upon the Turkey carpet.

MR GREATOREX: Did he say anything to you at that point?

ELIZABETH CREE: No, sir. I could see that he was breathing with some difficulty and that there was some sort of bubbling around his lips.

MR GREATOREX: And what did you do then?

ELIZABETH CREE: I called for our maid, Aveline, to watch him while I went for the doctor.

MR GREATOREX: So you left the house?

ELIZABETH CREE: Yes.

MR GREATOREX: And did you not say, to a neighbour whom you passed, 'John has destroyed himself'?

ELIZABETH CREE: I was in such a hot haste, sir, I do not know what I might have said. I had even forgotten my bonnet.

MR GREATOREX: Go on.

ELIZABETH CREE: I returned with our doctor as quickly as ever I could, and together we went into my husband's room. Aveline was bent over him, but I could see then that he had expired. The doctor smelt his lips and said that we must inform the police, or the coroner, or some such.

MR GREATOREX: And why did he say that?

ELIZABETH CREE: He believed from the odour that my husband must have consumed some prussic acid, or other poison, and that there would have to be a post-mortem examination. I was naturally very shocked at this, and I am told that I fainted away.

MR GREATOREX: But why had you shrieked out in the street, a few minutes before, and told your neighbour that your husband had destroyed himself? How could you possibly have reached that conclusion if, as you still then believed, he was merely suffering from a gastric illness?

ELIZABETH CREE: As I explained to Inspector Curry, sir, he had threatened self-murder before. He was of a very morbid disposition and, in my anxiety at the time, my mind must have carried me back to those threats. I know that, by his bedside, there was a book on laudanum by Mr De Quincey.

MR GREATOREX: I think Mr De Quincey is immaterial on this occasion.

Nine

A young man sat in the Reading Room of the British Museum and, as he opened the pages of that month's *Pall Mall Review*, noticed that his hand was trembling slightly. He put it up to his straggling moustache, smelled the faint traces of sweat upon it, and then composed himself to read; he wished to savour and to remember this moment when he first saw his own words printed between the thick covers of an intellectual London journal. It was as if some other and more glorious person were addressing him from the page but, yes, this was his essay: 'Romanticism and Crime'. After quickly scanning some opening remarks on the lurid melodrama of the popular press, which he had written at the request of the editor, he read his own argument with great pleasure:

'I might turn for a suggestive analogy to Thomas De Quincey's essay "On Murder Considered as One of the Fine Arts", which is justly celebrated for its postscript on the extraordinary theme of the Ratcliffe Highway murders of 1812 when an entire family was butchered in a hosier's shop. The publication of this essay in *Blackwood's* provoked criticism from those members of the reading public who believed that he had sensationalised, and therefore trivialised, a peculiarly brutal series of murders. It is true that De Quincey, like certain other essayists from the early part of this century (Charles Lamb and Washington Irving spring immediately to mind), could on occasion introduce passages of levity and even whimsicality into the most serious arguments; there are moments in his essay where he excessively glamorises the short career of the murderer John Williams, for example, and seems somewhat unsympathetic to the suffering of that man's unfortunate victims. Yet it would hardly be fair to assume, on this evidence alone, that the mere tendency to sensationalise these sanguineous events did in any pronounced way trivialise or demean them. Quite the opposite case might be inferred – the Marr murders of 1812 reached their apotheosis in the prose of Thomas De Quincey, who with purple imagery and soaring cadence has succeeded in immortalising them. Indeed the readers of *Blackwood's* would also have recognised the presence of beliefs and preoccupations just beneath the surface of De Quincey's ornate prose which are manifestly at odds with any desire to trivialise the deaths along the Ratcliffe Highway.' He stopped for a moment and inserted his finger between his neck and the stiff collar of his shirt; there was something chafing him, but then he ceased to feel the irritation as he read on.

'It is well known that murders, and murderers, are variously considered in various periods. There are fashions in murder just as there are fashions in any other form of human expression; in our own period of privacy and domestic insularity, poisoning is the favoured means of despatching someone into eternity, for example, while in the sixteenth century stabbing was considered to be a more masculine and combative form of vengeance. But there are various forms of cultural expression, as the recent work of Hookham has suggested, and this essay by Thomas De Quincey may be studied more appropriately in a quite different setting. It is perhaps worth remarking that the writer was associated with that generation of English poets who have by common consent been labelled "the Romantics" – Coleridge and Wordsworth had been his close friends. The term hardly seems appropriately attached to a man obsessed with murder and violence, and yet there is a network of most curious associations which brings the foul butcheries of Limehouse into the same world as that of *The Prelude* or "Frost at Midnight". Thomas De Quincey has, for example, created a narrative out of the Marr murders in which the killer himself emerges as a wonderful Romantic hero. John Williams is seen to be an outcast who enjoys a secret power, a pariah whose exclusion from social conventions and civilisation itself actually invests him with fresh strength. In truth the man was a nondescript ex-seaman forced to live in a mean lodging house, whose own absurd stupidity led to his eventual capture, but in the pages of De Quincey's account he is transformed into an avenger whose bright yellow hair and chalk-white countenance afforded him the significance of some primeval deity. At the centre of the Romantic movement was the belief that the fruits of isolated self-expression were of the greatest importance and were capable of discovering the highest truths; that is why Wordsworth was able to construct an entire epic poem out of his private observations and beliefs. In De Quincey's account John Williams becomes an urban Wordsworth, a poet of sublime impulse who rearranges (one might say, executes) the natural world in order to reflect his own preoccupations. Writers such as Coleridge and De Quincey were also heavily influenced by German idealistic philosophy, as were all men of culture at the beginning of this century, and they were as a consequence peculiarly interested in the concept of "genius" as the epitome of the intense, isolated mind. So it is that John Williams is transformed into a genius of his own particular sphere, with the advantage that he is also associated with the ideas of death and eternal silence: one has only to recall the example of John Keats, who was seventeen at the time of the Ratcliffe Highway murders, to understand how potent that image of oblivion might become.' An attendant brought two books over to his desk; the young man did not thank him, but glanced down at the titles before smoothing his hair with the palm of his hand. Then he put his hand to his nose again, and sniffed at his fingers as he continued to read.

'There are other very suggestive currents which swirl across the surface of De Quincey's prose. He is primarily concerned with the fatal figure of John Williams, of course, but he takes care to place his creation (for that is what the murderer essentially becomes) before the scenery of a massive and monstrous city; few writers had so keen and horrified a sense of place, and within this relatively short essay he evokes a sinister, crepuscular London, a haven for strange powers, a city of footsteps and flaring lights, of houses packed close together, of lachrymose alleys and false doors. London becomes a brooding presence behind, or perhaps even within, the murders themselves; it is as if John Williams had in fact become an avenging angel of the city. It is not difficult to understand the force of De Quincey's obsession. In his most notorious work, *Confessions of an English Opium Eater*, he recounts a period in his life (before he began to take laudanum) when he was an outcast upon the streets of London; he was then just seventeen, and had absconded from a private school in Wales. He travelled to the city, and at once became a prey of its relentless, powerful life. He starved, and began to sleep in a derelict house near Oxford Street where he found "a poor, friendless child, apparently ten years old" who "had slept and lived there alone for some time before I came". Her name was Ann, and she lived with a perpetual and inextinguishable fear of the ghosts who might surround her in that crumbling dwelling. But it is the great thoroughfare, Oxford Street itself, which haunts De Quincey's imagination. In his *Confessions* it becomes a street of sorrowful mysteries, of "dreamy lamplight" and the sounds of the barrel-organ; he remembers the portico where he fainted away from hunger, and the corner where he and Ann would meet in order to console each other among "the mighty labyrinths of London". That is why the city and his suffering within it became – if we may borrow a phrase from that great modern poet Charles Baudelaire – the landscape of his imagination. It is this interior world which he places within "On Murder Considered as One of the Fine Arts" – a world in which suffering, poverty and loneliness are the most striking elements. By chance it was in Oxford Street, also, that he first purchased laudanum – it could be said that the old highway led him directly to those nightmares and fantasies which turned London into some mighty vision akin to that of Piranesi, a labyrinth of stone, a wilderness of blank walls and doors. These were the visions, at least, which he recounted many years later when he lodged in York Street off Covent Garden.

'There is one other curious and chance connection between murder and the Romantic movement. De Quincey's *Confessions* were first published anonymously, and one of those who falsely laid claim to their composition was Thomas Griffiths Wainewright. Wainewright was a critic and journalist of great refinement; he was one of the few men of his time, for example, to recognise the genius of the obscure William Blake. He even praised Blake's last epic poem, *Jerusalem*, when all of his contemporaries considered it the work of a madman who had located Jerusalem itself in, of all places, Oxford Street! Wainewright was also a vociferous admirer of Wordsworth and the other "Lake Poets", but he has one further distinction which was celebrated by Charles Dickens in "Hunted Down" and by Bulwer-Lytton in *Lucretia*. Wainewright was an accomplished and malevolent murderer, a secret poisoner who despatched members of his own family before turning his attention to chance acquaintances. He read poetry by day, and poisoned by night.'

George Gissing put down the journal; he had not yet finished the piece, but he had already noticed three errors of syntax and several infelicities of style which disturbed him more than he could have anticipated. How could his first essay come so lame into the world? His melancholic disposition began to reassert itself, after the first great rush of enthusiasm and optimism, and he closed the *Pall Mall Review* with a sigh.

Ten

MR GREATOREX: Can you explain how it was, then, that your husband should commit suicide two days after you had purchased the prussic acid from the druggist in Great Titchfield Street?

ELIZABETH CREE: I had told him that evening, after I had returned home, that I had bought something for the rats.

MR GREATOREX: Now, these rats. Your maid, Aveline Mortimer, has already testified that there were no rats. Yours is a newly built house, is it not?

ELIZABETH CREE: Aveline hardly ever went down into the cellar, sir. She is of a nervous disposition, and so I did not tell her of my discovery. As for the house—

MR GREATOREX: Yes?

ELIZABETH CREE: Even a new house may harbour rats.

MR GREATOREX: Will you tell me now where you placed the bottle of prussic acid?

ELIZABETH CREE: It was in the scullery, beside the irons.

MR GREATOREX: And did you tell Mr Cree of its location?

ELIZABETH CREE: I presume I did. We had a general conversation at dinner that night.

MR GREATOREX: We will return to that conversation later, but I would like to remind you now of a remark you made earlier. You said that your husband was of a morbid disposition. Can you explain that a little more fully to me?

ELIZABETH CREE: Well, sir, he dwelled upon certain matters.

MR GREATOREX: What matters?

ELIZABETH CREE: He believed that he was condemned. And that demons were forever watching him. He believed that they would destroy his mind, before they destroyed his body, and that he would be then consigned to hell. He was a Romanist, sir, and this was his fear.

MR GREATOREX: Am I correct in thinking he had a substantial private income?

ELIZABETH CREE: Yes, sir. His father had speculated in railway shares.

MR GREATOREX: I see. And will you tell me now how a man of such uncommon anxieties managed to conduct himself through the day?

ELIZABETH CREE: He went each morning to the Reading Room of the British Museum.

Eleven

The early autumn of 1880, in the weeks just before the emergence of the Limehouse Golem, was exceptionally cold and damp. The notorious pea-soupers of the period, so ably memorialised by Robert Louis Stevenson and Arthur Conan Doyle, were quite as dark as their literary reputation would suggest; but it was the smell and the taste of the fog which most affected Londoners. Their lungs seemed to be filled with the quintessence of coal dust, while their tongues and nostrils were caked with a substance which was known colloquially as 'miners' phlegm'. Perhaps that was why the Reading Room of the British Museum was unusually crowded on that raw September morning when John Cree arrived with his Gladstone bag and his ulster neatly folded over his arm. He had removed his coat beneath the portico, as was his custom, but before stepping into the warmth of the Museum he looked back into the fog with a curiously mournful expression. Some wreaths of it lingered about him as he walked into the great entrance hall, and for a moment he resembled some pantomime demon rising onto the stage. But he bore no other resemblance to any such apparition: he was of middling height, as the phrase then was, and he had neat dark hair. He was forty years old, sturdily built, with perhaps a trace of stoutness, and his round bland face only served to emphasise the extraordinary paleness of his blue eyes: at first sight you might have thought him blind, so pale they seemed, but a second glance would convince you that he was somehow looking *into* you.

He had a customary seat in the Reading Room, C4, but on this particular morning it had already been taken by a pale young man who was nervously tapping the green leather desk with his hand while he read a copy of the *Pall Mall Review*. There was a vacant place beside him, in a room which was already very busy, and John Cree put his bag carefully upon it. On his other side sat an elderly man with what in those days was considered an unusually long beard. The fact that he was sitting between George Gissing and Karl Marx, if he had recognised it, would have meant nothing at all to John Cree; he would have known them neither by name nor by reputation, and his only sensation that morning was one of annoyance at being, as he put it to himself, 'hemmed in'. Yet Marx and Gissing would, within a very short time, have a place in his history.

What books had John Cree chosen to read on this foggy autumn day? He had reserved a copy of Plumstead's *History of the London Poor* and Molton's *A Few Sighs From Hell*. Both books were concerned with the life of the indigent and the vagrant in the capital, and for that reason they were of especial interest to him; he was fascinated by poverty, and by the crime and disease which it engendered. It was, perhaps, an unusual preoccupation for a man of his class and background; his father had been a wealthy hosier in Lancaster but John Cree himself, much to the disappointment of his family, had not been a success in trade. He had come to London in order to escape from the shadow of his father and also to pursue a literary career, as a journalist on *The Era* and as a dramatist; yet he had so far proved no more successful in these areas than in any other. But he believed that now, in the life of the poor, he might have found his great theme. He often recalled a remark by the publisher Philip Carew that 'there was a grand book to be written about London'. Why not release his own private misery within the general sufferings of so many?

On his right hand, Karl Marx was dividing his attention between Tennyson's *In Memoriam* and *Bleak House* by Charles Dickens; this might seem odd reading for the German philosopher but at the end of his life he had returned to his first enthusiasm, poetry. In his early years he had read fiction eagerly and had been moved, in particular, by the novels of Eugène Sue; but Marx had characteristically expressed himself through the medium of epic poems. Now he was once again contemplating the composition of a long poem, which was to be set in the turbulent streets of Limehouse and entitled *The Secret Sorrows of London.* That was why he had spent many hours in the neighbourhood of the East End, often in the company of his friend Solomon Weil.

On John Cree's left hand, George Gissing had put down the *Pall Mall Review* and begun to skim through a number of books and pamphlets on the subject of mathematical machines. The editor of the *Review* had a particular fascination for the work of Charles Babbage, who had died nine years before, and he had commissioned this ambitious young writer to compose an essay on the inventor's life and work. No doubt much of the technical detail would be beyond Gissing's comprehension but the editor, John Morley, had admired 'Romanticism and Crime' and trusted the young man to produce another 'bright' offering for his pages. Morley also paid well – five guineas for five thousand words, an amount which would keep Gissing for at least a week. So he had eagerly immersed himself in accounts of computing machines, differential numbers and modern calculus theory.

At this particular moment he was reading Charles Babbage's essay on artificial intelligence, while John Cree himself was studying an account of Robert Withers. Withers was a self-employed cobbler from Hoxton who had been so worn down by poverty that he had destroyed his entire family with the mallets and chisels which he employed in his meagre trade. Cree was disturbed by the details of malnutrition and degradation, but he probably could not have admitted to himself that, in reading of such misery, he felt more alive now than he had ever done before. Karl Marx, meanwhile, was making his own notes. He was reading the last instalment of *Bleak House*, and had reached that point where Richard Carstone asks, on his deathbed, 'It was all a troubled dream?' Marx seemed to find the remark interesting, and wrote on a sheet of lined paper, 'It was all a troubled dream'. At the same moment George Gissing was transcribing this arresting passage into his own notebook: 'The quest for machine intelligence must arouse fresh speculation in even the most orthodox mind: think of all the calculations which might be performed in the field of statistical enquiry, where we might find ourselves able to make many very intricate deductions.' Karl Marx had turned the pages of *Bleak House* – at his age, he tired of fiction too easily – and had come upon that passage where '. . . poor crazed Miss Flite came weeping to me, and told me that she had given her birds their liberty'.

And so the three men sat side by side on this autumn day, as unaware of each other as if they had been sealed in separate chambers. They were lost in their books, as the murmuring of all the inhabitants of the Reading Room rose towards the vast dome and set up a whispering echo like that of the voices in the fog of London.

Twelve

MR GREATOREX: You have said that your husband was of a morbid disposition. But he was regular in his habits, was he not?

ELIZABETH CREE: Yes, sir. He always returned from the Reading Room at six o'clock, in good time for dinner.

MR GREATOREX: And in the months before his death you observed no change in these habits?

ELIZABETH CREE: No. After he had returned from the Reading Room, he always went to his study and sorted out his papers. I would call him down at half-past seven.

MR GREATOREX: And who prepared the food?

ELIZABETH CREE: Aveline. Aveline Mortimer.

MR GREATOREX: And who served it?

ELIZABETH CREE: The same. She is a good maid, and looked after us well.

MR GREATOREX: Is it not odd to have only the one servant in a household such as yours?

ELIZABETH CREE: It was to spare Aveline's feelings. She had something of a jealous nature.

MR GREATOREX: Now, please tell us, what was your practice after dinner?

ELIZABETH CREE: My husband drank a bottle of port each night, and had done so for a number of years without any ill effects. He used to say that it calmed him. I would often play the piano and sing to him. He liked to hear the old ditties from the halls, and sometimes he would join with me in the vocalisation. He had a good tenor voice, sir, as Aveline will confirm.

MR GREATOREX: You were once in the music-hall yourself, were you not?

ELIZABETH CREE: I . . . Yes, sir. I was an orphan when I went upon the stage.

Thirteen

My mother descended into hell at last, having been taken there by the fever. I ran out of our lodgings and purchased a jug of gin; then I poured it all over her mouth and face to cover up the smell. The young doctor scolded me for that but, as I told him, a dead body is a dead body however you look at it. She was put into the earth of the paupers' graveyard by St George's Circus; one of the fishermen gave me a sail in which to wrap her body, and the ferrymen built a wooden box for her from some old ship planks. Little did they know where this new craft was sailing. I would have gladly helped them in their work but they still thought of me as 'Little Lizzie' or 'Lambeth Marsh Lizzie'. I smiled then when I thought of the names that my mother had called me, when she confessed to her god that I was one of her sins. I was the sign of the devil, the bitch from hell, the curse upon her.

They collected ten shillings for me after the funeral, when we gathered in the Hercules tavern, and I cried a little for the sake of it. I can always produce the goods. I left them as soon as ever I could and took the money back to Peter Street, where I hid it beneath one of the floorboards – but not before I had taken out three shillings and put them on the table. Oh what a dance I did then, among the litter of Bible pages which I had scraped from the walls, and when I could no longer dance I acted out the scene I had watched in Craven Street. I was Dan Leno mocking his naughty daughter; then I took my mother's stained pillow, cradled it, kissed it, and flung it to the floor. If I did not make haste I would have been late for the show, and so all at once I grabbed my mother's old coat from its hook on the door. I knew it would fit me snugly: I had measured myself against it even as she lay upon her bed in death.

The theatre in Craven Street was so brightly lit that I might have been watching it in a dream; all the gas lights flared around me, and in the brightness my mother's coat looked so faded and threadbare that I would gladly have exchanged it for any piece of outlandish stage gear. There was a small crowd outside, wondering at a poster – they must have been flower girls and cab touts and hawkers and such trades – and one boy was spelling it out for his father. 'It's Jenny Hill,' he said as I joined them. 'The Vital Spark. And then there's Tommy-Move-Over-For-Your-Uncle-Farr.'

'He dances with a skipping rope.' His father shook his head with immense satisfaction. 'And then it turns into a hangman's piece of cord. But where's that tiny one with the clogs?' He was there, billed on this night as 'The Infant Leno, the Whipper-Snapper with a Million Faces and a Million Laughs! Every Song Funny! Every Song in Character!' I could no more have prevented myself from walking towards the lights than I could have stopped breathing. All thoughts of Lambeth Marsh and of my mother disappeared as I took my ticket and went up into the gods. This was where I belonged, with the golden angels all around me.

The Dancing Quakers came on first, with a shuffle routine, and some peel was thrown at them from the pit. Then there were a couple of swagger songs from a lion comique, a pair of patterers called The Nerves who did some encores and 'obligings again', until Dan Leno made his appearance. He was dressed as a dairy girl, complete with a little apron and a bonnet frilled in blue, and he danced his way across the stage with a milk-pail on either arm. There was a lovely picture of the Strand behind him once again and, this time, I managed to pick out some of the signs and shop-windows which were much more glorious here than they were in reality. In my old life I had seen things darkly, but now they were most clear and brilliant. Even the dust on the stage seemed to shine, and the painted green door at the corner of Villiers Street seemed so inviting that I wanted to knock and walk in. But then Dan Leno dropped his milk pails and began to sing:

Our Stores! Our Stores!
Our nineteenth-century stores!
There's eggs overlaid,
And old marmalade,
In our nineteenth-century stores.

He came forward and started squirming and simpering, putting forward one dainty foot and then withdrawing it, advancing towards the pit and then retreating, with such a wistful, piteous, put-upon face that you could not help but laugh. 'This morning a lady came in and said, "How do you sell your milk, dear?" I said, "As quickly as possible."' Who would have thought that he was still a young boy? ' "And how do you go with those big buckets?" she asks me. "Well, believe me or believe me not," I says, "I goes natural."' There was some more patter and then, when the little orchestra struck up a tune, he began swaying across the stage and singing 'I'm Off to Get Milk for the Twins'. He came on next as Nelson and then as an Indian squaw: you never heard such laughter when he accidentally set fire to his pigtail by rubbing two sticks together. 'Kindly give me a few moments to change,' he said, joining in with the fun, although we all knew that it was part of his spoof. 'Just a very few moments.' And then he came back, in a battered old hat, and sang a cockney solo.

I had not had a bit to eat since my mother's death, but I felt so revived and refreshed that I could have stayed in the gods for ever. When it all came to an end, and when the last copper had been thrown upon the stage, I could hardly bring myself to leave: I think I would be sitting there still, staring down at the pit, if the crowd had not pushed and pulled me out into the street. It was like being expelled from some wonderful garden or palace, and now all I could see were the dirty bricks of the house fronts, the muck of the narrow street, and the shadows cast by the gas lamps in the Strand. There was straw scattered on the cobbles of Craven Street, and some pages from a magazine lying in a puddle of filth. A woman or child was crying in an upper room, but when I looked up I could barely see the silhouettes of the chimney stacks against the night air. Everything was dark, and the sky and the rooftops merged together. Now, with all my strength, I longed to be in the theatre once more.

There was an oil lamp gleaming at the corner near the river, with some people gathered around: I could see that it was some kind of pie-stall, and so I walked that way to purchase a saveloy for myself. It was a bitter cold evening, and the hot coals offered some comfort as well. I must have been standing there for a minute or two, shuffling my feet on the cobbles, when a beery-looking man in a bright yellow check suit ran over. 'Harry,' he said to the pie-seller. 'They're all in dire need of pies. Be a good boy and heat some up.' I knew at once that he had come from the theatre, and I stood in awe of this blessed creature who lived within the light; he saw me staring, I think, and tipped me a wink. 'Be a good girl,' he said, 'and help your uncle with these pies. Be careful, though. They're too good to drop, as the pregnant woman said to the midwife.' I followed him across Craven Street, holding some of the pies – I could scarcely feel them, hot though they must have been, and I could barely contain my trembling as we walked down a narrow alley by the side of the theatre, and then up a flight of iron steps into the building itself. He pushed open a door covered in green baize and we walked into a passageway that smelled of beer and spirits. My eyes were so wide that I noticed everything, even the faded purple carpet which curled up at the edges and the skipping rope which one of the shufflers must have left against the wall. 'Here's a little bit of what you fancy,' the man who had called himself my 'uncle' was saying now to a dancer who opened a door at the sound of his footsteps. 'Nice and hot as you like it, Emma dear. But perhaps not quite big enough.'

She seemed to look at me with disapproval but turned back into the room. 'Bring in the donkey meat.' I recognised the voice as that of the swaggering lion comique who had sung 'All Through a Little Piece of Bacon' to great applause. Then another door was thrown open and we entered a room full of people: there were two large mirrors propped against the walls, as well as some wooden stools and chairs which already had costumes and garments thrown across them in apparent confusion. I held out my hands, and the pies just went. The comedian-caroller who had sung 'The Whole Hog or None' took one, the Dancing Quakers grabbed three from me (they could not have been in the highest spirits, having been whistled from the stage) and then the Nerves took two more. There was only one left. I suppose I was meant to eat it myself, but then I noticed Dan Leno sitting on a stool in a corner of the room; he had his head cocked to one side, and gave me such a bright funny look that I walked straight over to him. Even as I spoke I was surprised by my own audacity. 'Here's the last one for you, Mr Leno.'

'*Mr* Leno, is it?' One of the Dancing Quakers had heard me. 'She should be in a green room, since she's such a green one.'

'Now, now.' It was my new 'uncle' remonstrating with her. 'What's the harm in doing us all a favour, as the cannibals said to the missionary?' Meanwhile Dan Leno had spoken not a word, but sat munching his pie with his eyes fixed upon me. 'Tell me, my dear,' said 'Uncle', coming over to me and patting me on the arm. 'What's your moniker?'

'I don't understand.'

'Your name, dear.'

'Lizzie, sir.' Then, as I looked around at all of them, I suddenly felt that I must also step into a character. 'Lambeth Marsh Lizzie.'

The wicked Dancing Quaker gave another low laugh and curtseyed to me. 'Are you mellow in the marshes? Are you a little light in the marshes, Lizzie?'

'Now then. Order, ladies and gents.' But my 'uncle' need not have remonstrated with them. All at once they seemed to have forgotten about me, and began talking to each other and eating their pies. Then Dan Leno came over.

'Don't let them dumb yer,' he said, very confidentially. 'It's just their way. Isn't that right, Tommy?' My 'uncle' was still hovering about me, and Dan Leno gave him a stern look before introducing him to me. 'Allow me to present Tommy Farr. Agent, author, actor, comic acrobat and manager.' 'Uncle' bowed to me. 'He's the one who hands out the spondulicks.'

'The dear girl doesn't understand, Dan. You see, dear, he means the backsheesh.'

'Sir?'

'The bustle. The bunce. The money.'

'Come to think of it, we owe you a little something.' Dan

took a shilling out of his pocket. 'As Tommy would say, you did extend to us a helping hand.' When I took the coin, he glimpsed my own hands – so raw, so pitted and so large that, even then, I think he felt sorry for me. 'We're at the Washington tomorrow night,' he said in a very gentle voice, quite unlike his stage scream. 'There may be a little job for you there. If you would oblige again.'

I recognised that line from the variety, and I laughed. 'Where is the Washington, sir?'

'It's in Battersea. In your immediate neighbouring vicinity. And if it's all right with you, I'd rather you called me Dan.'

I left them soon after, and I walked through the night. I could not have slept, because I was already in a dream. I drifted down the line of gas lamps, and sang as softly as I could the words I had heard in the Craven Street theatre:

Oh mother, dear mother, come home with me now,
The clock in the steeple strikes One.

I could not remember the rest of it, but it was enough for me to imagine myself dancing upon the stage with the beautiful picture of London behind me.

Fourteen

September 9, 1880: My wife sang to me after dinner. It was an old song from the halls and, when she did all the business in her usual droll fashion, it brought back those days so fresh that we both might have wept.

September 10, 1880: Very cold and foggy for the time of year. Spent the day in the Reading Room, where I made copious notes on Mayhew's *London Labour and the London Poor*. What a moralist that man is! I had been reading the newspapers ever since my first escapade, even though I knew that the death of such a chicken would cause no great stir in the world. Then I saw a paragraph in the *Morning Herald* – 'Self-Slaughter of Young Woman' – and I knew at once that the affair had been hushed up. The gay ladies would not want to spoil their trade in that quarter, and my little business might have scared away the swells. Yet I must admit that I felt somewhat humiliated; all that work gone for nothing and, in the face of this neglect, I made a pledge to myself that next time I would leave a mark that everyone would notice. Really, I was not to be trifled with in these matters.

I left the Museum that evening and waited in Great Russell Street by the cab stand, although the fog was still so thick that

I despaired of ever finding a driver. But then I saw a pair of bull's-eye lamps approaching from a distance, and I waved my bag; I shouted out 'Limehouse!' but my words could find no passage through the fog. Then, as the cab drew nearer, someone tapped me on the shoulder. I turned quickly, in case it were some thief set to rob me, but it was the old bearded gentleman who sometimes sits near me in the Reading Room.

'We are going the same way,' he said. 'And there is only one cab. May we ride together?' He had a foreign accent, and at first I took him for a Hebrew; I have a great reverence for their learning, and so I assented at once. It seemed delightful to me to spend a little time with such a scholar before pursuing my own researches. The cab stopped and we clambered inside; it smelled no more wholesome than a dogcart but, on a night such as this, I would willingly have travelled in a prison wagon.

'This fog,' I said to my companion, 'is as thick as I have known it. It might have come straight from hell.'

'From the furnaces and manufactories, sir. There was nothing like it even twenty years ago. Now all the coal that we consume literally surrounds us.'

He had a sharp voice, which I thought interesting in a man of his age. 'You are from Germany, sir?'

'I was born in Prussia.' He looked out at the fog as we slowly made our way down Theobalds Road. 'But I have lived in this city for over thirty years.' He had a noble forehead and, when we passed a gas lamp, I could see how fiercely his eyes gleamed in the light. It was at this precise instant that I surprised myself with a wonderfully new idea. Why should I lavish all my genius upon those who were unworthy of it, when to exterminate a fine scholar would be so easily within my power? Think of the glory in destroying a brilliant man, and then, in the exultation after the act, what if I were to take off the topmost part of his skull and examine a brain still warm with its exertions?

'I have seen you in the Reading Room,' I said to him at last.

'Yes. There is always more to learn. More books to devour.' He lapsed into silence again, and I understood that he was not accustomed to general conversation. But, still, he seemed disposed to talk to a stranger on such a night as this. 'I used to come to the museum before the Reading Room was first built. We had all grown so used to the old library that we thought we would never accustom ourselves to the new establishment. But we survived.'

'You came regularly?'

'I came every day. I lived in Dean Street in those days, and I walked there each morning. There was much illness in my house, and the museum became my retreat.'

'I am sorry to hear of it.'

'Well, well, these things are determined for us.'

We had come up into the City Road, before turning south towards the river, and in the light from the front of the Salmon Vaudeville I took the opportunity of inspecting his head in a purely scientific spirit. If I could break it open with one blow, then perhaps the accumulated knowledge of his years would fly from him in some tangible shape. 'You are a fatalist, then?' I asked.

'No. On the contrary, I wait impatiently for change.'

I looked out into the fog, reflecting to myself that it might come sooner than he thought. 'A fine night for a murder,' I said.

'If I may say so, sir, murder is a bourgeois preoccupation.'

'Oh? Is it so?'

'We dwell on the suffering of one, and forget about the sufferings of many. When we ascribe guilt to one single agent, then we can deny the responsibility of all.'

'I cannot follow you there.'

'What is one murder here or there compared with the historical process? And yet, when we pick up a newspaper, what do we find but murder alone?'

'You throw the subject in a new light, certainly.'

'It is the light of world history. *Weltgeschichte.*'

We were close now to our journey's end, and I could see the tower of St Anne's, Limehouse, with the fog swirling about it. What a good fortune for me that this Prussian philosopher lived in the theatre of my operations; to despatch him here, among the whores, would make a very neat piece of tomfoolery. 'Let me take you to your lodgings,' I said. 'It is too foul a night to walk far.'

'Scofield Street is my destination. It is close to the highway here.'

'Yes. I know it very well.' I knew it to be in the Hebrew quarter, too, and I was more delighted still. To murder a Jew – it had the wonderful flavour of some blood-and-thunder play although, as I have had cause to observe in the past, the drama upon the stage is sometimes no more than an intensification of the rituals within our own hearts. And speaking of hearts, I yearned to see that of the old man with the glittering eyes. I could hold it and cherish it. And then, perhaps, make it a part of myself? What are the lines of that unjustly neglected poet, Robert Browning?

> Had I been two, another and myself,
> Our work would have o'erlooked the world.

The cab-driver banged on the trap and asked for directions; he had taken us only reluctantly to this neighbourhood, well known for its dens and its flash houses, and now wanted to leave us here as quickly as he could. 'Scofield Street!' I shouted up to him. 'Turn left at the next corner, and it is on our right hand.' I knew Limehouse so well that it had become my own Field of Forty Footsteps. That was the notorious field behind Montague House where so much blood had been shed that no grass would ever grow, and, as I explained to my German scholar while we came up to his street, by curious coincidence that patch of fatal ground lies directly beneath the Reading Room of the British Museum. He did not find this of any great concern, and made ready to leave the cab. Well, my fine friend, I thought as I watched him gathering his coat about himself and wrapping his scarf around his throat, you will soon know for yourself how books and blood can be subtly joined together. We stopped on the dark side of the street, and I pressed half a crown into the driver's hand before escorting my companion to the door of Number 7. I wished to be able to recognise it again, at the appointed time. We saluted each other, and then I turned on my heel towards the river. The tide was out and there was such a stench that the fog itself seemed like some miasma of filth and effluence. But the gay ladies were still at their game, and I sought for one who stood apart from the rest. I was crossing Limehouse Reach in the direction of the seamen's mission, when I saw a shape ahead of me – whether of woman, or man, or something else, I could not tell; but I pressed my bag against my chest, and hurried after. It was a woman shivering with the damp and the cold, who looked at me gratefully enough.

'What is your name, my little bird?'

'I'm Jane.'

'Well, Jane, where do you go from here?'

'I have a room in that house, sir, with the yellow door.'

'All things look yellow in this fog, Jane. You will have to guide me there.' I took her by the arm, but then turned her about to face the river. 'Shall we take a walk before we retire? I wonder if we can see the Surrey shore.' Of course we could see nothing whatever, and by the time we came to some old steps there was a silence so profound that it seemed to be some material element of the fog. 'How do you take it, Jane?'

'I take it any way you care to give it, sir.'

'Will you say "when"?'

'Just as you like.'

'Let's go down the steps a little way. My home is down below, you see.' She seemed reluctant to follow me, but I coaxed her. 'I have something in my bag which might please you. Have you heard of the new protective sheath? Look here.' I opened the bag and then, with a quick movement, took my knife and cut her across the throat from left to right. It was a powerful start, although I say so myself, and she leaned back against the wall with an astonished look upon her face; she sighed and seemed eager for more, so I obliged her with a few deep cuts. Then, lost in the fog, I created such a spectacle that no eye seeing it could fail to be moved. The head came off first, and the intestinal tract made a very pretty decoration beside the womb. Along this part of the river, two centuries ago, malefactors were left in chains to rot with the movement of the tides – how rare an opportunity for a London historian such as myself to revive the old pastimes. What a work is man, how subtle in faculties and how infinite in entrails! Her head lay upon the upper step, just as if it were the prompter's head seen from the pit of the theatre, and I must admit that I applauded my own work. But then there came a noise from the wings, and I walked quickly by the riverside until I came out by Ludgate.

Fifteen

John Cree was wrong in assuming that the German scholar lived in Scofield Street. On that foggy night in early September, Karl Marx was simply calling upon a friend. He visited Solomon Weil once a week for an evening of philosophical discussion. They had met in the Reading Room of the British Museum eighteen months before, when they had found themselves sitting side by side: Marx had noticed that his neighbour was studying Freher's *Serial Elucidation of the Cabbala*, and all at once remembered reading it himself when he was a student at the University of Bonn. They had started speaking in German together, perhaps because they recognised some familial resemblance (Solomon Weil had been born in Hamburg, coincidentally in the same month and year as Marx himself), and soon enough they discovered a similar interest in theoretical enquiry and subtle disputes of learning. It is true that in his published writings, and in particular in the earliest of them, Karl Marx had condemned what he described as a degraded Judaism. In one of his first essays, 'On the Jewish Question', he had concluded '*ist der Jude unmöglich geworden*' or 'the Jew becomes impossible'. But Marx himself sprang from a long line of rabbis and was deeply imbued with the vocabulary and the preoccupations of Judaism. Now, at the end of his life, the sudden glimpse of a commentary upon the Cabbala was enough to launch him into a torrent of German conversation with Solomon Weil, and an almost inexplicable affection for this scholar who was studying one of the books of his youth. He had spent most of his life in persistent invective against all forms of religious belief but, as he sat beneath the great dome of the Reading Room, he was strangely moved and excited. They left the Museum together that evening, and agreed to meet the following day. It must be said that Solomon Weil himself was a little perplexed. He had heard of Marx through other German émigrés, and was surprised to find this atheist and revolutionary so charming and erudite a companion. He had, perhaps, been even too polite; but Solomon Weil assumed, correctly, that Marx was trying to atone for his vindictive assaults upon his own old faith.

During their second conversation, held in a small chop house off Coptic Street, Solomon Weil mentioned to Marx that he had acquired a large library of cabbalistic and esoteric learning: he had some four hundred volumes in his lodgings, and at once Marx asked if he might examine them. That was the origin of their regular weekly suppers in Limehouse, where the two men would exchange theories and speculations as if they were young scholars again. Weil's library was remarkable – many of the books in his collection had once belonged to the Chevalier d'Éon, the famous French transsexual, who had lodged in London in the latter half of the eighteenth century. The Chevalier had been particularly interested in cabbalistic lore, largely because of its emphasis upon an original divine androgyny from which the two sexes sprang. D'Éon bequeathed his collection to an artist and Freemason, William Cosway, who in turn had left it to a mezzotint engraver with whom he had collaborated in certain occult experiments. This engraver then converted to Judaism, and in gratitude for his newly awakened faith left his entire library to

Solomon Weil. So the old books were now shelved in his rooms at 7 Scofield Street, together with some of Weil's own acquisitions such as *A Second Warning to the World by the Spirit of Prophecy* and *Signs of Times, or A Voice to Babylon, the Great City of the World and to the Jews in Particular.* Weil had also purchased a collection of material devoted to the life and writings of Richard Brothers, the visionary and British Israelite who believed that the English nation represented the lost tribe of Israel. But there was one less predictable element in his library: he also had a passion for the popular theatre of London, and had acquired a collection of sheet music from a printer's in Endell Street which specialised in the newest songs from the halls.

In fact he had just been looking over the lyrics of 'That's What Astonishes Me', made famous by the male impersonator Bessie Bonehill, when on that foggy evening in September he heard the tread of Karl Marx upon the stairs. They greeted each other with a firm handshake, in the English fashion, and Marx apologised for arriving after the customary hour but, on a night such as this . . . They both employed an agreeable argot of German and English, with the occasional use of Latin and Hebrew terms for an exact or particular sense; that is why certain elusive textures and atmospheres of their conversation must necessarily be lost in an English reproduction. Their meal was simple enough – some cold meat, cheese, bread and bottled beer – and as they ate Marx was describing his failure to make progress on the long epic poem about Limehouse which he had recently begun. Had he not, as a young man, written nothing but poetry? He had even completed the first act of a verse drama when he was still at university.

'What did you call it?' Weil asked him.

'*Oulanem.*'

'It was in German?'

'Naturally.'

'But it is not a German name. I thought it was perhaps related to *Elohim* and *Hule*. Between them they represent the conditions of the fallen world.'

'That never occurred to me at the time. But, you know, when we look for hidden correspondences and signs . . .'

'Yes. They are everywhere. Even here in Limehouse we can see the tokens of the invisible world.'

'You will forgive me, I know, but I am still more concerned with what is visible and material.' Marx went over to the window, and looked down into the yellow fog. 'I know that, to you, all this is considered to be the *Klippoth*, but these hard dry shells of matter are what we are forced to inhabit.' He could see a woman hurrying down Scofield Street, and there was something about her nervous haste which disturbed him. 'Even you,' he said. 'Even you have an affection for the lower world. You have a cat.'

Solomon Weil laughed at his friend's sudden metaphysical leap. 'But she lives in her own time, not in mine.'

'Oh, she has a soul?'

'Of course. And when you live as much in the past and in the future, as I do, it is good to share lodgings with a creature who exists entirely for the present. It is refreshing. Here, Jessica, come here.' The cat uncurled itself among some scattered books and papers, and slowly advanced towards Weil. 'And it impresses my neighbours. They think I am a magician.'

'In a sense, you are.' Marx came back into the room, and resumed his seat by the fireside opposite Weil. 'Well, as Boehme taught us, opposition is the source of all friendship. Tell me now. What have you been reading today?'

'You would not believe me if I told you.'

'Oh, you mean some hermetic scroll long hidden from the sight of men?'

'No. I have been reading the song sheets from the music-halls. Sometimes I hear them sung in the streets, and they remind me of the old songs of our forefathers. Do you know "My Shadow is my Only Pal" or "When These Old Clothes Were New"? They are wonderful little ditties. Songs of the poor. Songs of longing.'

'If you say so.'

'But there is also an extraordinary gaiety within them. Look at this.' On the front of one sheet was a photograph of Dan Leno dressed as 'Widow Twankey, a Lady of the Old School'. He had a vast wig of curled brown hair, a gown that swirled down over his ankles, and he was holding a very large feather in his tightly gloved hands. The expression was at once domineering and pathetic; with his high arched eyebrows, his wide mouth, and his large dark eyes, he looked so droll and yet so desperate that Marx put down the music sheet with something like a frown. Then Solomon Weil took out from a pile of sheets another photograph of Leno beside a song entitled 'Isabella with the Loose Umbrella' in which he was dressed as 'Sister Anne' in *Bluebeard*. 'He is what they call a screamer,' Weil explained as he placed the sheet neatly back in its place within the pile.

'Yes. I might well scream. It is the *Shekhina*.'

'Do you believe so? No. It is not the shadow female. It is male and female joined. It is Adam Kadmon. The Universal Man.'

'I see there is no end to your wisdom, Solomon, if you can make a cabbala out of the music-hall. No doubt the gas lamps in the gallery become the *Sephiroth* of your vision.'

'But don't you understand why they love it so? For them it is so sacred that they talk of the gods and of the pit. I even discovered, quite by chance, that many of these halls and little theatres were once chapels and churches. You were the one who talked of hidden connections, after all.' So Karl Marx and Solomon

Weil continued their conversation into the night and, while Jane Quig was being mutilated, the scholars discussed what Weil called the material envelope of the world. 'It can assume whatever shape we please to give it. In that respect it resembles the golem. You know of the golem?'

'I have a vague recollection of the old tales, but it has been so long . . .'

Already Solomon Weil had gone over to his bookcase and taken down a copy of Hartlib's *Knowledge of Sacred Things*. 'Our ancestors thought of the golem as an homunculus, a material being created by magic, a piece of red clay brought to life in the sorcerer's laboratory. It is a fearful thing and, according to the ancient legend, it sustains its life by ingesting the spirit or soul of a human being.' He opened a page to the description of this creature, beside a large engraving of a doll or puppet with holes for the eyes and for the mouth. He brought it over to Marx, and then resumed his seat. 'Of course we do not have to believe in golems literally. Surely not. That is why I read it in an allegorical sense, with the golem as an emblem of the *Klippoth* and a shell of degraded matter. But then what do we do? We give it life in our own image. We breathe our own spirit into its shape. And that, don't you see, is what the visible world must be – a golem of giant size? Do you know Herbert, the cloakroom attendant at the Museum?'

'Of course I know him.'

'Herbert is not a man of any great imagination. I think you would agree with me there?'

'Only in the expectation of tips.'

'He really only understands coats and umbrellas. But the other day our friend told me a curious story. One afternoon he was walking with his wife down Southwark High Street – taking his constitutional, as he put it – when they passed the old alms-houses set back from the road there. Now Herbert and his wife happened to glance that way, when both of them glimpsed – just for a moment, you understand – a hooded figure bent over towards the ground. And then it was gone.'

'And what are you going to tell me about Herbert's story?'

'The figure was there. They did not imagine it. They could not have imagined anything so appropriate to a medieval dwelling.'

'So you, Solomon Weil, are telling me that it was a ghost?'

'Not at all. You and I do not believe in ghosts any more than we believe in golems. It was more interesting than that.'

'Now you are engaging. in paradox, like a good Hebrew scholar.'

'The world itself took that form for a moment because it was expected of it. It created that figure in the same way that it creates stars for us – and trees, and stones. It knows what we need, or expect, or dream of, and then it creates such things for us. Do you understand me?'

'No. I do not.' The fog had begun to disperse as they talked, and Marx roused himself from the fireside. 'How late it is now,' he said, going over to the window once more. 'Even the fog has decided to retire.' They parted with a handshake, and saluted one another, in German, for the last time upon this earth. Marx buttoned up his top-coat as he walked out into the street and looked in vain for a cab; he was passed by one or two inhabitants of the neighbourhood, who later remembered the small foreign-looking gentleman with the untrimmed beard.

Sixteen

MR LISTER: Now, Elizabeth. May I call you Elizabeth?

ELIZABETH CREE: I know you are defending me, sir.

MR LISTER: Tell me, Elizabeth, what possible reason could you have for murdering your own husband?

ELIZABETH CREE: None, sir. He was a good husband to me.

MR LISTER: Did he ever beat you, or strike you in any way?

ELIZABETH CREE: No, sir. He was always gentle with me.

MR LISTER: But you do profit financially from his death, do you not? Tell me about that.

ELIZABETH CREE: There was no life insurance, sir, if that is what you mean. We had an income from the railway shares, which he had inherited from his father. There was also a hosiery business, which we sold.

MR LISTER: He was a faithful husband?

ELIZABETH CREE: Oh, very faithful.

MR LISTER: I find that easy to believe when I look at you.

ELIZABETH CREE: I'm sorry, sir? Do you wish me to say something else?

MR LISTER: If you would oblige me a little, Elizabeth. I would like you to tell the court how you and your husband first met.

Seventeen

I found the Washington just by the old Cremorne Gardens, as Dan Leno had told me. I could hardly have mistaken it: its walls were painted with life-size figures of actors and clowns and acrobats, and I imagined myself as one of the pictures here, sauntering along the fresco with my blue gown and yellow umbrella, singing my own especial song for which the world loved me. But what song could that be?

'You must be giddy Godiva,' someone said behind me. 'The maid who was sent to Coventry.' It was my new 'uncle', Tommy Farr, but he no longer had the flash check jacket which had so impressed me. He was wearing a lovely black top-coat, with all its fur trimmings, and a silk hat. He must have seen my look of wonder, because he tipped his hat back a fraction and winked at me. 'At the Washington,' he said, 'we all have to be a bit of an artiste. It's not so free and easy. Can you read the English language, dear?'

'Yes, sir. Like a native.' My mother had taught me to do so, with her Jeremiahs and her Jobs and her Isaiahs, and now I could read as well as anyone living; I soon grew tired of spouting her nonsense, though, and read copies of the *Woman's World* which a neighbour passed on to me.

Uncle had appreciated my little joke about 'a native' and patted me on the shoulder. 'Well, read that there, then.'

There was a poster on the wall behind me, and so I turned to it and spoke in a clear, firm voice. 'At this unequalled establishment—'

'There aren't any capitals in your voice, dear. Put in the capitals.'

'At this Unequalled Establishment there will appear on Monday the twenty-ninth Miss Celia "She Can Be Rather Sultry" Day. Following the very successful reception of her ditty, "Hurrah for the Dog of the Fire Brigade", she will be joined for the chorus of that Renowned Confabulation with the Lion Comique himself, The White-Eyed One.'

'I wrote all that myself,' Uncle said. 'In the best possible style. I could have been another Hamlet. Or do I mean Shakespeare?' He seemed to be close to tears, and I felt quite alarmed for him. 'Alas, poor Celia, I know her well.' He sighed and raised his hat. 'She's an old-timer. She shouldn't be playing all this blue bag stuff.' His mood then changed abruptly. 'Tell me, dear, what does it say at the very bottom of the bill?'

'Tonight. A Benefit for the Friends In Need Philanthropic Society.'

'That's us, you see. We're the friends in need. And we're very philanthropic, if you know what I mean.' He raised his eyebrows like an old-style Harlequin, and took me firmly by the arm. 'Let's perambulate upon the stage.'

We walked into the Washington and, as we passed through the vestibule, I found myself in the most wonderful scene – finer by far than the one in the Craven Street theatre. There were so many mirrors and glass lamps all around me that I held onto his arm more tightly. I might have been in a cathedral of light, and I was afraid of losing all sense of myself among this brightness. 'That's a good girl,' he said, patting my hand. 'This really takes the bun, doesn't it?' We walked up some steps and onto the stage itself. It had not been swept, and

I glimpsed little pieces of star-dust lodged between the wooden boards. Someone had left three chairs and a table here, but they were so brightly painted that they did not resemble any furniture I had ever seen; they looked like children's toys, and I would have been afraid to sit on them in case they turned into something else. Suddenly I felt myself lifted off my feet and whirled around: Uncle was spinning me faster and faster, until his silk hat dropped off the stage and he dumped me on the painted table. I felt so giddy that I could hardly speak, and looked up at the ropes and the canvas floating above me. 'I had to feel the weight of you,' he said, gasping as he clambered from the stage to retrieve his hat. 'Just in case I can get you into a rope-dance. A spin does you good, anyway. It sends the blood racing, doesn't it, as the surgeon said to the jockey.'

'Don't let him chaff yer.' I looked down into the theatre and, to my surprise, saw Dan Leno standing at the back. 'He can be a terrible one for chaffing the ladies, can't you, Uncle?'

'That is my way, Dan. But it's only the way it's done on the stage.' He seemed abashed in the boy's presence and I knew, even then, that Dan was the one who mattered in this company. Yet he was such a little slip of a thing – even shorter than I had remembered him from the night before, and with such a wide mouth that he reminded me of a marionette or a juvenile Punch.

'We were talking about you last night,' he said, coming down the aisle with his pert little step. 'Are you out of a shop?'

'Sir?'

'Are you not currently engaged in employment? Are you workless?'

'Oh yes, sir.'

'My name is Dan.'

'Yes, Dan.'

'Can you read?'

'That's just the point I was putting to her myself, Dan.'

'I know what point you would like to put to her, Uncle.' Dan ignored him after that and carried on talking to me in his brisk, intense fashion. 'Our prompter ran off with a slangster comique the other day, and sometimes we need a bit of help from that quarter. Do you understand me? Otherwise we might get ballooned off the stage.' I understood well enough that I was being invited to join them, although I had no notion of what a prompter might be. Dan Leno must have seen the delight on my face, because he gave one of those infectious smiles which I came to know so well. 'It's not all lavender,' he said. 'You'll also have to be a general fetch-and-carry kid. A bit of dressing. A bit of this and that. Do you have a neat hand?' He blushed as soon as he had said it, and tried not to look at my large, raw hands. 'You can do some play-copying for us, you see. Now let's have a bit of fun, shall we?' He was wearing an overcoat which almost came down to his ankles, and from one of its many pockets he took out a small exercise book and a pencil which he handed to me with an elaborately low bow. 'Write it down,' he said, 'as I spoof it.'

He splayed his legs wide on the stage, put his thumbs in the pockets of his waistcoat, and then tweaked an imaginary moustache. 'I'll tell you who I am, Uncle, I'm a recruiting sergeant. The other day I was standing at the corner of the street when I saw you, Uncle, as is your wont.' Then Uncle stood up very straight, as Dan stalked over to him with as much ferocity as if he were eight feet high. 'Do *you* want to be a soldier?'

'I don't. I'm waiting for a bus.'

'Oh dear! Oh dear! My word! What a life! But it puts me in mind of a very delicate little story concerned with my profession. A fine young fellow came up to me the other day and said, "Governor, will I do for a soldier?" I said, "I think so, my boy," and walked around him. But then I noticed that he walked round *me* at the same time. When I got him before the doctor, the medicine man said, "Dan, you do find them." Then we discovered that he had only got one arm. I never noticed because we were perpetually walking around one another. Well, what a life!'

I wrote all this down as quickly as I possibly could; then, at the end, he jumped down from the stage and stood on tiptoe to look over my shoulder. 'That's a good girl,' he said. 'You're as neat as a shipping clerk. Uncle, will you sing a nice patter for Lizzie, just to see how fast she can go?' I understood now that part of my new employment was in writing down what Dan called 'extempore vocalisation', so that anything said 'off the cuff' could be used in later performances. Uncle took off his hat and then squatted upon it, just as if he were about to relieve himself. 'Now then,' Dan said, very sternly, 'none of your blue stuff here. Not in front of the girl. Do your patter song, or get off the stage.' I had never heard such authority in a young man, but Uncle dutifully put on his hat and, with his hands out in front of him, began to sing:

My love was no foolish girl, her age it was two score—

'Did you get that, Lizzie?'
I nodded.

My love was no spinster, she'd been married twice
before . . .

I was a quick study, and I soon caught up with the words when he started repeating the chorus. Dan was obviously delighted by my progress. 'How does a pound a week suit you?' he asked me after he had taken my notes and put them back in the pocket of his overcoat. It was as much as my mother and I had ever earned, and I did not quite know what to say. 'That's

70

settled, then. You get your packet from the money-taker at the entrance on Friday nights.'

'He's very cute in business, is Dan,' Uncle said. 'He's not in the nursery now.'

'And never was. What about diggings, Lizzie?' It was clear that I did not understand what he meant. 'Do you have a lovely palace to hide in, or only a hole in the ground?'

Now that I felt so transformed, I did not want to return to Lambeth Marsh. And I could see no harm in playing the orphan girl. 'I am quite alone in the world, and the landlord will not see his way to letting me stay unless I – share his rooms with him.'

'That's really rubbing it in. That's the kind of thing that makes me volcanically mad.' Dan walked around the stage for a moment, and then turned to me. 'We've got some nice little lodgings in the New Cut. Why don't you pack up your bag and join us?'

This was a wonderful chance, and of course I seized it at once: 'May I?'

'You may.'

'It will take me no more than an hour or so. I have only a very few possessions of my own.'

'Write it down now then. Number 10 at the New Cut. Ask for Austin.'

So all was settled, and I made haste to leave before I discovered that the whole business was some dream of my own. I had just reached the theatre entrance when I heard Uncle calling down to Dan. 'Couldn't we put her in a living picture, Dan? Now that Elspeth wants to try the wires?'

There was a moment's silence. 'Too soon, Uncle. Too soon. Anyway she might make a good gagger. You can never tell. She's got the dial for it.'

'You can say that again.'

'She's got the dial for it.'

*

71

I ran home as quickly as I could, across Battersea Fields, and as soon as I entered our lodgings I knew that my old life had already come to an end. I gathered the rest of my money from beneath the floorboards, and placed it neatly on my mother's dirty bed. There was an old tin trunk against the wall, which we used as a seat when we were sewing together; it held nothing but some scraps of her religiosity, some ragged hymnals and the like, which I gladly chucked out of the window. Then I took out all of our clothes, plain though they were, and folded them neatly within it. I could have carried it on my own shoulders, it was light enough, but I did not want to show myself as in any way unladylike; so I dragged it only as far as St George's Fields, where I hired a horse cab which took me to the New Cut for threepence.

Number 10, New Cut, was a neat little house in a new terrace, and I felt quite a princess as the cab came to a halt and I stepped out onto the pavement. The driver was a scrawny piece of meat, with a stove-pipe hat to hide his baldness, but very gallantly he carried my tin trunk to the door. He had a little moustache, and I could not resist making a joke out of it when I gave him an extra penny. 'Has your wife been punching you?' I asked. 'There's a bruise under your nose.' He put a hand up to his mouth, and rushed away.

'What is it?' As soon as I had knocked upon the door, I heard a female voice bellowing in the passage.

'It's the new girl.'

'What is her name?'

'Lizzie. Lambeth Marsh Lizzie.'

'Is she from Dan?'

'Yes. She is.'

The door was opened suddenly by a man wearing a seedy frock-coat and huge bow-cravat, just like the comic singers I had seen in the Craven Street theatre. 'Well, my dear,' he said.

'You look rather like a low-comedy granddaughter. Come.' Obviously I had been mistaken about hearing a woman's voice: it was his own, but so high and tremulous anyone would have judged it to be of the opposite sex. 'I'm putting you with Doris, the goddess of wire-walking. Do you know her?' I shook my head. 'Lovely party. She can spin upon a penny. Great friend of mine.' I could tell from his flushed face, and his trembling hands, that he was a drinker; he must have been no more than forty, but he looked too frail to last. 'I would carry your trunk myself, dear, but I'm prone to faintness of the arteries. That's why I gave up the profession.' He was mounting the stairs, talking as freely and as gaily to me as if we had known each other for many years. 'Now I'm a landman. Do you get it? Landlady. Landman. I don't like landlord, do you? It sounds too beery, too saloony. I'm known to all the hall folk as Austin. Simply Austin.' I ventured to ask him what he once did upon the stage. 'I was a blacked-up turn, and then a funny female. I only had to pop on a wig, and they would all yell. I killed them stone dead every time, dear. Here we are. Goddess? Are you in?' He put his ear to the door in a very extravagant manner, and waited there for a few seconds. 'And answer came there none. I think we'll just push our way through, don't you?' He knocked again, and then slowly opened the door upon a scene of great disorder: there were plumed hats and pieces of corsage, lace drawers and crumpled skirts, tights and shoes, littered all over the room. 'She is not a very neat creature,' Austin said. 'She has the soul of an artist. Your bed is over there, dear. In that corner.' There was indeed a second bed, although it was covered by clothes, hat boxes and clippings from the newspapers. 'I wondered what happened to that teapot,' he said, and removed a brown enamel article from what was now my pillow. 'Doris loves her tea.' He was about to leave the room when he suddenly turned upon his heels, in what I later discovered to be a comedy way, and said in an exaggerated whisper, 'It's ten shillings a week to share. Dan says he'll take it out of your packet. Is that all right?'

I nodded. I felt that I had already entered a new life, and was so delighted by my transformation that I even looked with pleasure upon the confusion of this little room. As soon as Austin had gone I cleared the bed and placed all my clothes upon a nearby chair and side-table. There were some withered flowers in pots upon the window-sill and, when I looked out, I could see the new railway and a row of warehouses beneath it. It was all so astonishing and so unfamiliar that I really felt as if I had been taken out of the old world and raised to some blessed place of freedom. Even the lines of the railway track seemed to glow.

'I know what you're thinking,' a woman said behind me. 'You're thinking, why ever did I leave my little back room in Bloomsbury?'

'I come from Lambeth. Lambeth Marsh.'

'It's just a song, dear.' I had turned around to find myself addressed by a tall young woman with very long dark hair. She frightened me a little, because she was dressed all in white. 'I'm the goddess of wire-walking,' she said. 'Doris to you.' She took my hand very kindly, and we sat down together upon her bed. 'Dan told me to expect you. Why, you look half-starved.' She went over to a little chest of drawers and came back with a bag of monkey nuts and a bottle of lemon fizz. 'I'll make us some nice toast and butter in a minute.' We sat together for the remainder of the afternoon; I told her that my parents had died when I was very young, that I had earned my living as a seamstress in Hanover Square, and that I had run away from a hard mistress before I had found lodgings with a sail-maker in Lambeth Marsh. After that, I had been found by Uncle and Dan Leno. Of course she believed my story – who would not? – and throughout my narrative she patted my hand and sighed. At one point she began to cry, but then wiped her eyes, saying, 'Pay no attention to me. It's just my way.' We were having a very comfortable cup of tea, after my story, when there was a tap on the door.

'Five o'clock, dears.' It was Austin's high, womanly voice. 'Overture and beginners, all down for the first scene.'

'Don't mind him,' Doris whispered to me. 'He's in the inebriate way. Do you know what I mean? Only the one?' Then she called out to him, 'All right, my darling! We're getting ourselves fully prepared!' She got up from the bed, and began undressing in front of me. My mother had always hidden herself when she washed, so furtive and ashamed of her flesh was she, and I stared at the sight of Doris's fair skin and breasts. She was what they call in our trade statuesque. I washed myself quickly as well, and, when she saw the plain gown I had put on, she gently draped a fine wool coat around me before we left the house together.

I did not know how or when I was to begin my work but, obedient as ever, I went with Doris to the Washington. It must have been near our diggings, but she put out her hand and waved to a brougham. At first I thought she had hired it but when the driver looked down, and addressed her familiarly as 'Goddess', I realised that he must have some connection with the company. 'Is it Effs tonight,' he said, 'or the Old Mo?'

'We're starting at Battersea, Lionel, and then we're working our way around.'

'Who's the new cub?'

'Never you mind, and keep your eyes on the road.' As soon as we had entered the brougham Doris whispered to me, 'Lionel may seem very nice to you, dear. But he is not a gentleman of the old school.'

We arrived at the Washington just a few minutes later and,

as we hurried towards the side-door, a young man approached Doris with a note pad. 'Can I have a word?' he said. 'I'm from the *Era*.' He was well-spoken, and his eyes were as pale as the marshes. Of course I could never have known that one day he would become my husband; that he was John Cree.

Eighteen

September 12, 1880: What a wonderful spread in the *Police Gazette*, although the rough engravings scarcely did justice to the business. They had depicted me with a top hat and cloak in general theatrical representation of a swell or masher – I suppose that I was grateful for the recognition, since only a member of my class could have performed such a delicate feat, but I would have preferred more authenticity in the composition. Dear Jane's body could also have been more perfectly drawn, and lacked certain subtle effects of light and shade; mezzotint or stipple are so helpful in conveying atmosphere without the general prettifying of colour, although I suppose that an act such as mine can be represented by the simple force of the engraver's old-fashioned burin. There was also something wanting in the style of the newspaper reports: they smacked too much of the Gothic, and were woefully inadequate in syntax. 'Two nights ago, a human fiend perpetrated the foulest and most horrid murder ever seen in this city . . .' and so forth. I knew that the common people preferred to turn their lives into the cheapest melodrama, with the taint of the penny gaff, but surely the more educated classes of the newspaper world might aspire a little higher?

And then I recalled the scholar. It was an easy thing to kill a whore, after all, and there could be no real or lasting glory in it. In any case, so strong is the public lust for blood that the whole city would be waiting in anticipation for the killing of another flash girl. That would be the beauty of the Jew: it would throw all into confusion, and lend such splendour and excitement to my progress that each new death would be eagerly awaited. I would become the model of the age.

September 16, 1880: By a stroke of luck my darling wife, Lizzie, decided to spend the evening with a friend in Clerkenwell – one of her old theatrical pals who, I suspect, has become an inebriate. But it gave me a wonderful opportunity to create my little surprise. I knew Scofield Street well enough, and I perfectly remembered the house where I had left the Hebrew on that foggy night, so I decided to spend the day in the Reading Room to complete my study of Mayhew before embarking on my quest. I saw him in his customary place; he did not notice me at all, but I marked him well. When he left his seat to consult the catalogue, I made my way over to his desk as casually as if I were merely walking by – who could resist the temptation of seeing the last book on earth such a man was about to read? He had left one volume open, and its title was obscured – I glimpsed only tables of cabbalistical and hieroglyphical figures which were no doubt the offspring of some Asiatic mind. But there was also a new book lying on top of a catalogue from Murchison's in Coveney Street, so I knew that he had just purchased it. It was entitled *Workers of the Dawn*; I could not make out the author's name as I passed by, but it seemed a peculiar choice for a German scholar. Then I returned to my own place and read Mayhew until my friend left the Reading Room and walked out into the dusk.

There was no need to follow him, since I knew his destination, and on such a fine night I decided to stroll towards the river with my bag of tricks. (Perhaps someone would need the services of a surgeon along my path!) I came up by Aldgate and the Tower before turning down Campion Street. It was so clear a night that I could see the towers of the churches of the East, and it seemed to me as if the whole city were trembling in anticipation of some great change; at that moment, I felt proud to be entrusted with its powers of expression. I had become its messenger as I walked towards Limehouse.

There was a gas lamp at the top end of Scofield Street where it comes out by the Commercial Road, but the patch which led down towards the river was now quite dark: Number 7, with the brown door, was situated just on the borders of light before the street melted into shadow. It was a common lodging house, and the door was still unbolted: I glanced up at an oil lamp gleaming within the upper storey, and judged pretty well where I would find my scholar bent over his books. I climbed the stairs softly so as not to disturb his labours, and then knocked gently on his door three times. He asked who it was.

'A friend.'

'I know you?'

'Surely.'

He opened the door a fraction, and I pushed it wide with my bag. 'Good God,' he whispered. 'What is that you want from me?'

It was not my Jew; it was another. But I showed no surprise and stepped forward with my left hand outstretched. 'I have come to make your acquaintance,' I said. 'I have come to discourse with you about death and everlasting life.' Then I held up my bag. 'Herein lies the secret.' He made no move, but watched me as I opened it. 'You and I both have a sense of the sacred, have we not? We understand the mystery.' I took out the mallet and, before he could cry out, I struck him down. I had given him a powerful blow but he was not dead yet; the blood soaked down through the threadbare carpet from his open wound, and I knelt beside him to whisper in his ear. 'In your cabbala,' I said, 'all life is an emanation from *Ain Soph*. So now flee from the dregs of matter, I pray you, and return to the light.' I took off his black robe and his cotton undergarments; there was a basin of water on a table beside his bed, and reverently I washed him with my own handkerchief. Then I brought out my knife and began the work. The body is truly a *mappamundi* with its territories and continents, its rivers of fibre and its oceans of flesh, and in the lineaments of this scholar I could see the spiritual harmony of the body when it is touched by thought and prayer. He lived yet, and sighed as I cut him – sighed, I think, with pleasure as the spirit rose out of the opened form.

I had a great desire to cut his penis, and so complete the rituals of his faith. I took it off and then, holding it up to the oil lamp, inspected its intricate curves and lines. Here, truly, was another work of God. There was an open book beside the lamp, and I placed the penis upon it – where better for the generative organ of a scholar to be found? But what was this? On the page was delineated the image of some might demon and, beside it, a short history of the golem. I knew that such a thing was fashioned like a homunculus, from red clay; but now I read with interest how it preserved its life by feeding from the human soul. Of course it was fanciful nonsense, one of those bugbears from the night of the world, but there was an amusing coincidence in the blood of the scholar running across the very name of the creature as if it were a richly delineated page from an illuminated manuscript. The severed penis and the golem had become one. I left the room and hurried down into the street; when I came to the corner of Commercial Road I was about to set up a cry of 'Murder! Oh God! Murder!' when a black cat of ill fortune crossed my path. So I shook my fist at the animal from hell, and kept my peace.

September 18, 1880: Lizzie has begged me to take her to the Canterbury, where Dan Leno and Herbert Campbell are appearing together, but I am tired of their sad exploits upon the stage. I see now, from the *Daily News*, that I have become known as the Limehouse Golem. What fools these people are.

Nineteen

And so Solomon Weil had been found, mutilated, among his
books. The brutal murder of the Jewish scholar, only six days
after that of the prostitute in the same area, provoked a fren-
zied interest among ordinary Londoners. It was almost as
if they had been waiting impatiently for these murders to
happen – as if the new conditions of the metropolis required
some vivid identification, some flagrant confirmation of its status as the largest and darkest city of the world. This probably
accounted for the eagerness with which the term 'golem' was
taken up and published; few people who used it could have
been aware of its exact significance, but cabbalists believe that
the very sound or letters of a word can themselves become
signs of its spiritual meaning. So in the intonation of 'golem'
the public may have divined the horror of an artificial life and
a form without a spirit – the cadence and inflection of the
word echoing and mocking 'soul'. It was an emblem for the
city which surrounded them and the search for the Limehouse
Golem became, curiously enough, a search for the secret of
London itself.

One of Weil's neighbours had remembered seeing a
foreign-looking gentleman with a beard leaving the house in
Scofield Street, although she could not be sure which night that

had been. In fact as the members of the recently established Criminal Investigation Department pursued their enquiries, they noted down other sightings of the same bearded foreigner; he had been seen lingering among the crowds outside the Pantheon song-and-supper rooms along the Commercial Road, for example, when it had also been noticed by one observant waiter that he had written something in a small pocket-book. The police were also able to find a more immediate witness: a hansom-cab driver came forward to testify that he had driven a gentleman of similar appearance to Scofield Street a few nights before. He remembered it distinctly as the night of the last great fog, and he had picked up the fare by his usual stand in Great Russell Street. He was sure that the gentleman had come from the British Museum, because he had seen him in that area before; unfortunately, he had forgotten the presence of John Cree on that same night. Two police detectives from 'H' Division visited the Superintendent of the Reading Room on the following morning, and from their description of the bearded foreigner the identity of Mr Karl Marx was quickly established.

Marx himself had been confined to his house since the evening John Cree had seen him in the Reading Room of the British Museum; he had contracted a severe cold, which had no doubt been exacerbated by his evening with Solomon Weil and his long walk homeward. He had seen no newspapers and so was quite unaware of the death of his friend – until, that is, Chief Inspector Kildare and Detective Paul Bryden visited his house in Maitland Park Road on the morning of September the 18th. They were shown into his study on the first floor by one of Marx's daughters, Eleanor, who at the time was also looking after her mother: Jenny Marx had been ill for some weeks, and would soon be diagnosed as suffering from cancer of the liver. The room which they entered was filled with books, scattered around as if the spirit had been drained from them and they had sunk exhausted to the floor; the atmosphere was heavy with the scent of cigar smoke and, for a moment, Bryden was reminded of the song cellars and Caves of Harmony which he had inspected when he first joined the Metropolitan Police Force. Karl Marx was sitting at a small desk in the middle of his study; he was wearing a pair of steel-rimmed spectacles which he removed as the two policemen entered. He was not particularly perturbed by their visit; he had been used to official attention for the last thirty years, and he greeted them with his customary mixture of gravity and self-assurance. But he was, perhaps, a little puzzled: in recent years the Home Office had seemed to lose interest in him. He was, after all, now an elderly revolutionary.

He invited both men to sit on a leather sofa beneath the window and, walking up and down on the small avenue of carpet left between his books, he politely asked them their business. Kildare wondered where he had been on the evening of the 16th, and he replied that he had stayed in bed with a chest cold from which he was now recovering. His wife and two daughters would confirm his presence in the house that night but, excuse me, had there been some kind of event? When they informed him of the death of Solomon Weil he stared at them for a moment, put his hand up to his beard, and muttered something in German.

'So you knew him, sir?'

'Yes. I knew him. He was a great scholar.' He took his hand from his beard, and looked at them gravely. 'It is an attack upon the Jew,' he said. 'It is not an attack upon Solomon Weil.' It was obvious that the police officers did not wholly understand him. 'If only you knew,' he continued, 'how in this world men can become the symbols of ideas.' Then he remembered his manners, and asked them if they would care for tea; Eleanor was summoned once again and, after she had left the room, the policemen questioned Marx more closely about his association with Weil. 'I am a Jew also, although perhaps you would not know it.' Kildare made no reply but he noticed that, although Marx was old, there was a defiance and even anger within him which he barely managed to keep in check. 'We spoke together of the old stories and legends. We discussed theology. We both lived in our books, you see.'

'But you have also been seen alone, sir, in the streets of Limehouse.'

'I love to walk. Yes, even at my age. When I walk, I can think. And there is something about those streets which excites contemplation. Shall I tell you a secret?' Still Kildare said nothing. 'I am writing a poem. In my earlier years I did nothing but compose poetry and now, in a place such as Limehouse, I can recall all the anger and sorrow of my youth. That is why I walk there.' He hardly noticed Eleanor when she brought in the tea, and she left the room as quietly as she had entered. 'But do you suspect me of being a murderer, as well? Do you think I have red hands?' The allusion was not lost upon them, since they had already examined the files on 'Carl Marx' in the Metropolitan Police Office – they had particularly noticed Detective Officer Williamson's Special Report, numbered 36228, written six years before, in which it was recommended that Mr Marx should be denied naturalisation on the grounds that he was 'the notorious German agitator, the head of the International Society, and the advocate of Communistic principles'. He had also been investigated at the time when Irish revolutionaries had attacked Clerkenwell Prison and the Home Secretary, Lord Aberdare, had placed him under surveillance after the fall of the Paris Commune in 1871.

'All I see upon your hands,' Kildare replied, 'is the ink that you use.'

'That is good. That is how it should be. Sometimes I believe that I am made of ink and paper. Tell me now, how was Solomon killed?' Kildare looked across at the door of the study, which Eleanor had left open, and Marx closed it very quietly. 'Is there something . . .'

'The details are unpleasant, sir.'

'Tell me everything, if you would be so kind.' Marx listened intently as Kildare explained how the skull of Solomon Weil had been crushed with a blunt instrument, probably a mallet, and how the body had then been mutilated. He also described how various organs had been draped around the room, and how the penis had been found on the open page of Hartlib's *Knowledge of Sacred Things* across the entry for 'golem'. That would be the name he would read in the newspapers. 'So now they call this murderer a golem, do they?' Marx was very angry, and for a few moments he allowed the full force of his nature to be revealed to the two detectives. 'So they absolve themselves of their responsibilities, and declare that the Jew is killed by a Jewish monster! Make no mistake about it, gentlemen. It is the Jew who has been killed and mutilated, not Solomon Weil. It is the Jew who has been violated, and now they wash their own hands clean!'

'But a prostitute has also been foully mutilated, sir. She was not a Hebrew.'

'But do you see how this murderer strikes at the very symbols of the city? The Jew and the whore are the scapegoats in the desert of London, and they must be ritually butchered to appease some terrible god. Do you understand that?'

'So you think it is some kind of conspiracy, or secret society?'

Karl Marx waved away the question with his hand. '*Die Philosophen haben die Welt nur verschieden interpretier.*'

'Sir?'

'I cannot interpret it for you in that sense, gentlemen. I am talking only of the real forces which have created these deaths. Murder is part of history, you see. It is not outside history. It is the symptom, not the cause, of a great disease. You know, in the prisons of England, more convicts die at the hands of their fellows than by the judicial process.'

'I don't follow you there.'

'I mean that the streets of this city are a prison for those who walk in them.'

At that moment there was a gentle tap upon the door and Eleanor, staying outside, asked if the gentlemen would care for more tea. No, they were refreshed and required no more; so she came in to remove the tray. She had something of her mother's poise and once indomitable energy but she had also inherited her father's innate theatricality – to such an extent, in fact, that, like her sister, Jenny, she was intent upon a career on the stage. She had already taken lessons from Madame Clairmont in Berners Street, but, although she had always enjoyed the low comedy of the halls, in such a respectable family as her own a career as *comique* or *danseuse* was quite out of the question. So she had begun to pursue a more serious course and in fact, earlier that week, had been promised her first part in *Vera, or the Nihilist* by Oscar Wilde. Her role was to be that of Vera Sabouroff, the daughter of an innkeeper, and she was mentally rehearsing one of her lines – 'They are hungry and wretched. Let me go to them' – when she came into her father's study to remove the tray.

Her father was accustomed to her presence, and simply continued with his conversation. 'The dramatists treat the streets as theatre, but it is a theatre of oppression and cruelty.'

'They are hungry and wretched. Let me go to them.'

'What was that, Lena?'

She had spoken out her line, without realising she had done so. 'Nothing, Father. I was thinking aloud,' she whispered as she left the room.

The two detectives were not disposed to stay much longer in the old man's company; but they listened to him politely enough, as he strode up and down the avenue of carpet. 'Do you know French, by any chance?' he asked them. 'Do you know what I mean when I say that *le mort saisit le vif*?'

'Has it something to do with death, sir?'

'It could be so. It can be translated in any number of ways.' He went over to the window; from here, he could see a small park where children came to play. 'It also has something to do with history, and the past.' He stared down at a small boy carrying a hoop. 'And I suppose that Solomon Weil was the last of his line.' He turned to face the police detectives. 'What will happen to his books? They cannot be dispersed. They must be secured.' They looked at him in surprise for asking such a question and now, at last, they rose to leave without answering him. They did not believe that they had found their murderer, although Marx's alibi would have to be thoroughly investigated and, for the next few days, he would be followed whenever he left the house in Maitland Park Road.

He remained in his study after they had gone, and tried to recall the details of his last conversation with Solomon Weil. He took up a sheet of paper and, still standing, made brief notes on all that he could remember. There had been one incidental exchange which still remained with him. They had been discussing the beliefs of a sect of Jewish Gnostics who flourished in Cracow in the mid-eighteenth century; their central article of faith concerned a form of perpetual reincarnation in the lower world, through which the inhabitants of the earth were continually reborn in other places and in other circumstances. The malevolent spirits of the lower air could sometimes divide a departing soul into two or three 'flames' or 'flashes', so that the elements of the same person might be distributed into more than one body of the newly born. The demons had one other power, granted to them by Jehovah who is the evil god of this world: certain remarkable men would be restored to earth in the full knowledge of their previous life and identity but, on pain of everlasting torture, they could never reveal that knowledge. If they managed to sustain another natural cycle of generation upon this earth, then their spirit would finally be released. 'Do you know that you are Isaiah,' Solomon Weil had asked Marx that night, 'or perhaps you are Ezekiel?'

He went over to the window once more, and looked down at the children. Was his old friend even now waking up to another life on earth? Was he one of the chosen, who would know that he had once been Solomon Weil? Or had his soul already been released? But it was all nonsense.

He walked to his shelves, and took down *Dialogues of Three Templars on Political Economy* by Thomas De Quincey.

Twenty

I believe that in a past life I must have been a great actress. As soon as I walked upon the stage with Doris, even before the gas had been lit, I felt quite at my ease. Of course in those early days I was merely the prompter and play-copier, no higher in station than the general utility man or the callboy – I never thought to sing or dance, any more than the limelight man would dream of becoming a comic patterer. But, as I said, the stage was my element.

My first days were spent watching Dan Leno in rehearsal with Charlie 'They Call Me Dizzy' Boyd, and my employment was to write down all the 'trimmings' and 'chaff' which occurred to them as they went through the script. I would hear Dan say, 'That wouldn't make a bad line, would it?' or, 'Can you see your way to adding this little bit of business?' and I knew that I would have to write furiously in order to keep up with what he called his 'spontaneising'. He was still very young but he could already draw upon an infinite fund of pathos and comic sorrow: I often wondered where it came from, not finding it in myself, but I presume that there was some little piece of darkness in his past. He was always laughing, he was never still, and he had a way of saying the most ordinary things so that you never forgot them. We were passing the Tower of London one day, on our way back from the Effingham in Whitechapel, and he leaned out of the window to look at it. He kept on staring until we turned down the next street, and then he settled back in the carriage with a sigh. 'Now that's a building,' he said, 'that satisfies a long-felt want.' It was the way he said it, too, not like a cockney slangster but, as he used to put it, in a melodious melancholy manner of mirth.

So I loved those early days, as I watched and listened to them gagging on the stage. 'Tell me, officer,' Charlie was saying, 'are you flying by the seat of your pantaloons or sitting on the fly of your pantaloons?'

'That's too strong.' Dan always came down hard on that type of humour. 'I'll bring you round to your song, don't you think? And then I'll come down to the pit and start my monologue.' That song was Charlie's speciality – 'Yesterday She Gave Me Twins, Just To Show There's No Hard Feelings' – and Dan took on the role of Charlie's much put-upon, much harassed wife. 'Yes, he took me to the hospital. Such a lovely place it was. Full of beds. The nurse comes up to me and says, "Are you here because of him?" "Well, dear," I said, "he paid the bus fare." Didn't we all laugh? Then I said to her, "If you'll just relieve me of this little burden, I'll be on my way." "When are you due?" she says."Not the baby, dear. Him." Oh, we laughed.' Dan stopped then, and looked over at me. 'It hasn't got that certain spark, has it?'

I shook my head. 'It's not quite motherly enough.'

Dan turned to Charlie, who was silently performing his favourite trick of walking backwards in perfect tempo. (I had once seen him on the stage of the Savoy Variety, trying to fool a constable on guard outside a grand party by walking backwards and pretending to leave rather than enter. It was memorable.) 'What do you think, Charlie? Was I motherly?'

'Don't ask me, dear.' He had become motherly himself, in

sympathy. 'I've had so many kids that I think Noah must have got to me. Something very old and hard, anyway.'

Of course there were often jokes and remarks which I pretended not to hear: it's natural for hall folk to bring out the blue bag, as they say, but I wanted to convince Dan that I was as innocent as any Columbine in the panto. I wanted to save myself for the stage. Doris, the goddess of wire-walking, was always very good to me. She had listened to my orphan's story, and had decided to 'keep an eye out' for me. We slept together on cold nights, and I would press up against her night-dress to get the beauty of her hot. And we used to talk as we snuggled – we used to dream of having the Prince of Wales out front, and how he would come round to shake hands with us after the performance, or of how some rich admirer would send us five carnations a day until we agreed to marry him. Our mutual friend Tottie Golightly, a warbler and funny female, sometimes joined us for a little bit of mash and sausage in our room. She was the most fashionably dressed creature, with high button boots that shone like diamonds in the gas lamp, but on stage she wore a battered yellow hat, a top-coat three sizes too big for her and a pair of ancient shoes. She always came on brandishing an old green umbrella like a gigantic lettuce leaf. 'Now what about this?' she used to say, waving it about. 'Stupendous, ain't it? Magnificent, ain't it? You could go into the Channel with this, and never get wet. Am I right, or is any other woman?' That was her catch phrase, and she could never begin it without the house shouting out the rest with her. Her famous song was 'I'm a Woman of Very Few Words'; after she had finished it she would leave the stage for a few seconds, and then return in gleaming frock-coat, trousers and monocle to warble 'I Saw Her Once at the Window'. I noticed everything, you see, and remembered everything; I think that, even then, I was waiting impatiently for the day when I could put on make-up and costume as well.

Little Victor Farrell was another artist who, unfortunately, took a shine to me. He was no more than four feet in height, but he made a great impression on the public with his character of 'The Midshipmite'. He used to follow me about everywhere, but when I told him to blow away he would give one of his sarcastic little smiles and pretend to wipe his eyes on a handkerchief which was almost as big as he was. 'Let's go down to the Canteen for a chop,' he said one night after we had been playing at the Old Mo. 'Do you feel like a bit of meat, Lizzie?' I had just finished cleaning out the green room, and I was too tired to give him the elbow; in any case, I was famished. So we went downstairs below the stage: it was like a refreshment cellar, but it was patronised only by artists and their friends. These 'friends' were the usual stage-door Johnnies and swells who went after any female in the business – but they never came after me, not when they had taken one look at me and realised that I would no more lift my skirts for them than I would for the devil.

There were no fancy frescoes or flowers in the Canteen, just a few plain tables and chairs with a big cracked mirror against one wall where they could all reflect upon their bleary faces. It smelled of tobacco and mutton chops, with a bit of spilled gin and beer to add savour. I hated the place, to tell you the truth, but, as I said, I was hungry. Little Victor Farrell would not let go of my arm, just as if he wanted to put me on show like the stuffed parrot he used in his 'Midshipmite' routine, and he steered me to a table where Harry Turner was brooding over a glass of stout. Harry rose from his chair when I came over – he always was a gentleman – and Victor asked if he would have another, to which he graciously assented. Harry was Statisti-con, the Memory Man, and there was never a date or a fact which he couldn't recall on the stage. He told me his story once – how he was almost crushed to death as a child in a street accident, by one of those old-fashioned postilions, and had to spend three months in bed. He decided to read everything he could and found himself memorising history dates, just for the pleasure of it; he never looked back. He still had a limp from where the wheel of the carriage went over his leg, but he had a sounder mind than anyone else I ever met. 'Tell me, Harry,' I said, just to pass the time while Victor went over to the bar. 'What was the date when the Old Mo was built?'

'Lizzie, you know I don't like to do it off the stage.'

'Just the one?'

'It was opened on the 11th November, 1823, having previously seen service as a chapel for the Sisters of Mercy. The original foundations were dug up on the 5th October, 1820, when they were found to date from the sixteenth century. Happy now?'

Victor had come back with the needful, and was already exchanging a few silent gestures with his friends – a wink and a nod go a long way with hall folk. 'Give us the use of that memory, Harry. Who's the old file over there?' Victor was looking towards an elderly party sitting very close to a lady comique, and looking altogether snug. 'Look at that ring,' he said. 'He must be putrid with money. Rolling in loof.'

'The oldest man in the country,' Harry said, 'was Thomas Parr who died in 1653 at the age of one hundred and fifty-three. You can't put a good man down.'

'I know where you can put a good man up,' Victor whispered to me. I took his hand gently, and then pushed his finger so far back that you could hear him screaming all over the Canteen. I only relented when the others stopped and looked at us; Victor explained that I had trod on one of his corns.

'Will that learn you?' I whispered fiercely to him.

'For a woman, Lizzie, you've got a lot of strength.' He paused to examine his bruised fingers. 'Do accept my most profound apologies. Do you think I put myself forward too much?'

'Don't you ever forget that I am an innocent.'

'You *must* be over fifteen, Lizzie.'

'No, I *mustn't*. Now go and order me a baked potato before I damage you again.'

Victor was one of those 'have-another-with-me' boys. I knew he did the low halls and was paid with what we called 'wet money'; he told me so himself, and he was proud of the fact that he could drink as much as any reasonably sized man – 'putting a quart into a pint pot' was his way of expressing it. That night he did himself proud; he was pitching and tossing all over the place and, when he slipped under the table, I allowed him to look up me for a few moments. But when he felt my ankle I gave him such a savage kick that he came out on the other side. I was about to get up and kick him again, when a young man came hurrying over to the table. 'Do you require any assistance?' he asked me. I recognised him at once: it was John Cree, the reporter from the *Era* who had come up to Doris when we were performing at the Washington.

'Please help me, sir,' I said. 'I should never have been led into this dreadful place.'

He escorted me up the stairs and took me out into the little alley by the side of the theatre. 'Are you perfectly well?' He waited while I composed myself. 'You look pale.'

'I have been very ill used,' I replied. 'But I think I must have some guardian angel who saves me from evil.'

'Can I escort you anywhere? The streets, in such a place as this . . .'

'No, sir. I can find my own way. I am accustomed to the night.' And so he left me, while I purged the tobacco smoke with lungfulls of London air. What a strange night it had become, and it was as yet far from over. For, just a few hours after I had met John Cree, at first light, the body of Little Victor Farrell was found in a basement area two streets away: his neck had been broken, no doubt because of some drunken fall. He had left the Canteen 'highly schmozzled', as one of his fellow inebriates had said, and it was believed that he had wandered through the night and somehow tripped down the stairs which led to the basement. 'The Midshipmite' was no more.

We had a matinee the following day, and Uncle was acting the inconsolable. 'He was a real mammoth comique,' he said to me, with a handkerchief poised in his hand, 'even though he was just a little one. I thought he could hold his drink but, alas, as Shakespeare used to say, I was very much mistaken.' At that moment drink was holding Uncle, since he had already been given 'just the one' out of sympathy by most of the artistes. 'He started as a busker, Lizzie. He was busking and pitching by the time he was two feet and a half.' He raised his handkerchief, but only to blow his fat nose. 'I remember when he first came on at the old Apollo in Marylebone. He was billed as The Shrimp With Feeling. Did he ever sing you "The Lodging House Cat"?'

'Never you mind, Uncle.' I gave him a little kiss upon his damp forehead. 'He was a great sparkler, and now he's moved on to the great stage in the sky.'

'I doubt if there will be variety there, dear.' He gave a little snort, halfway between a laugh and a sigh. 'Ah well, all flesh is grass.'

I sensed that my opportunity had come. 'I was wondering, Uncle. You know that Victor was like a second father to me—'

'Yes indeed.'

'—and I was hoping to pay a little tribute to him?'

'Go on, dear.'

'I was wondering if you would let me take on his act this evening. I know all his songs by heart.' He looked earnestly at me for a moment, and so I carried on talking more quickly. 'There is a gap in the bill, I know, and as I wanted to give him a proper send-off . . .'

'But you're a good few inches taller, Lizzie. Would it be right?'

'That would be the joke of it, you see. Wouldn't Victor laugh?'

'I don't know about that, dear. But I suppose you can show me.'

In fact I had studied Little Victor very carefully indeed, so I knew both the patter and the business. Even though I was not in costume I sang 'If Ever There was a Damned Scamp' in front of Uncle, and jumped up and down in the approved 'Midshipmite' manner.

'You've got the right bounce,' he said.

'Victor was training me. He said I had such a funny dial it was a pity to waste it.'

'And you certainly manage a warble.'

'Thank you, Uncle. Do you think Victor would have wanted me to have the chance to show it?'

He was silent for a minute, and I could tell that he was speculating on the novelty of it: what if he could make a funny female or a legmania dancer out of me? 'Do you think,' he said, 'we could pretend that you were Little Victor's daughter? Out of tiny acorns, you know . . .'

'I did always think of him as a second father. He was so good to me.'

'I know he was, my dear. He was very paternal.'

So, after a few tears were shed, it was agreed that I should go on that night with Little Victor's routine. I think Dan disapproved of the scheme but, when he saw the enthusiasm shining from my face, he could not bring himself to forbid it; I had been banking on that. You can imagine my nervousness as I dressed up for the first time: Little Victor's clothes were too small for me, naturally, but that was the joke of it. As I said to Doris while we were changing, it's a funny thing how seawater can shrink a midshipmite's duds. We were in the green room with some of the other girls and boys, all milling about and laughing with the kind of gaiety that comes after a death. No one had loved, or even really liked, Little Victor – in any case hall folk mourn another's passing by trying to be that little bit brighter.

'Quart – 'ervn – 'our.' It was the call-boy.

Doris opened the door and shouted after him, 'What's the house, Sid?'

'All pudding. Easy as you like.'

I was going on between the ballet dancers and the Ethiopian serenaders; the property man saw me shaking in the corner, so he came over and put his arm around me. 'You know what they say, Lizzie, don't you? A bit of chaff sets you up. If they give you the bird, you whistle back at them.' It was not the most reassuring speech, but no doubt he meant well.

When I was announced as Little Victor's daughter, the house went wild. Everyone knew about his accident – it was that kind of neighbourhood – and when I came on in his old clothes singing 'All for the Sake of Dear Father' I knew that I had got them. I milked the death a little, but then I put in some patter I had memorised from Victor's act, as well as some old comic business on the subject of lost handkerchiefs. But I also had a trick of my own. I knew how strange my hands were still, so large and so scarred, so I had put on a pair of white gloves which served to emphasise their size. I held my hands out in front of me and sighed, 'Look at them rotten cotton gloves!' They loved it, since it was one of those phrases which somehow strike a chord, and then I followed it up with that ditty which causes such a furore, 'It's Sunday All Over Again'. I suppose that I could have gone

98

on for ever, but I saw Uncle beckoning to me from the wings. I hurried over to him while they were still whistling and banging their feet.

'Give them one more refrain,' he said, 'and then come off when they ask for more.' So I skipped back onto the stage and sang the second verse.

> No duck must lay, no cat must kitten,
> No hen must leave her nest though sittin',
> Though painful is her situation
> She must not think of incubation,
> For no business must be done on Sunday,
> They'll have to put it off till Monday.

I sang it especially well because I remembered my mother, and the way she used to drag me off to the little tin-roof chapel and turn my own Sunday into a time of misery. And, as I danced upon the stage, I had the most pleasurable sensation that I was stamping upon her grave. How I exulted! They loved me for it. There was a shower of coppers and, despite Uncle's request, I 'obliged again' with a chorus of 'Up Goes the Price of Meat'. Then there was so much whistling and stamping that I could hardly hear myself thank them. I was in such a blaze of glory I might have died and gone to heaven. Of course, in a manner of speaking, I had died. My old self was dead and the new Lizzie, Little Victor's daughter with the rotten cotton gloves, had been born at last.

I believe that Dan was still annoyed with me for taking over Little Victor's act, but he realised that I had acquitted myself very well. I was still a pigeon in the world of the halls but, over the next few weeks and months, I steadily crept up the bills. I made one song my very own, 'The Hole in the Shutter, or I'm a Little Too Young to Know', but I soon realised that I had much more talent in the comic line than as an ordinary dancer or singer. I was a good spoofer, and very soon I had my own catch phrase printed after my name – 'Funny Without Being Vulgar'. I can still remember all my scenes perfectly well. I pretended to be a bathing machine, and sang 'Why Can't We Have the Sea in London?' and then I used to kill them with 'I Don't Suppose He'll Do it Again for Months and Months and Months'. I never saw the dirt in it, not me, and I delivered it as a harmless little song about a wife whose husband took her once a year on a steam-boat outing to Gravesend. It must have been the way I pronounced 'do', but they used to scream.

I never knew where the comedy came from. I was not a particularly funny female off the stage, and I suppose that in some ways I was even prone to misery. It was as if I had some other personality which walked out from my body every time I stood in the glare of the gas, and sometimes she even surprised me with her slangster rhymes and cockney stuff. She had her own clothes by now – a battered bonnet, long skirt and big boots suited her best – and, as I slowly put them on, she began to appear. Sometimes she was uncontrollable, though, and one night at the Palace in Smithfield she began to perform a burlesque medley of the Bible with the most wicked patter about David and Goliath. There was a large Hebrew element in that particular hall, and they loved it, but the next day a deputation from the Society For The Propagation of the Gospel complained to the manager. What they were doing there in the first place I do not know, but Little Victor's daughter had to drop that particular item. Of course I had my admirers: ask any artiste and she will tell you how pestered we all are with stage-door Johnnies. They came on strong, but most of them were no more than twopenny bus conductors or City clerks. Fortunately Doris and I were still sharing a crib off the New Cut, so we just used to march straight past them. 'I'm no

Blondin,' she said once, 'but I can walk in a straight line when I have to.' She was still the goddess of wire-walking, at least to her admirers, but Little Victor's Daughter was soon spoken of as quite 'the thing' in variety circles. We were still the best of pals, though, and liked nothing better, after the show, than to retire to our room and share a nice plate of bacon and greens. I was always overwrought after my performance – and, to judge by Doris's concern, sometimes a trifle hysterical – but after a while Little Victor's Daughter would fade away and Lizzie would come back. I had to be careful not to contradict the orphan story I had sold her when I first arrived in lodgings, but that was the easy part: I had invented a whole history which made me much more interesting to myself, and I really had no difficulty in sustaining it.

Sometimes Austin would join us with some bottles of stout, and he would reminisce about the old days when he was a boy soprano in the Caves of Harmony and the Shrines of Song. 'I had a lovely voice,' he told us confidentially one night, 'and when I appeared in the tea-gardens I was like an angel from heaven. I could have been legit, ducks, I could have been another Betty. But professional jealousy held me back. I was kept off the boards out of fear, you know. I was denied Drury Lane. Ah well, dears, shall I be Mother?' He poured us another stout, while he and Doris began to share the gossip of the day – how the ventriloquist was courting a young 'burnt cork' dancer from Basildon, and how Clarence Lloyd had been found in his dame's dress outside a seamen's mission dead drunk. Poor Clarence had been taken into custody for importuning, or so Austin said, and had been led to the station singing 'In My First Husband's Time'. But somehow our conversation always came around to Dan, or 'Mr Leno' as Austin insisted on calling him when he was drunk. Dan always remained something of a mystery to us, although his mystery was really his artistry which was obvious even to the lowest class of audience. 'They talk of Tennyson and Browning,' Austin used to say, 'and I am the last person to deny the genius of those two gentlemen, but believe me, girls, Mr Leno is *it*.'

It was true: Dan was only fifteen then, but he played so many parts that he hardly had time to be himself. And yet, somehow, he was always himself. He was the Indian squaw, the waiter, the milkmaid, or the train driver, but it was always Dan conjuring people out of thin air. When he played the little shop-keeper, he made you see the customers who argued with him and the street arabs who plagued him. When he murmured, in an aside, 'I'll just go and unchain that Gorgonzola' you could smell the cheese and, when he pretended to shoot it and put it out of its misery, you could see the rifle and hear the shot. How they all roared when he first appeared on the stage; he would run down to the footlights, give a drumroll with his feet, and raise his right leg before bringing it down with a great thump upon the boards. Then suddenly he was the sour-faced spinster on the look-out for a man.

'He is endless,' Uncle said to me one night as we were leaving the Desiderata in Hoxton. 'Completely endless.' He was holding my arm rather too tightly but, since he had been so good to me in the past, I disengaged myself very gently. He did not seem to notice. 'What would you say, Lizzie dear, to a nice parcel of fish and chips? Put something hot inside you, do.' I was about to plead tiredness, when who should we see coming out of the shadow of Leonard's Rents but the young man who had saved me from little Victor's attentions so many months before. I had glimpsed him on other occasions since then, and had been expecting him to interview me for the *Era*. Unfortunately, he was always very respectful and kept his distance. He raised his hat to me when we passed and, perhaps thinking that Uncle was becoming a little too close and friendly, he asked me how I was.

Uncle gave him a 'heavy swell' look and was about to pass on, but I stopped for a moment. 'It is good of you to ask, Mr . . .'

'John Cree of the *Era*.'

'I am very well, Mr Cree. My manager is just escorting me to my brougham.' I was very dignified indeed, and even Uncle was impressed. But, from that time forward, I often thought of Mr John Cree.

Twenty-One

On the morning Karl Marx was interviewed by the police detectives, George Gissing was sitting in his customary place beneath the dome of the British Museum Reading Room. There were two long tables reserved for ladies, and Gissing always sat as far away from them as possible. This was not because he was in any sense a misogynist – far from it – but he was still young enough to maintain the illusion that the pursuit of knowledge must be a cloistered and self-denying activity, in which the mind itself must suffuse or overpower the body. In any case he came to the Reading Room partly to escape what he termed, in homage to Nietzsche whom he had just been reading, 'the presence of the Female Will'. This was not some theoretical interest on his part, since in fact he believed that his entire life had been destroyed by the presence of one particular woman.

He had been eighteen years old at the time; he had been an eager and promising student at Owens College in Manchester, and was preparing for his entrance examinations to the University of London when he met Nell Harrison. She was seventeen, but was already an alcoholic who earned her drink by prostitution. Gissing became infatuated with her after a chance meeting in a Manchester public house; he was an idealist who believed that, in the best theatrical tradition, he could 'rescue' Nell. Literature was everything to him then, and in the shape of this young woman he invested all of his instincts for narrative and for pathetic drama. It is also possible that her name evoked childhood memories of Little Nell's doomed wanderings in Dickens's *The Old Curiosity Shop*, but it is more likely that the romantically inclined literary young man became obsessed with her because of her drunken prostitution – here was a modern outcast, who might have come from the pages of Emile Zola. In that sense he was wrong to blame her for all of his misfortunes, because they were in part the result of his own delusions.

The tragedy of his life happened soon after their meeting. He used his scholarship funds to feed and clothe her; he even bought her a sewing machine (then a relatively new invention) so that she could earn a proper living as a seamstress. But she drank away the shillings he found for her and, as a result of her constant demand for money, he began to steal from his contemporaries at Owens College. In the spring of 1876 he was caught by the college authorities, arrested, and sentenced to a month's hard labour in Manchester Prison. He had been the most gifted and learned student of his generation but, at a stroke, all hope of academic and social advancement seemed to have gone for ever. He travelled to America after his release, but found it impossible to survive. And so he returned to England or rather, more pertinently, to Nell. He could not escape her (perhaps he did not wish to escape her) and together they came to London; they moved from cheap lodging to cheap lodging, always moving on when Nell's trade was discovered. Yet still he clung to her. This sounds like a mere melodrama from the London stage, something which might be performed on the boards of a 'theatre of sensation' like the Cosmotheka in Bell Street, but it is a true story – the truest story George Gissing ever completed. He was an avid scholar, an accomplished classicist and linguist who in other circumstances would already have been a member of one of the ancient universities or a lecturer at the new University College in London; but instead he was attached to a vulgar prostitute, a drunkard and a slattern who had destroyed all hopes he might have harboured for conventional advancement. This was how Gissing viewed his whole life and yet, in the spring of 1880, he married Nell. Now, as he sat in the warmth of the Reading Room, he realised that not even this formal union had been able to divert her from her customary ways.

He had not altogether lost his own literary ambitions, however; he managed to earn a living as a tutor, but he was also hoping to write essays and reviews for the London periodicals. 'Romanticism and Crime' had been judged a great success by the editor of the *Pall Mall Review*, for example, and Gissing was now ready to complete the first draft of his article on Charles Babbage. He had also, with the help of some small savings, managed to arrange the publication of his first novel in the spring of this year (just a few days after his marriage to Nell); it was entitled *Workers in the Dawn* and opened with a sentence which was later to have a peculiar resonance in his own life: 'Walk with me, reader, into Whitecross Street.' By the autumn, however, it had sold only forty-nine copies, despite some modest praise in the *Academy* and the *Manchester Examiner*, and he realised that in the immediate future he would have to rely upon the more certain rewards of journalism. So now he laboured over the remarkable inventions of Charles Babbage for the sake of an article.

But Gissing was not a scientist, and at this moment he was struggling to understand Babbage's principles of numerical form in the context of Jeremy Bentham's notion of 'felicific calculus'. The connection may appear a fortuitous and even strange one but, in the intellectual culture of the period, science, philosophy and social theory were more readily joined.

Gissing was even now attempting to relate the concept of the 'greatest good' with recent experiments in social statistics, with special emphasis being placed on those formidable figures which had emerged from what Charles Babbage called his Analytical Engine. This was in many respects the forerunner of the modern computer since it was a machine, or engine, which combined and dispersed numbers over a network of mechanically related parts. The particular motive for combining the research of Bentham and Babbage (as far as Gissing could understand the literature upon the subject) was to calculate the greatest amount of need or misery in any given place, and then to predict its possible spread. 'To be exactly informed about the lot of humankind,' one Benthamite had written in a pamphlet entitled 'The Elimination of Poverty in the Metropolitan Area', 'is to create the conditions in which it can be ameliorated. We must know before we can understand, and statistic evidence is the surest form of evidence currently in our possession.'

Of course Gissing himself was acquainted with poverty, and even degradation; he had lived among them ever since he had come to London with Nell. He was now only twenty-three but had already written, 'Few men, I am sure, have led so bitter a life.' And yet he could hardly believe that, if men were 'informed' of his condition, his lot would in any sense be improved; for him, to be a statistic or an object of enquiry would mean that he was degraded still further. He understood that this was no doubt an aspect of his already shrinking and sensitive temperament, when any reminder of his condition encroached upon him as a fresh agony, but he also had more general reservations. To be informed by statistical evidence was neither to know nor to understand; it was an intermediate stage, in which the enquirer remained at a distance from which the true reality could not properly be seen. To be informed merely – well, it meant having no sense of value or principle but only a shadow knowledge of forms and numbers. Gissing could easily imagine a future world in which the entire population was attuned to Bentham's 'felicific calculus' or to Babbage's calculating machines – he even considered writing a novel upon the subject – but by then they would be no more than the dumb witnesses or passive spectators of a reality which would wholly have escaped them. This was the reason for his difficulties with the article.

The day before, he had visited the manufacturing works in Limehouse where the last calculating machine had been assembled. As early as the 1830s Charles Babbage had managed to construct a 'Difference Engine' which could perform simple sums, but he soon became preoccupied with the far more complicated 'Analytical Engine' which could add, subtract, multiply and divide as well as solve both algebraic and numerical equations; it had also been able to print out the results of its calculations onto stereotype plates. This was the engine which Gissing had come to see. He was a novelist rather than a philosopher, and had decided that the best way of understanding Babbage's concepts was to look upon the great object itself. The manufactory, which housed both the calculating engine and two workshops, was situated at the lower end of Limehouse Causeway just beyond the church of St Anne's. It was said that Babbage had chosen this location because of his fascination with the large white pyramid which had been erected in the church grounds, and he is supposed to have remarked to a friend that 'the number of stones combined in a triangular pyramid can be calculated by simply adding successive differences, the third of which is constant'. But the friend did not understand him and, in any case, the truth is more prosaic: Babbage had worked before with Mr Turner, a maker of machine tools, and had purchased the building near that gentleman's house along the Commercial Road in order to expedite his work. Gissing found it easily enough and was greeted by a now very elderly Turner whose present function, according to the terms of Babbage's will, was to maintain the engine 'until the public mind is fully prepared for its use'.

Gissing presented him with a letter from the editor of the *Pall Mall Review* which confirmed his identity, and his intention to write about the work of Charles Babbage; such precautions were necessary because there had, all that year, been rumours of industrial spies sent over from France to glean the latest mechanical intelligence. Mr Turner took an inordinate amount of time reading the letter, which he seemed to regard as a document of the utmost complexity, and then he returned it to Gissing with an old-fashioned bow. 'Would you care to see the engine at once?' was the first question he put to him.

'I should very much like to see it. Thank you.' Gissing had a harsh and nervous manner of speaking which, perhaps, reflected the chaos which he sensed within himself.

'Then if you would follow me.' He took Gissing through an old workshop which had obviously not been used for some time: it was perfectly neat and, with its wooden tables scrubbed and its instruments highly polished, had become a finished memorial to the work of Babbage and of Turner himself. Here they had laboured together over the wheels and cogs which comprised what was called the 'mill' of the calculating engine. Samuel Rogers, the famous wit, professed to believe that it had been named in honour of John Stuart Mill; but Babbage assured him that it was a reference to the Albion Mills by the Westminster Bridge Road which he had first seen as a child. Those flour-making devices had convinced him even then of the benefits of mechanical advancement.

'If you care to go through, sir. Do mind your step, for the stone can be treacherous.' The old man led Gissing into the great room which housed Babbage's calculating engine; a row of neo-Gothic windows decorated the upper level of the chamber, and their light filtered downwards onto the glistening machine. This was the dream of Charles Babbage – a computer built more than a hundred years before any of its modern counterparts, which now gleamed like a hallucination in the light of September 1880. The scientists and professional mechanics of the nineteenth century had instinctively turned away from it, without realising why they had done so: this engine was not in its proper time and, as yet, could have no real existence upon the earth.

So how had it come to be created? Charles Babbage had once been found in the reading room of the Analytical Society, poring over a table of logarithms, and a colleague asked him what problem he was considering. 'I wish to God,' he replied, 'that these calculations could be accomplished by steam.' It is one of the most wonderful sentences of the nineteenth century, and in an oblique fashion confirms another of Babbage's extraordinary suppositions. He had once declared that 'the pulsations of the air, once set in motion by the human voice, continue into infinity', and he went on to speculate about this constant movement of atoms. 'Thus considered,' he wrote, 'what a strange chaos is this wide atmosphere we breathe! Every atom, impressed with good and with ill, retains at once the motion which philosophers and sages have imparted to it, mixed and combined in ten thousand ways with all that is worthless and base. The air itself is one vast library, on whose pages are for ever written all that man has ever said or woman whispered.' Charles Dickens read this account, which was published as part of Babbage's 'Advertisement' for an edition of his *Ninth Bridgewater Treatise*, and was profoundly impressed by a vision which so closely resembled his own. Certainly it seemed to correspond with Dickens's understanding of London, amplified in *Bleak House* and *Little Dorrit*, but in fact

Babbage's ideas were most effectively conveyed in *The Mystery of Edwin Drood* – Dickens's unfinished novel which was preoccupied with the themes of death and murder and which opened, curiously enough, in the very area of Limehouse where George Gissing now stood.

'Here, sir, are the cards.' Mr Turner took from his pocket a number of perforated pieces of zinc. 'Some are variable cards. The rest are numerical or combinatorial. Mr Babbage got the notion from the workings of a loom, and he applied it here.' But Gissing was staring at the mechanism itself. It seemed to be in four separate sections, with a central engine rising some fifteen feet towards the roof; to Gissing it was a giant form of rods and wheels and squared pieces of metal, so imposing and yet so alien an artifice that he was tempted to kneel down and worship it as if it were some strange new god. How could such a thing have been erected in the middle of teeming Limehouse? 'The heart of the engine is here, sir.' Mr Turner walked over to the largest section of the machine, and gently touched a tall vertical axis of wheels and cards. 'Mr Babbage devised a mechanism which allowed the engine to anticipate the numbers which had to be carried over. It stored the operations it had already used, and could then predict the movement of the figures. Do you see the beauty of it?'

'It is a very ingenious contrivance.' Gissing hardly understood what he was being told but it already seemed to him, as to his contemporaries, some eccentric monstrosity; he had just been reading Swinburne's study of William Blake, for an article he had proposed to the *Westminster Review*, and the parallel that occurred to him was with Blake's Prophetic Books. These works – the Analytical Engine and Blake's mad verses – seemed equally the work of curious and obsessive men who laboured in the production of designs which only they themselves could fully comprehend.

'The mill itself has ten distinct features, which include the digit counting apparatus, the repeating apparatus and the combinatorial counting apparatus. By means of these racks and cages, sir, the carriages of the engine can step down or step up. The cards here push forward the levers, which in turn cause the motion of these wheels.'

'I am afraid it is baffling to someone like myself. It requires too great a leap into the mysteries of mechanism.'

'But if you wish to write—'

Gissing anticipated the criticism. 'That is true, of course. But I intend to discuss Mr Babbage's social philosophy which, I am sure, lay behind all of these calculations. He was a philanthropist, was he not, who believed in the greatest good of the greatest number?'

'Oh, that was always his concern. He came here two days before his death, sir, to superintend the making of some new number cards out of zinc. He was as busy as ever. Always the same. Always with his energy.'

'He died eight or nine years ago?'

'October 1871. I had been his foreman for twenty years, sir, and knew how he was harassed and frustrated on every side by officials and scientists who could not understand him. He was highly intelligent, sir, and so he was an object of suspicion to lesser men. He had the dream of a grand analytical engine to assist in the affairs of the entire nation, but it came to nothing. Now, you see, I am getting to your point.' Gissing realised that he was not dealing with a mere foreman; this man had obviously shared in the aspirations of his employer. 'There are many problems and difficulties in Limehouse, sir, as you must have realised. You need only to have walked through the streets to this manufactory, and you would have seen what no man in a Christian country should see. The loose women even ply their trade against the walls of the church opposite.' Turner

112

could hardly have suspected that the man he addressed was married to one such woman. 'And then there have been these terrible killings.'

'Corruption exists everywhere, I know. But surely it is the poverty and misery in a place such as this which bring it on?'

'That was going to be my own precise point, sir. That was what Mr Babbage also believed: if only we could calculate the incidence and growth of the poor, then we could take proper measures to alleviate their condition. I have lived along the Commercial Road for many years, sir, and I know that with notation and data we might take away all the sorrow.' Turner was not here directly quoting his employer, who had in fact written that 'the errors which arise from unsound reasoning neglecting true data are far more numerous and more durable than those which result from the absence of facts.' Babbage went on to describe the virtues of 'mechanical notation' which might be used to create tables concerning 'the atomic weight of bodies, specific gravity, elasticity, specific heat, conducting power, melting point, weight of different gases and solids, strength of different materials, velocity of flight of birds and speed of animals . . .' This was his vision of the world, in which all phenomena were notated and tabulated; it had been conjured up like some golem here, in Limehouse, among the disease and suffering.

Gissing has been looking intently at the giant machine – could this voluminous and intricate engine truly be the agent of progress and improvement? No, it could hardly be so. For why was it that he felt a shrinking uneasiness in its presence? He was tired and hungry (all he had eaten that day was a slice of bread and butter), and in his enfeebled condition he was suddenly invaded by a further and more acute sense of anxiety. It seemed to him, for a moment, that this machine was like some metal demon summoned by the sullen appetites of men.

But then the panic passed, and he was able to consider it more soberly. He no more believed in progress than he believed in science, and he could not imagine a world in which either of them proved to be an irresistible force. He had been a poor man all of his life, and was even now living with Nell in a garret room off the Tottenham Court Road, but he placed no faith in those who considered that urban poverty could be miraculously removed or even alleviated. He knew enough of London to realise that its condition was irredeemable. He thought of himself as an 'individualist', in the idiom of the time, who understood the true nature of the world. In fact, despite the connotations in the title of his first novel, *Workers in the Dawn*, Gissing was neither a radical nor a philanthropist; he had no real pity for the sufferings of the poor, except as a form of self-pity, and at a later date he was to write: 'I have always regarded as a fact of infinite pathos the ability men have to subdue themselves to the conditions of life.' He wrote, too, that 'suffering and sorrow are the great Doctors of Metaphysic'. He may have been condoning here his own failure to pursue an academic career but, in any case, was such a man likely to be convinced of the efficacy of the Analytical Engine? But then why, when he observed it glistening in the autumn light of East London, was he filled with a sense of fear? He had seen enough now. He thanked Mr Turner for showing him the engine, and stepped out into Limehouse Causeway.

A man and woman were fighting in the street and, as he passed, he smelt the unmistakable aroma of spirit drinkers; he knew it well. Then a window opened above him, and he heard a woman calling, 'As long as you live in this 'ere 'ouse, it shan't go on!' These were what Gissing knew to be the 'conditions of life', but he ought to have understood that these same 'conditions' had created the giant machine which he had just examined. There was an intimate connection between the vast computer lodged in the manufactory and the very atmosphere of Limehouse. He might have noticed, for example, the white pyramid in the grounds of the church of St Anne's which had so impressed Charles Babbage himself. A journey towards the mysteries of London might then begin with an examination of that pyramid and the Analytical Engine; both stood in some direct relation to sorrow, and to the desire for purgation or escape. Indeed this might be how the modern computer was conceived, as part of a narrative far more extraordinary and capacious than *Workers in the Dawn*.

In the novels which Gissing subsequently wrote, there are often coincidental events and chance encounters; when asked about these devices he generally declared that 'this is what happens' or 'this is the way life is'. He may have been correct in this assumption but he was also speaking from direct experience: as he now walked through Limehouse Causeway towards Scofield Street, for example, he saw his wife running across the road ahead of him. He had not seen her for three days, but he was accustomed to her sudden absences. He hardly had time to consider what she might be doing in this place, and he shouted out 'Nell!' The woman turned, and then stepped into an alley. He followed as quickly as he could, but by the time he came to the entrance of the alley she had disappeared into a warren of dilapidated lodgings which hung over it. He could not just leave her here and walk away: he guessed that she was pursuing her old profession in a fresh locality, if only to earn the money for her drink, and without any certain sense of direction he entered the house closest to him. He peered up a narrow staircase and began to climb the first flight, but then he turned around and through the porch saw his wife hastening back into the street. Once more he followed and observed her moving quickly northwards; it became a long pursuit but he kept her in sight until she came out into Whitecross Street by Fore

Lane, where she entered a mean tenement. Gissing stood on the opposite side of the street, in the shadow of a derelict coffee-shop. A German band passed as he waited there expectantly, and caused such a distraction among the taverns and beer parlours of the neighbourhood (where any diversion was welcomed) that Gissing was afraid Nell had somehow managed to slip away into the surrounding courts and alleys. He approached the house slowly but then, in a sudden moment of fury at the behaviour of his wife, he banged very loudly upon the door. It was opened at once by a small, pretty young woman who was curiously dressed in a riding outfit.

'There's no need to wake the dead,' she said in a flat, London voice. 'What is it that you want?'

'Is Nell here?'

'Nell who? Nell Gwyn? I don't know no Nell.'

'She is of middling height, with brown hair. And she has a brooch upon her dress, in the shape of a scorpion.' It was the brooch he had bought her on their wedding day just a few months before. 'She wears it on her left side.' He put his hand up to his own breast. 'Just so.'

'Many women come and go here. But not a Nell I can think of.'

'Please. She is my wife.' She had been looking past his shoulder at a crowd who had gathered beside the German band, now playing outside a chop-house, but he thought he detected the smallest expression of sympathy; still, she said nothing. 'Listen. If you see her, or learn anything about her, will you send a message to me?' He took out the pocketbook in which he had made notes about Babbage's Analytical Engine, wrote down his name and address, and then tore out the page. 'Of course I will pay you for any such service.'

She took the piece of paper, and folded it into the pleated pocket of her riding outfit. 'I will do what I can for you. But I can promise nothing.'

116

He left her then, and made his way homewards towards Tottenham Court Road in the melancholy knowledge that his entire future life was likely to be bound by these decaying streets and by his forced acquaintance with the low women who walked them. What good was literature, or literary ambition, in the face of obstacles such as these? Of what use was the Analytical Engine, with its tables and notations? Or perhaps it did possess a use – it served to remind him of what he was, a number, one of the 18 per cent of city dwellers who were sick at any given time and one of the 36 per cent who earned less than five guineas a week. He was not a man of letters, not when this dreary march homewards (to save the price of an omnibus ticket) marked the limits of his world.

But in fact Gissing had accomplished more than he knew. His subsequent essay on Charles Babbage in the *Pall Mall Review* aroused much speculation, most fruitfully in the mind of H. G. Wells who read it while still a schoolboy. But it was also seen by Karl Marx who, in the last year of his life, wrote three short paragraphs on the benefit of the Analytical Engine for the progress of international communism. His words, preserved among his posthumous papers, were taken up some forty years later when the communist government of the Soviet Union established a Science Ministry and decided to subsidise the development of an experimental arithmetic machine. The journey of a half-starved novelist to Limehouse might in that sense be said to have affected the course of human history; it may also be interesting to note that when H. G. Wells and Stalin met in Moscow in 1934 they discussed Karl Marx's notes upon the invention of Charles Babbage.

But Gissing's visit to the East End had more immediate consequences. The third attack of the Limehouse Golem, after the murders of Jane Quig and Solomon Weil, was upon the woman who had greeted Gissing at the door of the house in

Whitecross Street. It was she who was left, savagely mutilated, upon the white pyramid outside the church of St Anne's, Limehouse. The police report upon the killing noted that she was gazing at the church itself when she was found: this was a period when, perhaps under the unacknowledged influence of old superstitions, the position of the eyes of the murdered victim was considered important. Even in later years, they were photographed in case there was any truth in the belief that they would reflect the face of the murderer. But on this occasion the police report was wrong. Alice Stanton had not been gazing at the church but at a building beyond it: she had been gazing at the workshop where the Analytical Engine waited to begin its life.

Part of the riding habit was still upon her body, and the other items of that ensemble were scattered beside the dismembered limbs. It was not known why she had chosen to wear that outfit, unless it was to arouse her more depraved clients, and at the time it was not clear where she had obtained it. In fact it had belonged to Dan Leno; it was the costume he wore for his role as the female jockey, when he rode side-saddle upon an imaginary horse called 'Ted, The Nag That Wouldn't Go'. The dead woman had purchased it from the second-hand clothes dealer, whose shop upon the Ratcliffe Highway had already been visited by John Cree.

Twenty-Two

September 20, 1880: So they found her by the church, a true bride of Christ strewn across the stones in an attitude of humble worship. She had been born again. I had baptised her in her own blood, and had become her redeemer. Perhaps the identity which the public prints have given me is appropriate; after all the 'Limehouse Golem' has a somewhat spiritual connotation. I have been named after a mythological creature, and it is reassuring to know that great crimes can immediately be translated to a higher sphere. I am not committing murders. I am invoking a legend, and anything will be forgiven me as long as I remain faithful to my role.

I strolled down to the site of my last visitation yesterday afternoon, and was delighted to see some young men picking up tufts of grass and pieces of stone where the blood had been shed. I suppose they may have been in the service of the police detectives, but I prefer to believe that they were engaged in the fine art of divination. The dried blood of the slain was once used to ward off misfortune, and I left the scene in the happy knowledge that these patient labourers were earning a few pence as a result of my own exertions. I consider them my followers who, in their toil, achieve more than those policemen who demean me with their calculations and investigations.

What do they know of the real nature of murder when they surround it with coroners and bloodhounds? What happened to the hounds of hell?

My path took me down the glorious Ratcliffe Highway – soon, I hope, to be made more glorious still and as renowned as Golgotha or that field of Aztec sacrifice which Mr Parry depicted so vividly in the July issue of *The Penny Magazine*. I made my way, like any priest, to the site of the offering where the Marr family had already been put into a sound sleep. The clothes-seller was there as before, bustling among his shirts and dresses, and I greeted him cheerfully as I entered his shop. 'I remember you well, sir,' he said. 'You wished to purchase something for a maidservant, but could find nothing to your liking.'

'Well now, you see, I am here again. Our servants rule us these days.'

'I agree with you there, sir. I have one of my own.'

At that I pricked up my ears. 'And a wife? I recall that you told me of a wife.'

'One of the finest.'

'And you mentioned children?'

'Three, sir. All well and healthy, thank God.'

'Infant deaths are so common in this quarter, you must count it a great blessing. I have studied many fatalities in Limehouse.'

'You are a doctor, sir?'

'No, I am what is called a local antiquary. I know this area very well.' He became a little furtive, I thought, and so I decided to broach the subject at once. 'Perhaps it is known to you that this house has its own particular history?'

He looked towards the ceiling for a moment, where no doubt the happy family were lodged, and put a finger to his lips. 'Not to be mentioned, sir, if you please. I purchased the house cheap because of its unfortunate circumstances, but my dear wife is still uneasy in her mind. What with these latest killings—'

'Shocking.'

'That's exactly what I said myself, sir. Shocking. What is it that they call him? The Limehouse Golden?'

'Golem.'

'It must be some Jew or foreigner, sir, with such a name as that.'

'No. I don't believe so. I believe this to be an Englishman's work.'

'I can hardly believe it, sir. In the old days perhaps so, but in modern times—'

'All times are modern to those who live in them, Mr – what may I call you?'

'Gerrard, sir. Mr Gerrard.'

'Well, Mr Gerrard, enough of our idle talk. May I purchase something for my maid?'

'Of course. There are some fine articles just recently brought in.'

So I played my game with him, and examined various items of female foolery. Eventually I came away with a shawl of dyed cotton, but I knew that I would return sooner than Mr Gerrard expected.

September 21, 1880: A clear cold day with no trace of fog or mist. I surprised my wife with the gift of the shawl, but she is such a loving devoted object that I cannot resist spoiling her. So when she begged me once more to see Dan Leno at the Oxford, I surrendered. 'I have a little work to do next week,' I said. 'But when that is completed, we shall go.' It was then the strangest fancy took me: what if I allowed her to witness one of my own great acts? Would she make a good audience?

Twenty-Three

MR LISTER: I am grateful to you for your account of your early life, Mrs Cree. Everyone now perfectly understands that an association with the stage does not necessarily lead to a disordered life. But may I return to another subject? You have explained that your husband suffered from troubled fancies. Do you have anything further to add to that subject?

ELIZABETH CREE: Only that he seemed to be more than usually – I cannot find the word – more than usually disturbed during that month.

MR LISTER: You are referring to September of last year, are you not?

ELIZABETH CREE: Yes, sir. He came to me and pleaded for forgiveness. 'Forgiveness for what?' I asked him. 'I do not know,' he replied. 'I have done nothing wrong, yet I am all wrong.'

MR LISTER: And have you already stated that he was a Roman Catholic of morbid temperament?

ELIZABETH CREE: Yes, sir, I have.

MR LISTER: And so it is your considered belief, after many years of marriage, that he committed suicide while labouring under certain delusions?

ELIZABETH CREE: It is.

MR LISTER: Thank you. I have nothing more to ask you at this time.

The transcript in the Illustrated Police News Law Courts and Weekly Record *continued with the cross-examination of Mrs Cree by the barrister acting for the prosecution, Mr Greatorex.*

MR GREATOREX: Did you see him administer the poison to himself?

ELIZABETH CREE: No, sir.

MR GREATOREX: Did anyone see him do so?

ELIZABETH CREE: Not as far as I am aware.

MR GREATOREX: Now your maid, Aveline, has told this court that you generally mixed a night cordial for your husband immediately before retiring.

ELIZABETH CREE: It was just something to soothe him, sir. To ease his troubled dreams.

MR GREATOREX: Quite so. But surely if, on your testimony, he drank a bottle of port each night he had no need for a cordial?

ELIZABETH CREE: He found it useful to him. He told me so on numerous occasions.

MR GREATOREX: Were there any particular medicinal compounds in this soothing cordial?

ELIZABETH CREE: There was a soporific, sir, which I always purchased at the druggists. I believe it is called Dr Murgatroyd's Mixture. It is considered quite harmless.

MR GREATOREX: You must leave that for others to judge, Mrs Cree. And I take it that this mixture was the one about which your maid has testified?

ELIZABETH CREE: Sir?

MR GREATOREX: She informed the police detectives that she saw you mixing a white powder with the cordial.

ELIZABETH CREE: Yes. Dr Murgatroyd's is of a white nature.

MR GREATOREX: But far from soothing him in his last days, this cordial or something like it provoked violent stomach pains and profuse sweating. Is that not so?

ELIZABETH CREE: As I said before, sir, I believed that he was suffering from gastric fever.

MR GREATOREX: You have a great inheritance, have you not?

ELIZABETH CREE: A modest competence, sir, no more.

MR GREATOREX: Yes, I have heard you call it that before. But £9,000 per year is more than modest.

ELIZABETH CREE: I mean to say that I retain only a modest competence on my own behalf. I am a member of the Society for the Preservation of the Infant Poor, and most of my inheritance is devoted to the impoverished and the distressed.

MR GREATOREX: But you yourself are now neither impoverished nor distressed?

ELIZABETH CREE: I am neither of those, except for the distress I feel at the death of my husband.

MR GREATOREX: So let us return to that fatal evening, when he collapsed on the floor of your villa in New Cross.

ELIZABETH CREE: It is not a happy memory, sir.

MR GREATOREX: I am sure that it is not, but if I may encroach upon your patience for a little longer? Yesterday, I think, you mentioned that you held a long conversation with your husband at dinner just before he retired to his room?

ELIZABETH CREE: We always talk, sir.

MR GREATOREX: Do you remember the subject of your discussions?

ELIZABETH CREE: I believe we conversed about the topics of the day.

MR GREATOREX: I have nothing more for you at this time. Can Aveline Mortimer now be called?

The transcript in the Illustrated Police News Law Courts and Weekly Record *described how Aveline Mortimer was now brought to the witness box, where she began her testimony with the usual oath upon the Bible and certain routine questions about her name, age, marital status and address. There was even an illustrative woodcut of her standing in the box, wearing a demure hat and carrying her gloves in her right hand.*

MR GREATOREX: Were you present, Miss Mortimer, on the night that Mr Cree was found in his room?

AVELINE MORTIMER: Oh yes, sir.

MR GREATOREX: You had served at table that evening?

AVELINE MORTIMER: It was stuffed veal, sir, because it was Monday.

MR GREATOREX: And did you happen to hear any of the general conversation between Mr and Mrs Cree on that occasion?

AVELINE MORTIMER: He called her a devil, sir.

MR GREATOREX: Oh did he? Do you happen to recall the circumstances of that particular remark?

AVELINE MORTIMER: It was at the beginning of dinner, sir, just after I had been called in with the tureen. I think they were discussing something which had appeared in the news-papers because, when I entered the room, Mr Cree had thrown a copy of the *Evening Post* upon the floor. He seemed very agitated, sir.

MR GREATOREX: And then he called Mrs Cree a devil? Is that correct?

AVELINE MORTIMER: He said, 'You devil! You are the one!' Then he saw me enter the room, and he said nothing more while I remained with them.

MR GREATOREX: 'You devil. You are the one.' What do you think he might have meant by this?

AVELINE MORTIMER: I cannot say, sir.

MR GREATOREX: Could he perhaps have meant, 'You are the one who is poisoning me?'

MR LISTER: This is highly improper, my lord. He cannot ask this woman to make inferences of that kind.

MR GREATOREX: I apologise, my lord. I withdraw that question. Let me then ask you this, Miss Mortimer. Do you have any notion at all why Mr Cree should refer to his wife as a 'devil'?

AVELINE MORTIMER: Oh yes, sir. She is a very hardened woman.

Twenty-Four

George Gissing returned to his lodgings in Hanway Street, by the Tottenham Court Road, without any hope of finding his wife returned; he had seen Nell upon the streets of Limehouse and knew well enough that, despite their recent marriage, she would now be in the vicinity of some wretched public house. He was not sure how long they could remain in their present place if she came back drunk again; their landlady Mrs Irving, who lived on the ground floor, had already suggested that they find 'dwellings elsewhere'. She had rushed out of her rooms one evening to find Nell lying upon the stairs in a stupor, trailing a cloud of gin, and demanded 'what this 'ere was' – to which Gissing had replied that his wife had been knocked down by a hansom and was given drink to recover herself. He had, over the years, proved an adept liar. He also realised that Mrs Irving was afraid that they would, in the phrase of the period, 'shoot the moon' and cheat her by absconding after dark; he suspected that she listened carefully every night for any sign of sudden removal.

It was not as if she entertained her tenants on a lavish scale, however; some bare wooden furniture, a bed and a sink were the sum of their comforts. It might be thought that a young man of Gissing's abnormal sensitivity would find such conditions intolerable, but he was accustomed to very little else. Some people accept the circumstances of life with a resignation and sense of defeat which are rarely, if ever, lifted; Gissing himself had created a man of that sort in his first novel, and had described how he had eventually sunk to the level of his surroundings. But others are so buoyed by energy and optimism that they pay very little attention to such things and are, as it were, blind to the manner of their present life in the constant struggle towards the future. George Gissing, curiously enough, represented both of these attitudes; there were occasions when he was so weighed down by depression and lethargy that only the prospect of imminent starvation forced him back to work, but there were also times when he was so exhilarated by the idea of literary fame that he quite forgot his poverty and luxuriated in the promise of eventual respectability and renown.

But there was another element involved in his recognition of his surroundings; sometimes he looked upon them as a form of experiment, with his own life as a self-conscious exercise in realism. He had been reading Emile Zola's volume of essays, *The Experimental Novel*, published a few months earlier, and it had confirmed all his latent faith in '*naturalisme, la vérité, la science*' – to the extent that he congratulated himself on leading a thoroughly modern and even literary life. In such a light even Nell could be considered a heroine of the new age. There was only one difficulty and it was, appropriately, a stylistic one; despite Gissing's interest in realism and unstudied naturalism, his own prose encompassed the romantic, the rhetorical and the picturesque. Within the narrative of *Workers in the Dawn*, for example, he had bathed the city in an iridescent glow and turned its inhabitants into stage heroes or stage crowds on the model of the sensation plays in the penny gaffs. Even now, as he settled down in his small room and began looking through his notes on Charles Babbage's Analytical

Engine, he might have noticed that he referred to it as a 'towering Babylonian idol' which 'faces out towards the heaving masses'. This was not the language of a realist.

He could not begin writing this essay, however, until he had eaten. There was nothing in his lodgings except a suspect piece of ham left beside the sink, so he permitted himself a visit to a chop-house on the corner of Berners Street where he knew he could dine for less than a shilling. Of course it was not a fashionable setting – it was the haunt of the local cab-drivers who came in at midday for their pies and porter – but it served its purpose. Gissing could sit here undisturbed (except for the occasional, sporadic raids of a young waiter) and write, or dream, or reminisce. This chop-house was also a favourite resort for the performers who appeared at the Oxford Music Hall down the road, and on many occasions Gissing noticed how those 'out of a crib' were supported by their more fortunate colleagues; he had even thought of writing a novel upon a music-hall theme, but realised just in time that the subject was too light and frivolous for a serious artist. Instead he spent this particular evening sitting in the chop-house and contemplating the inventions of Charles Babbage. Even as he waited to be served, he began a paragraph on the nature of modern society which anticipated almost exactly the words of Charles Booth who nine years later, in *Life and Labour of the People of London*, defined 'the numerical relation which poverty, misery and depravity bear to regular earnings and comparative comfort'. This was the statistical grid about to be stretched across London, and over the next two days George Gissing composed an essay in which he attempted to explain the role of data and statistics in the modern world. Here, against his better instincts, he also extolled the virtues of the Analytical Engine.

Nell did not come home that night, and so he slept very soundly amid the noises of the Tottenham Court Road. He woke up at dawn, breakfasted on bread and tea, and then at ten minutes before nine set off for the Reading Room of the British Museum. He had in fact chosen these lodgings because of their proximity to the library, and he always considered this area of London to be his true home. He had been born in Wakefield, he had lived for a while in America, he had lodged in the East End and south of the river, but only within this small neighbourhood of Coptic Street and Great Russell Street did he feel entirely at ease. It was the spirit of the district itself which, he supposed, affected him so profoundly. Even the tradesmen he passed on his walk to the museum – the map seller, the umbrella man, the knife-grinder – seemed to share his sense of place and to accommodate themselves to it. He knew the porters and the cab men, the strolling musicians and the casual street-sellers, and he considered them as part of some distinctive human family to which he also belonged.

Of course the interpretation of any area is a complicated and ambiguous matter. It was often remarked, for example, how magical societies and occult bookshops seemed to spring up in the vicinity of the British Museum and its great library; even the Superintendent of the Reading Room in this period, Richard Garnett, was attached to the practice of astrological forecasting and had remarked, very sensibly, that the occult is simply 'that which is not generally admitted'. Mr Garnett might even have speculated on the coincidence of this particular September morning, when Karl Marx, Oscar Wilde, Bernard Shaw, and George Gissing himself, all entered the Reading Room within the space of an hour. But such speculations are nevertheless hazardous; the connection between occult bookshops and the British Museum might simply be explained on the grounds that libraries are commonly the home of lonely or thwarted people who are also likely to be attracted to magical lore as a substitute for real influence or power.

Gissing was one of the first to enter the Reading Room when its doors were opened at nine; he went immediately to his customary seat, and continued work upon his essay on Charles Babbage. He hardly thought of Nell at all while he sat over his desk, since in this place he felt himself to be protected from the vulgar life he was constrained to lead beyond its walls; here he could mingle with the great authors of the past, and imagine a similar destiny for himself. He wrote until evening, covering the pages of his bound notebook with the thin black ink which the library provided; he always signed and dated the first drafts of his essays as soon as they were finished and, after he had completed his signature with a flourish, strolled beneath the dome to recover himself.

It was already dusk by the time he left the Museum, and he bought some chestnuts from the street-seller who stood with his brazier beside the gates during the autumn and winter months. He passed a boy selling newspapers, but paid no attention to the 'Terrible murder!' he was announcing in a hoarse voice. Then, when he turned into Hanway Street, he saw two policemen outside the door of his lodgings. He realised that something must have happened to his wife and, curiously enough, he felt quite calm. 'Do you wish to see me?' he asked one of the officers. 'I am the husband of Mrs Gissing.'

'So you are Mr Gissing?'

'Naturally. Yes.'

'Could you come with us then, sir?'

Gissing, to his surprise, found himself being escorted up the stairs of his lodgings exactly as if he were under arrest; then, even before he could reach his door, he could hear Nell's voice raised in argument with some other person. 'You fucker!' she was screaming. 'You fucker!'

He closed his eyes for a moment before they led him into the room he knew so well, but which now seemed quite changed.

There was another police detective with his wife but Nell was not, as he had feared, under any form of restraint. She had been crying, and Gissing knew that she had been drinking gin, but as soon as he entered the room she looked at him with an interest that he found peculiar. 'Are you Gissing?' the detective asked him.

'I have already told these gentleman my name.'

'Are you acquainted with an Alice Stanton?'

'No. I have never heard of any such woman.'

'Were you aware that she was unlawfully killed yesterday evening?'

'No, I was not.' Gissing was becoming more and more puzzled; he glanced across at his wife, who shook her head from side to side with an expression he did not understand.

'Can you tell me where you were, yesterday evening?'

'I was here. I was working.'

'Is that all?'

'All? That is a great deal.'

'I gather that your wife was not with you?'

'Mrs Gissing—' It was a delicate matter, but he assumed that the police already knew her profession. 'Mrs Gissing was with friends.'

'I believe she was.' It was clear to Gissing that these men did not know how to address him. He was sensitive about such matters and guessed, correctly, that they were surprised by his manner: he was the husband of a common prostitute, and yet his speech and dress (threadbare but clean) were those of a gentleman. But he was also in an anomalous position: they had come to his lodgings, and he still could not discern their purpose. 'There are several questions we must put to you, Mr Gissing, but we cannot do so here. Would you be so good as to come with us now?'

'Have I any choice?'

'Not in this matter. None.'

'But what is this matter?' They did not answer him but took him down at once into the street, where a closed cab was waiting for them. Nell did not accompany them and, when he turned around to look for her, they simply told him that she had already 'identified the body'.

'What body? What do you mean?'

They led him into the cab, saying nothing else, and Gissing sank back into the stale leather seat with a loud sigh. He closed his eyes and did not open them again until the cab stopped and its door was opened quickly; he found himself in a small courtyard and heard someone shouting, 'Take him through.' He was escorted into a building of dark yellow brick, and followed the three policemen into a narrow room lit by a row of gas-jets. There was a wooden table in front of him, with a cheap cotton cloth laid across it. He knew well enough what it covered, even before Detective Paul Bryden pulled it away. The face had been partially disfigured, and the head lay in an unnatural position, but Gissing recognised her at once: it was the young woman who had come to the door in Whitecross Street when he was searching for his wife. 'Do you recognise this person?'

'Yes. I recognise her.'

'Will you follow me, Mr Gissing?' He could not resist looking down at the face again. Her eyes, which had been turned towards the home of the Analytical Engine in Limehouse, were now closed; but her expression, sealed at the time of her death like some hieroglyph upon a tomb, was one of pity and resignation. Bryden led him away, and together they walked down a brightly lit passage; there was a green door at the end, and Bryden cleared his throat before knocking gently upon it. Gissing had heard no one reply, but Bryden opened it and then suddenly pushed him forward. He was inside a room which

133

had barred windows; another police detective was seated at a desk and he directed Gissing to sit opposite him.

'Do you know what a golem is, sir?'

'It is a mythical creature. Something like a vampire, I believe.' He was no longer surprised by anything which was happening to him, and answered as naturally as if he had been in a schoolroom.

'Exactly so. And we are not men to believe in mythical creatures, are we?'

'I hope not. May I ask your name? It would make our conversation so much easier.'

'My name is Kildare, Mr Gissing. You were born in Wakefield, were you not?'

'I was.'

'Yet you retain no trace of your native accent.'

'I am an educated man, sir.'

'Quite. Your wife' – there seemed to Gissing to be no particular emphasis upon the word – 'tells us that you have written a book.'

'Yes. I have written a novel.'

'Would I have seen it? What is its title?'

'*Workers in the Dawn.*'

Kildare looked at him more sharply. 'Are you a socialist, then? Or a member of the International?' The police inspector had glimpsed some fatal connection between Karl Marx and George Gissing and, even in that moment, contemplated the possibilities of an insurrectionary conspiracy.

'By no means am I a socialist. I am a realist.'

'But your title has such a ring to it.'

'I am no more a socialist than Hogarth or Cruikshank.'

'I know of these men, of course, but—'

'They were artists, like myself.'

'Ah, I see. But there are not many artists who can boast that

134

they have been to prison.' Gissing felt that he ought to have anticipated their knowledge of his crime but, even so, he could not meet the man's eyes. 'You served one month's hard labour in Manchester, Mr Gissing. You were convicted of theft.'

He had thought it forgotten, erased from every memory except his own; when he had moved to London with Nell, he even began to experience what he was later to describe as 'a time of extraordinary mental growth, of great spiritual activity'. It may seem odd to talk of 'spiritual activity' within the dark city, but Gissing knew well enough that it has always been the home of visionaries. He had already written down some words of William Blake, which had been quoted in Swinburne's recent study of that poet, 'the spiritual Fourfold London eternal'. But now George Gissing sat with his head bowed before a police detective. 'Can you please tell me why I am here?' Chief Inspector Kildare took something out of his pocket, and handed it to him. It was a piece of notepaper, stained with blood; on it was written Gissing's name and address. 'This is my hand,' he said quietly. 'I gave it to her.'

'So we supposed.'

'I had been looking for my wife.' He realised, at last, exactly why he was being questioned. 'Surely you cannot believe that I am in any way connected with her death? It is absurd.'

'Not absurd, sir. Nothing to do with such a crime is absurd.'

'But do I seem to you to be a murderer?'

'In my experience, prison hardens a man considerably.'

'You must have learned some flash tricks.' This was another voice, coming from behind him; there has been a second policeman in the room throughout this interview. For Gissing, their suggestions were unendurable. He knew well enough that, in the idiom of the day, he was suspected of being a 'moral degenerate' who was living with a prostitute and whose first taste of crime and punishment must inevitably lead to more

135

and more outrageous assaults upon virtue and good order. It might even result in murder.

'The dead woman was a good friend to your wife,' Kildare was saying. 'And I expect you knew her very well. Am I correct in supposing that?'

'I had never seen her before. I knew nothing of her.'

'Don't you like to meet your wife's friends?'

'Of course not.' He could stand this no longer. 'You know very well what kind of woman my wife is. But you do not understand what kind of man I am. I am a gentleman.' He looked so defiant, and yet so frail, in the glare of the gas that even these two policemen might have been inclined to believe him. 'At what time, precisely, was she killed?'

Kildare hesitated, unsure whether he should volunteer such information. 'We cannot be certain, but she was found at midnight by one of her trade.'

'Then I am not your man. Go to the chop-house on the corner of Berners Street, and enquire about me. I sat at a table there until after midnight. Ask Vincent, the waiter, if he remembers Mr Gissing.'

Kildare leaned back in his chair with an expression of consternation. 'You told my officers that you were working.'

'And so I was. I was working in the chop-house. In all the sudden alarm and confusion I quite forgot that I had been there last night. It is one of my habitual places.'

There was a knock upon the door, which so startled Gissing that he rose from his chair for a moment. A policeman came in, and whispered to Kildare; Gissing could not hear him, but in fact he was providing further exoneration. No blood had been found upon the novelist's clothing in Hanway Street, and the knives were all clean. This was truly disappointing to Kildare, who believed that he was at last on the track of the Limehouse Golem. What better suspect could there be than the husband of a shameless prostitute – a former convict – who found himself being endlessly compromised by her and by her associates? What kind of vengeance might such a man seek? He left the room with the police officer who had conducted the search of the lodgings, and instructed him to visit the chop-house which Gissing had mentioned. He would have been less agreeable if he had known that the same officer had enjoyed sexual congress with Nell Gissing only an hour before – on the very same bed where Gissing had lain last night and dreamed of the Analytical Engine. The policeman had given her a shilling, and she had gone immediately to a gin shop in the Seven Dials.

Gissing sat perfectly still, and in the silence became aware once again of the corpse which lay only a few yards away. Since childhood he had entertained fantasies of suicide – particularly of death by drowning – and for a moment he tried to imagine that it was he who was lying upon the wooden table. He had always believed that his purpose was to endure life with as little suffering as possible, and to think of death with affection – but now, as he sat in this police office, he was also beginning to realise that the shape of his destiny might not lie within his own power. Here, in the course of one day, he had gone from the wonderful seclusion of his books in the British Museum to the degradation of arrest and the possibility of a criminal's death by hanging. And on what action had these events turned? A casual meeting in Whitecross Street, and the chance decision to write down his name and address in the search for Nell. And yes, of course, there was a more enduring reason for his present suffering – his wife had brought him to this. He would never have encountered the dead woman if Nell had not led him that way; he would never have been suspected, if he had not already been branded as a convict and an outcast because of her. What a thing it was, to be bound from head to foot by another person!

Bryden tapped him on the shoulder (he flinched, because at that moment he had been contemplating the possibility of Nell's own sudden death) and led him out of the room towards a flight of stone steps. He descended into a basement corridor, and found himself being taken into a small cell. 'Am I to be kept here?' he murmured, almost to himself.

'Just for this night.'

There was a piece of flat stone projecting from the wall, and Gissing sat down upon it slowly. He had trained himself to think, and to analyse his sensations, in moments of solitude; but he could contemplate nothing now except the stone wall in front of him. It had been painted light green.

The hero of *Workers in the Dawn* was described by Gissing as 'one of those men whose lives seem to have little result for the world save as a useful illustration of the force of circumstances'. Now, in the police cell, sat another prey of 'circumstances' trapped in a narrative over which he had no control. There was a bucket in the corner, to be used by the prisoners, and for a moment he considered putting it over his head and beginning to moan. But then his thoughts took another turn. He had read in a recent copy of the *Weekly Digest* that part of the ancient city of London had been found during the building of certain warehouses by Shadwell Reach. Some stone walls had been uncovered, and it occurred to Gissing that this cell might have been constructed from the remnants of them. Perhaps the old buried city extended as far as Limehouse with the Analytical Engine as its god or *genius loci*. So now he might be its sacrifice, waiting in an antechamber for the doom prepared. And was that the secret of the golem which the police detective had mentioned? Perhaps Charles Babbage's creation was the true Limehouse Golem, draining away the life and spirit of those who approached it. Perhaps the digits and the numbers were little chattering souls trapped in the mechanism, and its webs of iron no less than the web of mortality itself. What monstrous creation might it bring forth in years to come? What had begun in Limehouse might then spread over the entire world. But these were only Gissing's disordered thoughts as he sat, exhausted, in his prison cell.

He was released the following morning, after the policeman had confirmed that he had indeed sat in the Berners Street chop-house until after midnight. Vincent, the young waiter, had been particularly forceful; he alluded to Gissing sitting there 'all the bleeding night' while doing nothing but 'doodling', and accused him of being 'stuck up' despite the fact that 'he don't have sixpence'. A customer also remembered seeing him that evening, and corroborated Vincent's other testimony by describing Gissing as 'shabby genteel'. This was a popular expression but one less than just to the novelist; he always tried to dress well, and his gentility was not of manner but of mind.

He came out of the courtyard of the police office, and stood uncertainly in the Limehouse air. He had resigned himself to a long process of investigation and humiliation, but his unexpected release did not afford him any real sense of freedom. Certainly he had experienced an exhilarating moment of relief when he finally left the building of dull yellow brick, but that was followed by a more persistent sense of threat. His whole existence in the world had been suddenly and quickly called into question. If he had not visited the chop-house he might well have been convicted and executed; it was as if his life were now revealed as a paltry and tenuous thing which the slightest misfortune might destroy. He blamed his wife for his situation, as we have seen, but up to this time she had never threatened his very survival. That was a new consideration. His night in the cell had revealed to him that he had no real protection against her, or against the world.

He walked home by way of Whitechapel and the City, although he knew well enough that he was returning to no 'home' at all. He was like a condemned man going back to his cell. He could hear the argument as soon as he turned into Hanway Street: Nell was leaning down from the first-floor window and screaming at the landlady who stood in the street below. 'Such things,' Mrs Irving was shouting, 'such as should not happen in this 'ere 'ouse.' Nell replied with a volley of foul words, at which the landlady accused her of being a 'dirty 'ore'. His wife disappeared for a moment and then returned with a chamber-pot, the contents of which she directed at Mrs Irving's head. Gissing could bear no more of this. Neither woman had seen him, so he retreated quickly down the Tottenham Court Road and made his way to the British Museum. If there was to be rest for him anywhere in this world, it was among his books.

Twenty-Five

Within two years I had become a seasoned performer, and Little Victor's Daughter had developed a life and a history which I quite believed when I went upon the stage. Of course I had my *modèles*, as Uncle used to say. I had watched Miss Emma Marriott in *Gin and Limelight* and had heard 'Lady Agatha' (alias Joan Birtwhistle, a most unpleasant party) singing 'Get Back to your Pudding, Marianne', and I took a little inflection from both of them. There was another serio-comic lady, Betty Williams, who had started as a big-boot dancer but had developed into a real artiste with her rendering of 'It's a Bit of Comfort to a Poor Old Maid'. She had a certain way of tilting herself, so that she always seemed to be on the deck of a ship or struggling in a high wind – I borrowed that effect, too, for a number of my own entitled 'Don't Stick It Out So Much'. How they roared, even when I was at my most genteel. Little Victor's Daughter was the young virgin who said quite innocent things – how could she help it if she was open to misconstruction? Dan thought I was getting too blue and I became truly indignant with him – could I be blamed for all the chaff and the laughter in the gallery? I didn't think her history deserved it. Here she was, having been brought up by Little Victor after her parents had perished in a fire in a sausage shop; of course she had to earn her keep as a maid in Pimlico, and what was she to do if all the men in the house kept on giving her presents? As she used to sing, 'What's a Girl Supposed to Say?' What a performance it was!

It was not until my third year on the stage, with all the usual hurry from hall to hall, that I grew sick of Little Victor's Daughter. She was just too sweet, and I longed to kill her off by some violent action. When she was on the stage now I used to beat her about a bit – 'I'll give you the biggest scratch on the face,' the cook would say to me, and then I would land myself such a thump that I was almost knocked over. (Of course I played the cook as well, since it was part of what Dan called my 'monypolylogue'.) But she was no longer the right girl for me. So I was sitting in the green room one weekday evening, feeling pretty sorry for myself 'at my time of life', when I noticed that Dan had dropped one of his costumes on a chair. It was not his way to be untidy, so out of old habit I picked up the duds and began dusting them down. He had left a battered beaverhat, an old green top-coat, check trousers, boots and a choker; I was about to fold them away, when suddenly it struck me as quite a funny thing to try them on. There was a tall mirror propped against the wall, by the make-up basket, and I dressed as quickly as I could. The hat was a little too big and came over my eyes, so I tilted it on the back of my head like a coster; the trousers and coat fitted me perfectly, and I realised that I would be able to swagger in them ever so well. But what a picture I made in the mirror – I had become a man, from tip to toe, and there might have been a slangster comedian standing there; it was a perfect piece of business and, even then, I think I began to consider ways of getting up a new act.

Dan came into the room while I was standing in front of the mirror and practising some gestures. 'Hello,' he said as if to a stranger. 'Do I know you when you're at home?'

'Of course you do.' I turned around and smiled at him, although I was perhaps a little embarrassed at what I had done. He was always quick, and he recognised me at once. 'Good God,' he said. 'This is a funny thing.' He carried on staring at me. 'What a funny thing.'

'I could make it a scream, Dan. I could be Little Victor's Daughter's Older Brother.'

'A swell?'

'A shabby swell.'

I could see that he was contemplating the possibilities. There is always room in the halls for a good male impersonator and, somehow, I looked the part. 'I suppose,' he said, 'that it could be worked up. It could be quite a diversion.'

And so it proved. At first I went on as Little Victor's Daughter's Older Brother, but the name was too big for the bills and I settled for The Older Brother. The beaver-hat was always a success when it came down over my eyes, and even fell off my head, but I decided to compromise with a nice little felt-top number without any brim; then I found myself a frock-coat and some white trousers, before finishing off the mammoth ensemble with a high collar and big boots. I used to swagger on the stage like a leonine comique, and then somehow manage to have my hat knocked off by a gasman's pole; that set them roaring because I started to quiver – literally *quiver* – with rage before very carefully taking the gasman's cap and flinging it into the gutter. It was all mime, of course, and in the beginning Dan took me through the steps and gestures as if I were about to become a regular Grimaldi. But I was a good gagger, too, and after a while I developed my own masculine slanguage. ''Arf a mo', cocky' and 'will you just a wait a tic?' – uttered like they had never been uttered before – were two popular favourites: I sang them out just before I was about to run off the stage, and then I froze in the act of running with one leg stretched in the air behind me. The 'Older Brother' was a terrible scamp, and was courting a fat old pastry cook who was supposed to have hidden a fortune somewhere. 'She's a fine figure of a woman is my Joan,' he would say. 'It's the dough that does it.' (Dough in those days was the latest morsel of lingo for backsheesh.) 'Her hair's another thing altogether, and there are some who would say it's a home for old spiders. But not me.' I had another piece of foolery. When the new regulations came in, I used to gag them by marching across the stage with a banner saying 'Temporary Fire Curtain'. That always got them going and, while I had them in the mood, I would hit them with the latest of my ditties. I made a success out of 'I'm a Married Man Myself' and 'Any Excuse for a Booze', but I always ended my masculine turn with a song which Uncle originally found for me. It was entitled 'She Was One of the Early Birds and I Was One of the—', and there were many times when I would have to 'oblige again' before they would let me go on to the next hall. Of course everything was timed perfectly in advance, and my turn lasted thirty minutes before I got into the brougham and went on to the next set of doors. One evening's programme would take me to the Britannia in Hoxton at a quarter past eight, Wilton's in Wellclose Square by nine, the Winchester along the Southwark Bridge Road at ten, and rounding off with the Raglan in Theobald's Road at eleven. It was a hard life in some ways, but I was earning seven guineas a week plus supper. The 'Older Brother' had become a great draw, and within a very short time I had taught him how to be cocky and yet naive, knowing yet innocent. Everyone knew that I was also 'Little Victor's Daughter', but that was the joy of it. I could be girl and boy, man and woman, without any shame. I felt somehow that I was above them all, and could change myself at will. That was why I perfected the art of running off the stage, five minutes before the end, and coming back as Little Victor's Daughter while they stared at me in surprise. Uncle was acting as my dresser now, and had my feminine rags in his hand as I came off; he would always pat me on the you-know-what while I changed, but I pretended to ignore him. I recognised all his tricks by now, and I knew that I was equal to them. In any case I was preparing myself for that old pathetic number, 'I Wonder What It Feels Like to be Poor'. How the coppers rained down from the gods for that one! As I used to say, as I stood there as the lonely orphan, these were really 'pennies from heaven'.

It must have been two or three months after the Older Brother was born that I had a sudden fancy of my own: it might be a piece of fun to take him out into the streets of London and see the other world. I had a room to myself in our diggings now, just next door to Doris, and after the show was over I would go back in my own clothes as if I were about to toast a slice of bread and retire. But then I would quietly dress myself as the Older Brother, wait until the lights were dimmed and the house was quiet, and then creep out of the back window by the staircase. Of course he never wore his stage clothes, which were a trifle too short and too shabby, and he had bought for himself a whole new set of duds. He was a scamp, as I said, and liked nothing better than to stroll through the night like a regular masher; he would cross the river down Southwark way and then wander by Whitechapel, Shadwell and Limehouse. He soon knew all the flash houses and the dens, but he never set foot in them: he had his fun by watching the filth of the town flowing along. The females of the street would whistle to him but he passed them by and, if the worst of them tried to touch him, he would grip their wrists with his big hands and thrust them away. He was not so rough with the game boys, because he knew that they lusted after him in a purer fashion: they were looking for their double, and who could reflect them better than the Older Brother? No one ever saw Lambeth Marsh Lizzie or Little Victor's Daughter – she had gone away, and I liked to think of her sleeping peacefully somewhere. No. That is not precisely true. One man did see her. The Older Brother was walking through Old Jerusalem, just by the Limehouse church, when a Hebrew passed him by gaslight – they almost collided, since the Jew was walking with his eyes fixed upon the pavement. When he looked up, he saw Lizzie beneath the male and recoiled. He muttered something like 'Cab man' or 'Cadmon' and, in that instant, she struck out and knocked him to the ground. Then she went on her way as a swell of the night with her frock-coat and fancy waistcoat; she even made a point of tipping her hat to the ladies.

Doris caught me one night when I returned to the New Cut. She must have been drinking porter with Austin for longer than usual, because she was a little bit 'round the houses'. 'Lizzie, love,' she said. 'Whatever are you wearing?'

I had to think fast, even though I guessed that she would remember nothing in the morning. 'I'm rehearsing, Doris. I've got a new bit of business, dear, and I need the practice.'

'You look the spitting image of a dear old pal.' She kissed the collar of my frock-coat. 'A dear old pal. Long departed. Sing us a song, darling, do.' She was quite dazed with the drink, so I took her back to her room and gave her the refrain of 'My Sweet Mother Looks After Me Still, Though I Long to be with Her in Heaven'. How she loved that song. She recalled nothing the next morning, as I expected, but it really did not matter: three weeks later, the poor dear died of drink. She started sweating and trembling while we were sitting in Austin's nice little parlour; by the time we got her to the Free Hospital down the Westminster Bridge Road, she was all but gone. Drink is a slow poison, so they say, but it can always strike quickly when the body is weakened. We buried her on the Friday afternoon, just before our matinée at the Britannia, and Dan gave a little speech by the graveside. He called her the 'female Blondin' who aspired higher and higher. She never fell, he said: she was someone we all looked up to. It was a very nice oration, and we shed a few tears. Then we put her wire in the coffin, and cried some more. I shall never forget it. I was at my best that night, after the funeral, and the mirth of the Older Brother had them roaring. But, as I said to Dan at the time, we have to remain professionals. That same night I dreamed that I was dragging a corpse behind me with a rope but, after all, what do dreams matter when we have the stage?

That is what I should have told Kennedy, the Great Mesmerist, who was on a bill with me two weeks later. 'How is it done?' I had asked him, after I had seen him put several under the 'fluence. A fisherman had come down from the twopenny gallery and danced the fandango all over the place, while a coster and his donah were mesmerised into a clog dance which, being Londoners, they could not have known naturally. 'Is it just a wheeze?'

'No. It's a feat.' We were having a parcel of fish and chips on a licensed premises, not far from the hall in Bishopsgate, and he held up his glass so that he could look at me through it. We were in a snug little corner, where no one could see us, and I noticed a fire in his eyes – although I think now that it may just have been a reflection of the fire in the parlour.

'Go on, then,' I said. 'Astonish me, Randolph.' He took from his pocket the flash gold watch which he used on the stage, and read the time before putting it back again. At that moment I saw the fire gleaming inside the dial. 'Do that again.'

'Do what, ducks?'

'Let me see it burning.' So slowly he takes out the watch again, and holds it up to the firelight. I could not take my eyes from it, and all at once I remembered how my mother used to hold up a candle to light me to bed in our Lambeth Marsh lodgings. That was all I knew before I fell asleep. It seemed like sleep, at least, but when I opened my eyes the Great Kennedy was looking at me in horror. 'What on earth is the matter?' was all I could think of saying.

'It couldn't have been you, Lizzie.'

'What couldn't have been me?'

'I don't want to say.'

I was afraid for a moment of what I might have revealed. 'Go on. Do tell a girl.'

'All those terrible things.'

Then I laughed out loud, and raised my glass. 'Here's to you, Randolph. Don't you know when you've been spoofed?'

'You mean . . .'

'You never had me under at all.' He still looked at me doubtfully. 'Can you think so badly of your Lambeth Lizzie?'

'No. Of course not. But you were that genuine.'

'That's the game, you see. Keep them guessing.' We left it there but, afterwards, he never treated me quite the same.

Twenty-Six

MR LISTER: What is the evidence against Mrs Cree, after all? She purchased some arsenic powder for rats. That is the sum of it. If that were grounds for the charge of murder, half the women of England would be standing in this place. The plain and certain truth is that the prosecution has failed to provide any convincing reason why Mrs Cree should wish to kill her husband. He was a mild and studious man afflicted with some kind of brain disorder of an obsessive nature – reason enough for him to kill himself, as Mrs Cree has suggested, but no reason at all for him to be murdered by his own wife. Had he been a good husband to her? Yes, he had. Had he provided for her? Yes indeed, and to suggest that she killed him for an inheritance is the plainest folly when we consider how comfortable her life had been. Was John Cree some kind of beast who tyrannised his wife? If he had been some fiend in human shape, why then there might have been a possible motive for such a crime. But in fact we have heard that he was, despite his mental infirmity, a kind and loving husband. There was no possible reason in the world why Mrs Cree should wish to destroy him. Just look at her. Does she seem to you a monster incarnate, a veritable terror, as Mr Greatorex has implied? On the contrary, I see all the womanly virtues in her face. I see loyalty, and chastity, and piety. Mr

Greatorex has made great play with the fact that she was once a performer in the halls, as if that were necessarily the mark of a bad character. But we have heard from several witnesses that she led an exemplary existence while employed upon the stage. And of her life in New Cross, we have heard much praise from her neighbours for her wifely deportment. The maid, Mortimer, has said that she was a hardened woman – I wish to quote her exactly – but is that not often the way servants talk about their employers and especially, if I may say so, maids about their mistresses? Mrs Cree has told us that on several occasions she had threatened this Mortimer with a possible removal from her duties and expulsion from the house. We may have taken a different view of the maid's opinion after that. Certainly it would be enough to embitter that young woman against her employer. Now imagine the real scene within the Cree household, with this morbidly religious man being comforted and supported by his wife . . .

Twenty-Seven

September 23, 1880: My dear wife still wishes to see Dan Leno in pantomime next week. The season begins earlier and earlier, but I presume that the citizens of London need some diversion from the horrors in their midst. How much more charming to see Bluebeard kill twenty women in his chamber than to think of it being performed upon the streets! I am not so urgently inclined to see Leno again. I am as fond of display as any man, but the thought of him dressed as a princess or fishwife disturbs me as much as it ever did. It is against nature and, for me, nature is all. I am a part of nature, like the frost on the grass or the tiger in the forest. I am not some mythological figure, as the newspaper reports continually suggest, or some exotic creature out of a Gothic novel; I am what I am, which is flesh and blood.

Who ever said that life was dull? I went back to the Ratcliffe Highway at dusk, having told my wife that I was dining with a friend in the City. In the cool of the evening I stood outside the shop of the clothes-seller, and watched a young woman lighting the lamps in the upstairs apartments; then, after a moment, I saw the shadow of a child crossing the window. Once more I knew that I was on hallowed ground, and I gave thanks on behalf of the shopman and his family. They were about to become patterns of eternity, and in their own wounds reflect the inflictions of recurrent time. To die on the same spot as the famous Marrs – and to die in the same fashion – why, it is a great testimony to the power of the city over men.

I had already devised a means of entering silently and invisibly; I still stood on the opposite side of the street, and observed Gerrard come downstairs to his place of business. He picked up some coins, took a few items of cloth from the counter, and then began climbing the stairs. I hurried into the shop, and looked around for a place to conceal myself: there was another door beneath the stairs and, when I opened it, I realised from the odour that it led into an earth cellar. I love the smell of the underworld and, on an impulse, I smeared my face with some of the dirt that lined these dark walls; here I waited, the door shut, until I heard the sound of the shop being closed and bolted. I lingered a few minutes more in the seclusion of the cellar, but even there I could hear the murmur of voices in the rooms upstairs. Of course I could not come upon them at once, since in the consternation of that fatal moment a child or servant might escape, and I contemplated the means of taking them one by one. There were, as I guessed, some four or five above me. How had the Marrs been despatched?

A young woman was singing 'In Vauxhall Gardens' from that perennial favourite, *A Night in London* – I supposed it to be a servant girl or perhaps a daughter, and I came from my hiding place to savour the melody. There was a small wooden step-ladder by the side of the counter, and I knocked it to the floor; the sudden noise disturbed her song, and a few moments later I heard her foot upon the staircase. She grew more bold in the silence (although I could hardly restrain myself from bursting out in laughter) and descended the stairs. I was standing in the shadows just beside them and, when she came down into the shop, I took the mallet from my pocket and struck her down. She did not cry out – she did not even sigh – but, cradling her wounded body, I took my razor and cut her from ear to ear. It was hot business indeed, with the blood welling over the sleeves of my coat, and so I dragged her down into the earth cellar.

'Annie? Are you down below, Annie?'

It was Gerrard. I was tempted to reply in the voice of the servant, but I bit my tongue and said nothing. Slowly he came down the stairs, calling her name once more, until I reached out and took him with my razor. I had his head almost off his body before he made any noise, and then there was only a low moan as if he had always known what fate lay in wait for him. 'That servant of yours was a bad girl,' I whispered to him. 'She gave herself too willingly.' He seemed to look at me in wonder, and I patted his cheek with my hand. 'You have missed nothing else,' I whispered again. 'The play has just begun.'

I mounted the stairs, with the open razor in my hand – what a sight I must have made, all bathed in blood and with my face besmeared in dirt like an African tribesman. The child saw me first, and stared at me. 'Do you have a baby brother?' I asked her very gently. Then the mother rushed towards me, and set up a screaming such as I had never heard before. It was necessary for me to stop that noise at once and so, in defiance of all right ceremony and proceeding, I moved for her with my mallet and clubbed her down. Then I looked towards the children, now cowering in the corner.

Twenty-Eight

The brutal murder of the Gerrard family, by the hands of the Limehouse Golem, provoked the public to an even greater level of fury and exultation. As soon as the newspapers published the details of the 'latest atrocity', no one could talk of anything else. It was as if some primeval force had erupted in Limehouse, and there was an irrational but general fear that it would not stop there but would spread over the city and perhaps even the entire country. Some dark spirit had been released, or so it seemed, and certain religious leaders began to suggest that London itself – this vast urban creation which was the first of its kind upon the globe – was somehow responsible for the evil. Reverend Trussler, of the Holborn Baptist Church, compared the murders to the smoke of the London chimneys and denounced them as the necessary and inevitable results of modern existence. So why, then, should this taint not spread? Would it soon reach Manchester, and Birmingham, and Leeds? Other public leaders called for the detention of all prostitutes, ostensibly to save them from the activities of the Limehouse Golem; but such demands were part of a more general desire for some kind of ritual purification and cleansing. It was even suggested that the entire eastern portion of the city should be razed and estates of model dwellings erected in its place. The government of Mr Gladstone considered the idea, but it was eventually rejected as both impractical and expensive. Where, in particular, would the former inhabitants of the East End be housed while their new city was being constructed? And if these people were in some way responsible for the presence of the Golem, in the way that putrefying matter was thought to breed flies, they might simply spread the contagion if they were dispersed over the capital. The police themselves were not untouched by the feverish speculation, and even the detectives pursuing the case seemed to believe that they were on the trail of some genius or god of murder. They had not chosen to call him the Golem – that had been the invention of the *Morning Advertiser* – but now they used the term even in conversations among themselves. How, otherwise, could he have escaped detection for so long?

The sister of Gerrard, the clothes-seller, had been asleep in the attic storey of the house during the course of the murders; she had taken laudanum for a toothache and had consequently heard nothing. It is not easy to imagine her horror when she first came upon the bodies of the slain but, even as she saw her brother and his family lying dead, she noticed one thing: nothing in the house or shop had been disturbed, not one item of furniture or domestic object had been moved from its place. (She could not have known that the step-ladder, knocked over to arouse the servant's attention, had been put back in its original spot.) Somehow it was as if the family had been murdered without the assistance of any outside agency – almost as if it had *murdered itself* under the power of some dominating impulse. So the panic spread throughout London.

It even touched those who were not generally moved by public sensations, and who even affected to despise them. The murders in Limehouse led indirectly to *The Picture of Dorian Gray*, written by Oscar Wilde some eight years later, in which the opium dens and cheap theatres of that area play a large part in a somewhat melodramatic narrative. They also inspired the famous sequence of paintings by James McNeill Whistler, 'Limehouse Nocturnes', in which the brooding presence of the riverine streets is conveyed by viridian green, ultramarine, ivory and black. Whistler also described them as 'Harmonies upon a Theme', although they were conceived in the most disharmonious fashion – he spent one evening sketching the vicinity but, with his dark cloak and 'foreign' appearance, he was suspected of being the Golem and chased by a large crowd until he ran to the safety of the divisional police station where George Gissing had been questioned a few days before. Several plays were also written upon this murderous theme by hack writers, and were performed at the various 'blood tubs' or 'blood and thunder' playhouses where 'shockers' were the customary entertainment. At the Effingham in Whitechapel, for example, *The Limehouse Demon* became a standard of the horror repertoire together with *The Death of Chatterton* and *The Skeleton Cabman*. Small cardboard characters of the victims of the Limehouse Golem were also constructed, penny plain and twopence coloured, for use in booths and miniature theatres. It was in conditions such as these that Somerset Maugham and David Carreras, then young children, first became aware of their fascination for drama – and indeed Carreras himself in the 1920s wrote a play based upon the Limehouse killings entitled *No Man Knows My Name*.

And yet – in one of those coincidences that are so much part of this, or any, history – one theatrical figure of the 1880s was far more directly connected with the killing of the Gerrard family in Ratcliffe Highway. Gerrard had once been the 'dresser' of Dan Leno (in fact Leno had given the man some of his old female costumes when he started his business), and the great comedian had actually visited the Gerrard family only three days before their deaths. On that inauspicious occasion he had given them an impromptu rehearsal of his new song, 'The Boneless Wonder', during which he pretended to be made entirely of indiarubber.

Twenty-Nine

September 25, 1880: Elizabeth and I attended the panto-mime at the Oxford by the Tottenham Court Road. She insisted upon seeing Dan Leno play Sister Anne in *Bluebeard* but, as we stood by the entrance for a few minutes, I was delighted to hear everyone discussing my own little piece of business along the Ratcliffe Highway. Londoners love a good killing, on stage or off, and two of the wittier gentlemen were comparing the Limehouse Golem with Bluebeard himself. I was longing to approach them and introduce myself. 'I am he,' I would have said, 'I am the Golem. Here is my hand. You may shake it.' But I contented myself with a smile and a bow; they believed that they knew me, and bowed in return. Of course the commoner sort of people were also there – the mechanics and the small tradesmen went trooping up to the main hall, together with a few city clerks and their girls. Elizabeth asked me to purchase a book of words as we stood in the grand foyer. 'Old habits the hard,' I said to her.

'But some things have changed, John. Do you see the fres-coes? And all those flowers? We had nothing of the sort at the Washington or the Old Mo.'

'No more winkles and watercress, dear. Now it is chops and ale.'

The manager was at the door in a scarlet waistcoat; he was becoming agitated and waved his bejewelled hands in the air. 'Please to take your seats. Sixpence the body of the 'all, ninepence the gallery which is more select.' So we went up to the gallery and, as soon as Elizabeth saw the stage, she gripped my arm in her excitement; no doubt she could remember herself as the Older Brother or Little Victor's Daughter. The gas flares may have gone, and the audience were now more clean and wholesome, but for a moment she breathed the atmosphere which she had once loved so much. She hardly had time to point out the grand piano and the harmonium, when the pantomime boys came on. Then Dan Leno made his entrance, running down to the edge of the stage just like the old days, and my wife joined in the screaming laughter when he announced himself to be 'Sister Anne, the woman who knows'. I laughed as loud as anyone, because I knew that there was a murder in the air.

Thirty

It was not the first time that Dan Leno had taken on the role of Sister Anne, and in any case he had become accustomed to playing the dame. He was no longer the anxious but hopeful young comic whom Lambeth Marsh Lizzie had first met in 1864; now, sixteen years later, he was the established star of the halls who was billed as 'The Funniest Man On Earth'. In many respects he had become public property: his activities were chronicled in the newspapers, his appearance was disseminated throughout the country in countless photographs, and his 'funny female' impersonations were copied by the less successful comiques in a hundred low halls. He was well known as Dame Durden, as the Queen of Hearts in *Humpty Dumpty*, as the Baroness in *Babes in the Wood*, and as Widow Twankey in *Aladdin*; but his most famous, and ultimately most tragic, role was to be Mother Goose. Something then affected his mind, and he retired to a private asylum for a while – he never fully recovered, and there are some theatrical historians who claim that Mother Goose herself effectively destroyed him.

Sister Anne appeared for her main entrance in the middle of the first act; she was riding in a cart, which was pulled by two donkeys, and was dressed as a lady of the old school with towering wig and décolleté costume. It was not immediately clear why she was sitting in a donkey cart, but all was explained when a decrepit railway guard brought up the rear of the procession. The train had broken down, and she had been the only passenger.

'I say, missus, you *are* a swell.' This was the guard, speaking very loudly to be heard over the laughter of the audience.

'Do you think I look expensive enough?'

'Rather! You look like a walking vault.'

'Of course in *my* position I have to look wealthy.'

'That dress must have cost a lot of eggs.'

'I don't care about that, but I do grudge having so many expensive things underneath I daren't show.' At this point she raised herself gently from a sack of corn, and looked behind her with a puzzled expression.

'What, missus, ain't yer nothing to sit down on?'

'It's too bad. I have plenty to sit on, but nowhere nice to put it.'

The railway guard mopped his forehead until the laughter had subsided. 'So are you coming out in a minute?'

'*Au contraire*, I'm coming out in a rash.'

It was broad humour, of the kind the audience loved, but when it was delivered by Leno it seemed to become the essence of comedy itself; he was so plain and yet so haughty, with such a grand air and such a pitiful sniffle, ebullient in defeat and absurd in victory. The plot of the pantomime, rewritten by a journalist on the *Glow-Worm*, consisted of Sister Anne trying recklessly to capture the attentions of Bluebeard – she refused to hear anything 'untoward' about him, and was so desperate for a man that nothing would stop her. She was of a 'coming on' disposition and believed, in the words of one of her famous songs, 'I Don't Think I Put Myself Forward Too Much'. She had even learned to play the harp to attract 'Bluey', but of course her fingers, her arms and her dress managed to get entangled in the strings so that she ended up wrestling with the instrument upon the floor. Then she did a clog dance to entice her man, only to be told by him that she was 'as elegant as a steamroller'. But she never gave up hope and was always explaining to her beautiful sister, Fatima, the arts of seduction. One of the scenes which most entertained the audience occurred in the second act, when Sister Anne is changing behind a very small screen. Fatima came onto the stage and asked her gently, for fear of offending her feelings, 'Have you anything to do this evening, dear?'

'No,' Sister Anne replied. 'I have nothing on.'

It was a 'bit of fun', as Dan had said at the rehearsals, and the audience roared. There is perhaps no better indication of the taste of an age than its sense of humour, when the most painful or serious subjects can be so lightly handled that the joke itself becomes cathartic. That is why, even at the height of the Limehouse murders, many funny stories were being told about the 'Golem' and his victims. But if humour acts as a relief or release, it can also become an unacknowledged common language by which the worst aspects of a group or society can be made respectable. Perhaps that accounts for one of the scenes in the third act of *Bluebeard* when Sister Anne, having been tied to a chair by 'Bluey' for several days, faints away from want of food. At this point the villain unties her, lays her on the stage, and then begins to trample upon her in a pair of clogs. Sister Anne rouses herself for a few seconds, lifts her head and asks feebly, 'Whatever are you doing, dear?'

'It's my treatment. My doctor told me to take a walk every day on an empty stomach.'

It was not a bad bit of business, and the audience appreciated the joke. But it did suggest the extent to which Londoners of the period were eager to see the more forward or lecherous females punished for their behaviour. It would not be going too far to suggest, in fact, that there was some link between the murder of the prostitutes in Limehouse and the ritual humiliation of women in pantomime. John Cree certainly laughed very loudly when Sister Anne found herself being boiled alive with a dozen potatoes. 'Bluey!' she called. 'Bluey! I'm just slipping out to buy some carrots!' Very carefully she extricated herself from the tin bath, carrying a potato in each hand which she began to eat. This was Dan Leno as Elizabeth Cree still remembered him – with that melancholy face ('all the tragedy that is written on the face of a baby monkey', as Max Beerbohm described it), with that poignant glance, with that nervous rush of words lapsing into hoarseness, the shrug of the shoulders, and then with the sudden comic remark like a shaft of lightning in a storm, he had retained all the pathos and the ardour of his youth.

Sister Anne had finally realised that 'Bluey' was not 'quite her cup of tea', and was sitting in the comfort of her own parlour with an old friend and confidante. The role of Joanna Screwloose was played by a large and imposing comic actor, Herbert Campbell, whose matronly presence was the perfect foil to Leno's diminutive but vivid character.

'There is one thing, Joanna, which does rather hurt me.'

'What is that Anne, ducks?'

'I was good for another ten years, if Bluey had changed his ways.'

'But a woman in your position . . .'

'What position is that?'

'Let's not go into it now, dear.'

And so it went on. Elizabeth Cree realised that on several occasions the two comedians were 'gagging' one another and delivering lines extempore, but that only increased her pleasure in their performance and revived memories of her own old life upon the stage.

Thirty-One

All this time I had never really thought about my mother – she must already have rotted away, thank God – but there were occasions when I saw her still. Not in the flesh, of course, but in the spirit of the funny females whom Dan impersonated. There was one in particular who used to make me scream – Miss Devoutly, a lily-white virgin who was such a religious enthusiast that she made a habit of swooning in the arms of her vicar. I helped him in that, and gave him some of the references – 'Judges, chapter fifteen, verse twelve!' she would cry out before having one of her 'turns'. It was just like the old days in Lambeth Marsh. In the same way Dan would assist me with the Older Brother, and once even taught me a special kind of walk; it was that of a drunken waiter pretending to be sober and, as Dan said, it was a 'tip' that 'served' me well. But I also liked to pick up hints on my own account, and there were times when I would dress up in my masculine duds and hang around the docks or the markets to pick up some more of the 'slanguage'. The costers liked to speak it backwards among themselves, as I discovered one night in Shadwell when I was asked to have 'a top of reeb' instead of a pot of beer – Dan laughed when I told him, although I suspect he knew all the lingo already. Codger slang was much more delicate, and I found that to order a glass of rum I had to say, 'a Jack-surpass of finger and thumb', and to smoke a pipe of tobacco was to 'blow your yard of tripe of nosey-me-knocker'. Sometimes I believe that the race of Londoners is quite apart from the rest of the world!

One afternoon, the Older Brother went back to my old haunts in Lambeth. I passed the lodgings in Peter Street, and instinctively turned into the doorway just as if I still lived there with the dead woman; it gave me the strangest pleasure to know that, if she had been alive still, she would not have recognised me at all. I was a stranger in life and in death. Her grave was in the paupers' cemetery by St George's Circus; I knelt before it and took up the attitude known on the stage as 'horror upon horror's head'. 'I have changed everything,' I whispered to her. 'If you can see me from the cinder-heap, you will know. Do you remember the old song, Mother?' I expect that she would have liked to have heard one of her hymns, and drag me down into her own evil world, so instead I came out swaggering with the drinking song from the Coal Hole in the Strand:

> Then the hangman will come too,
> Will come too,
> Then the hangman will come too
> With all his bloody crew,
> And he'll tell me what to do
> Damn his eyes.

> And now I goes upstairs,
> Goes upstairs,
> And now I goes upstairs,
> Here's an end to all my cares,
> So I spit on all your prayers
> Damn your eyes.

We were never permitted to sing it on the stage, but Uncle repeated it to me until I had learned it by heart – what a piece of tomfoolery it was, and the best antidote ever concocted to the religious frenzy.

That night I was at my best and, after the performance, Charles Weston of the Drury Lane asked me if I would care to play one of the principal boys in that season's *Babes in the Wood*.

'*Would* I?'

'*Wood* you?'

'Yes, indeed.'

I suppose that might have marked the beginning of a little sourness between Dan and me. He was not particularly over-joyed when one of the regular artists left the halls for the seasonal pantomime, but he never said anything directly; he was always the perfect gentleman off the stage, and yet he was no longer quite so ready with his fun. There had been times when, to amuse the others after a rehearsal, Dan and I would do our own version of the *poses plastiques*, or plastic poses as we called them. We would drape our arms around the props in a series of unnatural attitudes depicting 'The Sultan's Favourite Returning From The Bath' or 'Napoleon's Rash Vow'. But his heart did not seem to be in it now, and we screamed no more. Still, I was a great success as the principal boy; I think I was the first to wear spangled tights upon the stage and, not for the first time, set up a trend. Walter Arbuthnot was the Baroness, while that laugh-a-minute duo, Lorna and Toots Pound, were the children. I can still remember the tears welling up in my eyes as we clasped each other's hands at the last performance and sang the familiar refrain:

In the panto of old Drury Lane,
We have all come together again,

165

And we hope to appear
For many a year
In the panto of old Drury Lane.

But it was not to be, alas, and my last year in the halls was to
be filled with woes and troubles.

They really began when I was back with Dan at the Standard in Clerkenwell; we knew that a large part of the audience
was of the Hebrew persuasion, so we had put in a few Yiddish
comiqueries that set them roaring. I had just finished my ren-
dition of 'Flossie the Frivolous' and hurried off to the sound of
great applause; some coins were thrown upon the stage, but I
was so tired and breathless that I simply could not bring myself
to sing again. 'I'm good for nothing,' I told Aveline Mortimer,
a rather bitter simultaneous dancer who specialised in 'Merry
Moments'. 'Whatever shall I do?'

'Just go on, dear, and wish them *Meesa Meschina*. It's their
holiday.'

So I went back on the stage, threw my arms wide, smiled
and spoke out very clearly. 'Ladies and gentlemen, and especially those gentlemen not utterly unconnected with a certain
historical chosen race—' That set them laughing, and so I
paused for a moment to get my breath. 'May I wish you, from
the bottom of my heart, *Meesa Meschina*!' There was a sudden
silence, and then such a pandemonium of whistling and hiss-
ing that I felt compelled to leave the stage.

Uncle hurried up to me as I stood, bewildered, in the wings.
'Whatever did you say that for, ducks?' He signalled to Jo to
pull down the curtain. 'Don't you know what that means in
their lingo? *Meesa Meschina* means SUDDEN DEATH!'

I was horrified and when I saw my erstwhile friend, Aveline
Mortimer, slipping away I could have indulged in a piece of sudden death on my own account. She had always been envious of

my success, but it was the most spiteful act she could possibly have performed. Fortunately Dan was equal to any kind of theatrical emergency and, since he was still in the costume of the Beautiful Landlady – with corkscrew ringlets and all – he went straight on and began to perform 'Man, by One Who Hates 'Em'. That quietened them a little, and when he followed it up with 'I'm Back on Licensed Premises' they were perfectly settled.

I was still a little shaken, as you can imagine. I never normally touched a drop but, after the show was over, Uncle took me 'next door' and bought me a large glass of shrub. 'It was that cow Aveline,' I told him. 'She will never dance on the same bill with me again.'

'Don't take on so, ducks. It's all forgotten, as the executioner said to the hanged man.' He patted my hand, and then held it for a minute more than was proper.

'Get me another glass, Uncle. I'm in that kind of mood.'

At this moment Dan sauntered in, wearing the latest fashion of broad check suit. 'I bet you could kill her,' he said.

'I could.'

'That's good. Keep in that state. I think I've got a little part for you.'

I should explain that sometimes we did 'incidentals' between the turns; it might be a burlesque medley of Shakespeare (Dan did a screamingly funny Desdemona), or a 'shocker' like *Sweeney Todd* played for the laughs. I'll never forget the time when the famous '"Over" Rowley' played one of Sweeney's victims who escaped by doing a series of gag somersaults; the audience would cry out, 'Over, Rowley!' and then he would turn another one of them until he finally vanished from the stage. Anyway, Dan had a plan for another 'incidental'. He knew that Gertie Latimer was about to put on *Maria Marten, or the Murder in the Red Barn* as her new horror at the Bell in Limehouse, and he had decided to guy it with a little something

167

of his own. He was going to play Maria, the unfortunate victim or murderee, while he intended me to play the sweetheart who strangles her and then hides her body in the notorious barn. Hugo Stead, well known as 'The Dramatic Maniac', was going to play Maria's mother who has visions of her daughter's death: the point was that Hugo had developed a wonderful little routine known as 'The Perfect Cure' whereby he simply jumped up and down, his arms pinned to his sides and his legs locked together, while he sang. So, whenever Mrs Marten had one of her visions, she would jump up and down in her excitement. 'Over' Rowley was going to be introduced somehow, just for the fun of having two of them capering about the stage. This was Dan's plan, in any event, and we sat in the public house discussing the tricks and the business. I had never played a murderer before, let alone a droll murderer, and I was a trifle nervous about the way it would go.

The curious point is that my future husband, Mr John Cree, was actually sitting very close to us in conversation with two patter comedians known as 'The Evening Shadows'. We had exchanged one or two words since that dreadful night when Little Victor Farrell 'met his doom', as they say on the bills, so I felt quite at my ease when Uncle beckoned him over to our table. 'John,' he shouted. 'Come over here. Dan has decided to go legitimate.' It was always our aim to have something 'placed' in the newspapers and, if possible, to have our names mentioned. So I smiled very sweetly when he brought up a chair.

'Mr Cree,' I said, 'thank you for joining us. Dan is planning something very serious.'

'What is that to be?'

'A shocker. I am to become a very masculine murderer.'

'I don't believe such a part will suit you at all.'

'Oh, you know, Mr Cree, stage folk are capable of anything.'

But then Dan spoiled the fun by explaining that it was a spoof interlude. Nevertheless John Cree did write, in the following week's issue of the *Era*, that 'The great comic funster, Lambeth Marsh Lizzie, better known to her countless admirers as The Older Brother, will be entertaining the public in an entirely new and sensational part which we believe to have some connection with a celebrated crime.' I think even then that John was partial to me, but I can honestly say that I never led him on; he was a gentleman, too, and would not take advantage of our snug little chats about the business after he had put me in his column. He told me that he had always lived in the shadow of his father, who was some kind of businessman in Lancaster, and I sympathised very strongly. 'But at least,' I added, 'you know your parents. I wish I could say as much for myself.' He took my hand for a moment, but I disengaged myself very gently. Then he told me that he was a Roman Catholic, and I shook my head in disbelief. 'That is quite a coincidence, Mr Cree. I have always yearned for religion, too.' He confided in me that he had always wanted to be a literary man, and that the *Era* was just the first step. I told him that it was exactly the same for me, and that I had joined the halls only that I might one day become a serious actress: so we became quite pally, and after a while he showed me a play that he had been writing. It was called *Misery Junction*, in honour of that famous spot on the York Hotel corner of the Waterloo Road; this was the place where the artistes out of a shop congregated and waited for the agents. I suppose that was why he was so interested in me and all my little affairs; I was flattered by his attentions, I admit it, but I never expected anything further.

Rehearsals for our spoof interlude were hellish, because all the fun was held in reserve: 'Over' Rowley did not roll over, except in a very half-hearted manner indeed, and 'The Dramatic Maniac' kept his jumps less than manic. I had my lines by heart, of course, but I was always being caught out by Dan's high spirits and general excitement. 'What a lot of cows,' he said when he first saw the farmhouse set. 'We might as well be in the green room.'

'Are you ready at last, Dan?' Uncle was the stage manager and liked to keep good order, although he was the first to laugh at Dan's remarks.

'No. I'm not ready. I've no particular reason for being any-where. In fact I'm going somewhere else.'

'Come on, Dan. Play the game. We haven't got time for the chaff.'

So then, with the galley pulls in our hands, we spent two afternoons learning the script as well as all the trimmings we devised as we went along. Uncle had written a nice set of verses for the murderer, when he is standing alone in front of the red barn, and I sang them out with gusto:

> I will be a mad butcher, they will call me insane,
> But I was driven to this by my false Mary Jane
>   Marten—

Dan was meant to come on at this point and say 'Parten?' instead of 'Pardon?' but he just stared down at the galleys.

'Go on,' I said, quite put out by the silence. 'It's your turn now.'

'I'm waiting for my cue.'

'Dan, I gave you your cue.'

'Whatever do you mean? My cue is – "Lizzie says Marten, and then laughs wildly".'

'I did laugh.' I turned to Uncle for support. 'Didn't I?'

'Yes, Dan. She laughed.'

'Was that a laugh? I thought she had the croup.' Then he turned the galley sheets over, and somehow managed to get entangled with them. 'There's something very wrong here. I seem to be leaving the stage with a goose. Where did the goose come from?'

Uncle was always very patient, and went over to help him. 'What page are you on?'

'Nine.'

'You've turned over three pages at once. There you are. Go on.' So then Dan recited Maria Marten's last words. 'I rue the day when he wooed me. Yes I do. I woo the day that he rued me. I was sitting on the step thinking of life – or was I sitting on life and thinking of the step? – with my usual flair in the following manner. Oh what is woman? Who is she? Is she imperative?' At some point in this monologue – which I am quite sure Dan could have continued for ever – I was supposed to creep up behind him and, much to the delight of the gallery, strangle him with my bare hands. Then I had to drag him into the barn, bury his body beneath some straw, and turn to the audience with 'It was all very restrained, wasn't it?'

'You know,' Dan said, after he had finished the rehearsal. 'I do think that scene is becoming very funny. I can see a lot of bounce in it.' And so it proved – except that, on one night, there was a little bit too much of the bounce. Dan was just finishing Maria's soliloquy, having added some remarks about the new laws on marrying a deceased wife's sister (he could find humour in anything), when I crept up behind him and began to put my hands around his throat. 'Be philosophical about it,' he was saying to no one in particular. 'Don't give it another thought.' A child screamed somewhere in the gallery as I closed on him: the noise must have disturbed me, because I had my hands around his throat for far too long. He was too much of a professional to stop the scene but, when I dragged him to the barn, he really had gone limp on me. I could see that his face had turned grey beneath the make-up, and he hardly seemed to be breathing. Of course I still retained my presence of mind, even with a thousand faces watching me, and I called out, 'Come here, Mr Marten. Something is very wrong with your girl.' Uncle was playing Dan's father, and was already in his mourning dress for the final burial scene. So he ran out, carrying his black hat in his hand, and together we took Dan off the stage: the crowd thought it was all part of the fun, and began to laugh. The fiddler had the presence of mind to jump up and begin a musical interlude, while Uncle and I tried to revive Dan with smelling salts and brandy. Then 'Over' Rowley and 'The Dramatic Maniac' improvised with a series of jumps and somersaults. Dan came round at last, and gave me a look that I will never forget. 'The last thing I felt,' he said, 'were those big hands of yours. Whatever did you think you were doing?'

'I suppose I don't know my own strength, Dan.'

'You can say that again.' He could see that I was about to burst into tears and so, weak though he was, he got me laughing with a remark about his 'indiarubber neck'. Then he insisted on going back to the performance: he was, as I said, always the professional.

But I think he remained nervous of me, and never again did he involve me in any knock-about farceries. Uncle took my side, naturally, and blamed it all on my eagerness; he had become quite a favourite with me now, and sometimes I even allowed him to pat my hand or stroke my knee. He was never permitted any other familiarities but he called me his 'little Lizzie', and once took the liberty of addressing me as his 'darling girl'.

'I am not your darling, Uncle, and I am not your girl.'

'Have a heart, Lizzie. Don't play so innocent with me.'

172

'I am not playing. I am real.'

'If you say so, Lizzie, if you say so.'

Uncle did not live in diggings but had purchased a smart new villa in Brixton; Dan and I, with one or two of the others, would sometimes make up a tea-party there. What fun we had in those days, with Dan pretending to be overawed by Uncle's signs of gentility. He would point at a silver teapot or a piece of lovely ebony furniture and ask us, in cockney slang, 'Don't it dumb yer?' Then our new resident turn, Pat 'It's All In The Patter' Patterson, would take up the business with a running commentary on the plush curtains, the ormolu clock, the paper flowers and everything else. Uncle always laughed when we spoofed his possessions but, as I was soon to discover, he kept his choicest items to himself.

I happened to be visiting him for tea one day, a few hours before a performance, when I realised that I was to be the only guest. 'My dearest niece,' he said. 'Come into the parlour.'

'Isn't that a nursery rhyme, Uncle?'

'It may be, Lizzie, it may be. But come in nevertheless.' He pronounced the last word in a deep, rich voice like some lion comique. 'Sit down and rest your pegs.' He filled me up with tea and cucumber sandwiches (I can never resist a nice bit of cucumber) and then, quite out of the blue, he asked me if I would like to know a secret.

'I love mysteries, Uncle. Is it a shocker?'

'Well, my dear, I believe it is. Come upstairs for a moment and we'll see.' So I followed him up to the attic regions. 'This is my dark room,' he whispered, tapping one door. 'And here is the surprise!' He opened the door, and I barely had time to notice the extraordinary expression upon his face before he ushered me into what I took to be an office: there was a desk and chair in a corner but then, of all things, in the middle of the room was a camera with its cloth and tripod.

He was such a darling man I would have expected him to take up water-colours, or something of the kind. 'Whatever do you want with this, Uncle?'

'That's the secret, Lizzie.' I could smell spirits on his breath, now that he was close to me, and I supposed that he had been taking a little something with his tea. 'Can I count on you to keep mum?' I nodded, and drew my hand across my mouth like the old servant in *The Great Fire of London*. 'These are some of my girls. Over here.' He went across to the desk, unlocked it, and took out some papers. At least they seemed to be papers but, when he handed them to me, I saw that they were photographs – photographs of women, half-naked or entirely nude, with whips and rods in their hands. 'What do you think of them, Lizzie?' he asked me eagerly. I was too surprised to say anything at all. 'It's just my fun, Lizzie. You understand. I like a good beating now and again. Doesn't everyone?'

'I know her.' I held up one of the photographs. 'That's the girl who used to assist the great Bolini. She used to be sawn in half.'

'That's her, ducks. What a performer.' Of course I was horrified by Uncle's dirty little secret, but I was determined not to show it. I think I even smiled. 'And you know, dear, I have a favour to ask of you.' I shook my head, but he preferred not to notice and went over to the camera. 'Would you oblige me with a pose plastique, Lizzie? Just a tableau?'

'I would rather be destroyed first,' I said, unconsciously repeating a line from *The Phantom Crew*. 'It is very disgusting.'

'Come on, dear. There's no need to play your games with me.'

'Whatever do you mean?'

'Oh, darling. Uncle knows all about precious Lambeth Marsh Lizzie.' I suppose he must have startled me, because I felt myself blushing. 'That's right. I've followed you, dearest, when you've put on your male duds and strolled down Lime-house way. Do you prefer to be a man, Lizzie, and attract the women?'

'It is nothing to you what I choose to do.'

'Oh dear, I quite forgot. And then there was that business with Little Victor.'

'What nonsense is this now?'

'I saw you and him in the Canteen that night. You gave him quite a kick, didn't you, Lizzie? It just so happened to be the night that he fell down a flight of steps and left his mortal coil. Surely you remember that, Lizzie? You were so heart-broken at the time.'

'I've got nothing to say to you, Uncle.'

'You don't have to *say* anything, dear.' What could I do? Some foul-minded people might listen to his stories about me, and I was only a defenceless artiste. Half the men and women of London would already have branded me as shameless for doing the halls, and the rest would be happy to believe the worst. It was in my interest to keep Uncle sweet. So that is why, every Sunday afternoon, I would take a cab to Brixton and in his attic room administer a very sound beating to the dreadful man; I was rather rough with him, I admit, but he never seemed to mind. In fact every time I drew blood he would shout 'Go on! Go on!' until I was quite exhausted. That is the penalty of my nature, you see, since I always do everything to the utmost of my ability. I am a professional. But I don't think that Uncle's heart was up to it: he was very friendly with the bottle and, being such a heavy man, he was bound to feel the strain.

About three months after he had persuaded me to wield the lash, he was taken poorly with palpitations. I remember the occasion well: he had come to our rehearsals of *The Mad*

Butcher, or What's in this Sausage? when he suddenly fell against the scenery. He was sweating and shaking so much that I urged Dan to call for a doctor but, by the time he arrived, it was too late. Uncle was gone to his reward, but I had the satisfaction of knowing that the last word he breathed was my name.

Thirty-Two

MR GREATOREX: So this is Elizabeth Cree. She stands here, according to the account you have just had the pleasure of hearing, as a much wronged and much maligned woman. She is an exemplary wife who has been charged with the foul crime of murder on the evidence of circumstance and gossip alone. You have been told that her unfortunate husband, John Cree, destroyed himself by eating arsenic powder. And why did he willingly embrace such a painful and protracted death? It seems that he was a Romanist who, according to his wife, was so afflicted by morbid piety that he believed he was condemned by God and watched by demons. Self-murder was his deliverance, although it might strike you as a trifle odd that he should thereby deliver himself to those same demons for eternity.

But let us leave religious speculation on one side for a moment, and contemplate the facts of the matter. Elizabeth Cree visited a druggist's shop in Great Titchfield Street a few days before the death of her husband. 'For the rats', she said – although the maid of the house, Aveline Mortimer, has testified that the newly built residence in New Cross harboured no vermin of any kind. Then her husband is found dead of arsenic poisoning. The corner has already testified that the victim must have imbibed quantities of that substance for at least a week before his untimely and unfortunate demise. You may find this unusual in the suicide of a desperate man. And then we have the evidence of a fatal dose, on the evening of October the 26th last year, when the maid has testified that she heard John Cree exclaiming to his wife, 'You devil! You are the one!' Only a short while later, as he lay upon the Turkey carpet in his bedroom, Mrs Cree ran into the street shouting 'John has destroyed himself' and other such words. It may seem odd to you that she already knew that this was the intention and the act of her husband – more peculiar still that she realised he was dying of arsenic poisoning without having examined him – but, in any case, it was not until some minutes later that she was able to rouse Doctor Moore. It was he who pronounced John Cree dead, at which point Mrs Cree fainted into the arms of her maid.

Let us consider Mr Cree now. His wife has informed you that he was a morbid papist, but no other witness has given evidence to that effect. We are, in other words, supposed to rely upon the sole testimony of Mrs Cree in order to account for her husband's self-murder. The maid, who lived in the same house for some years, has denied each one of Mrs Cree's allegations. On the contrary, she tells us, Mr Cree was a kind and liberal employer who gave no sign of any religious obsession at all. Once a week he attended the Catholic church of St Mary of Sorrows in New Cross with his wife, but this was at Mrs Cree's urging; she had a great desire, according to the maid, to appear respectable. And since Mr Cree's temperament and state of mind are so important in this case – indeed it is the sole point of the prisoner's defence – it will be appropriate to consider his life and character in a little more detail. His father was a hosier in Lancaster, but he came to London in the early 1860s to seek his fortune as a literary man. He wished to be a playwright, it seems, and so naturally he was inclined towards the world of the theatre. He found employment as a reporter on the *Era*, a journal devoted to the stage, and it was in this capacity he met and eventually married the woman who stands in the dock before you. Some time after this marriage John Cree's father died of a gastric fever, and his only son came into a large fortune. This is the fortune, of course, which his wife has now inherited. He gave up his post on the *Era* and from that time forward devoted his life to literary pursuits of a more serious nature. He frequented the Reading Room of the British Museum, as you have heard, and continued writing his drama. He is also, from the notes found in his possession, supposed to have been compiling a record of the London poor. Is this the kind of man who would succumb to religious delusions, as his wife has stated? Or perhaps John Cree was some evil domestic tyrant, some Bluebeard, who promised a life of unendurable misery? But this is not the case. By all accounts he was a quiet and courteous man who had no reason to kill himself, and against whom his wife could have no possible complaint. He was not, to use a modern analogy, some kind of Limehouse Golem.

Thirty-Three

September 26, 1880: My dear wife loved the pantomime so much that, last night in the carriage back to New Cross, she sang the reprise with which she and Dan used to close in the old days. As soon as she entered the house, she clasped the maid's hand and recounted the business of the whole performance. 'And then Dan did a little bit of back-walking with Bluebeard. "I'm going out and then I'm coming in again, just so you'll know I'm here." Do you remember it, Aveline?' My wife even imitated the hoarse voice of Sister Anne. I went upstairs to my study in order to settle an argument I was having with myself; I seemed to remember an essay on the pantomime by Thomas De Quincey, but I could not recall its name. Was it something like 'Laughter and Screaming', or 'The Trick of Screaming'? I had only remembered it as a very fine title indeed, but the precise wording now escaped me. So I went through the great writer's works and, by curious coincidence, found it in the same volume as my other cherished piece, 'On Murder Considered as One of the Fine Arts'. Its exact title was 'Laugh, Scream and Speech' and I discovered that I had even marked a passage in the margin, where pantomime is described as 'the short for fun, whim, trick and atrocity – that is, clown atrocity or crimes that delight us'.

What a wonderful phrase that was – *crimes that delight us* – and of course it quite explained all the popular interest in my own little dramas on the streets of London. I could even see myself appearing before the next whore with a mallet in my hand, exclaiming 'Here we are again!' in the right tone of screaming excitement. I might even put on costume before I slit them. Oh what a life it is! And of course the audience loves every minute of it – was it not Edmund Burke, in his very suggestive essay on the Sublime and Beautiful who explained how the greatest aesthetic sensations come from the experience of terror and danger? Horror is the true sublime. The common people and even the middling classes profess to be sickened or alarmed by my great career but, secretly, they have loved and admired each stage of it. Every newspaper in the country has dwelled reverentially upon my great acts, and sometimes they have even exaggerated them in order to satisfy the public taste – in a sense they have become my understudies, who watch every move and practise every line. I once worked on the *Era*, and I know how absurdly gullible newspaper reporters can be; no doubt they now believed in the Limehouse Golem with the same fervour as everybody else, and willingly accepted that some supernatural creature was preying upon the living. Mythology of a kind has returned to London – if indeed it ever really left it. Interrogate an inhabitant of London very carefully, and you will find the remnants of some frightened medieval churl.

I hired a cab to Aldgate, and then took a stroll towards Ratcliffe Highway; there was a policeman outside the house of the beautifully slain, and a small crowd who stood in the street with no other purpose than to gape or to gossip. I joined them readily enough, and was pleased to hear the evidence of their great respect and admiration. 'He did it without a sound,' said one. 'He cut their throats before they even knew it.' That was not strictly true, since the wife and children had seen me on the stairs, but, still, it is the thought that counts. ''E must be invisible,' a woman was whispering to her neighbour. 'Nobody saw 'im come or go.' I wanted to thank her for her flattering report but, of course, I was compelled to be invisible among them again. 'Tell me,' I asked an odd-looking fellow with a red scarf knotted around his head, 'was there much blood?'

'Tubs of it. They were washing it down all day.'

'And what of the poor victims? What will happen to them?'

'The cemetery in Wellclose Square. The same grave for them all.' He opened his eyes very wide as he imparted this interesting information to me. 'And I'll tell you what will happen to the Golem when they find *him.*'

'If they find him.'

'They'll bury *him* underneath the crossroads. With a stake through his heart.'

It sounded almost like a crucifixion, but I knew it to be the old penalty for extravagant crime: better that than to be left in chains by the riverside, while the tides washed over my body. Infinite London would always minister to me in my affliction.

I went back to New Cross and listened to my wife playing a new tune by Charles Dibdin on the piano.

Thirty-Four

When the police detectives came to interview Dan Leno on the subject of the Gerrard murders in the Ratcliffe Highway, only a few hours after John Cree had been consulting Thomas De Quincey's essay on pantomime, they happened to discover a copy of that author's 'On Murder Considered as One of the Fine Arts' in the great comedian's drawing room. But Leno had no interest in death of any kind (in fact he was thoroughly frightened of the topic), and the presence of this volume in his house had a much more unlikely explanation; it was a result of his passion for Joseph Grimaldi, the most famous clown of the eighteenth century.

The history of pantomime had been Leno's study ever since he had made his name in the music-hall; it was as if 'The Funniest Man On Earth' wished to understand the conditions which had, in a sense, created him. He collected old playbills as well as such items of memorabilia as the harlequin's costume from *The Triumph of Mirth* and the wand from *The Magic Circle*. Of course he knew of Grimaldi from the beginning – forty years after his death, he was still the most famous clown of all – and one of the first theatrical souvenirs he purchased was a colour print of 'Mr Grimaldi as Clown in the Popular New Pantomime of Mother Goose'. He had been 'the most wonderful creature of his day', according to one contemporary, because 'there was such *mind* in everything he did'. The phrase had appealed to Leno when he first read it, because it seemed to summarise his own performance; for him, too, it was a question of 'thinking through' (as he used to put it) an entire character. It was not enough to dress as Sister Anne or Mother Goose; it was necessary to become them. He also relished the famous story of Grimaldi's visit to a doctor while he was performing in Manchester; he was already in the grip of that nervous exhaustion which would eventually destroy him, and the doctor took one look at the poor man's face and gave his verdict: 'There is only one thing for you,' he said. 'You must go and see Grimaldi the clown.'

But Dan Leno knew very little else about his great predecessor until a few weeks before when, on the advice of Statisticon, 'The Memory Man', he visited the library of the British Museum. Here, in the catalogues beneath the vast dome, he discovered *The Memoirs of Joseph Grimaldi*, edited by 'Boz'. Leno was a literate, if not an educated, man – he always said that his school had been a travelling trunk – and he knew well enough that 'Boz' was the late Charles Dickens. This afforded him greater pleasure still, because he had always admired Dickens's portrayal of theatrical folk in *Nicholas Nickleby* and in *Hard Times*; he had once even met the great novelist, when he was playing at the Tivoli in Wellington Street and Dickens had come around afterwards to congratulate him on his performance. Dickens himself was always an admirer of the halls, and divined in Leno some bright image of his own desperate childhood.

Of course Leno immediately ordered the edited memoirs, and spent the rest of the day reading the narrative of Grimaldi's adventures. He had come naked and piping into the world on December the 18th, just two days before the date of Leno's own birth – whether they had both emerged under a lucky or unlucky star was, as yet, uncertain. He discovered that Grimaldi was born in Stanhope Street, Clare Market, in 1779 and had first appeared upon the stage three years later; Clare Market was not very far from Leno's own birthplace and he, too, had started work at the age of three. Here, then, was a kindred spirit. With increasing enthusiasm and excitement he noted down the details of Grimaldi's characteristic costume of white silk with variously coloured patches and spangles; Grimaldi, generally being mute upon the stage, would point to the colour which symbolised his mood. Leno wrote down the details of an entire scene between Guzzle the Drinking Clown and Gobble the Eating Clown; then he transcribed the words of Grimaldi's most famous and popular song, 'Hot Codlins', and even went so far as to memorise certain sentences from the clown's last speech to the theatre-goers of London: 'It is four years since I jumped my last jump, filched my last oyster and ate my last sausage. I am not so rich a man as I was then for, as some of you may remember, I used to have a fowl in one pocket and sauce for it in the other. Eight and forty years have passed over my head, and I am sinking fast. I now stand worse on my legs than I used to do on my head. So tonight has seen me assume the motley for the last time – it seemed to cling to my skin as I took it off a few moments ago, and the old cap and bells rang mournfully as I quitted them for ever. I have overleaped myself at last, ladies and gentlemen, and I must hasten to bid you farewell. Farewell! Farewell!' At this point, as Dickens records in a footnote, he was assisted from the stage. Dan Leno thought it the most wonderful speech he had ever encountered and, under the dome of the Reading Room, he recited it again and again until he had got it by heart. And as he whispered it to himself he thought of all the poor lost people who haunted the streets of the city, the children without a bed and the families without a home; for some reason Grimaldi, in his last days, seemed to represent them and console them. He remembered the speech, too, when he himself lay sick and dying; then Dan Leno spoke it aloud, word for word, while those around his deathbed believed that he was delirious.

During the course of that spring day in 1880, however, he still saw only the light and glory of Grimaldi's genius. He paid particular attention to Dickens's suggestion that 'his Clown was an embodied conception of his own', since he believed that the novelist had hit upon a characteristic which he himself also possessed; and when Dickens went on to describe 'the genuine droll, the grimacing, filching, irresistible, flinching Clown', he knew, without any arrogance or presumption, that he had truly inherited Grimaldi's spirit. Whether it was the strange coincidence of birth dates, or the very atmosphere of London from which they both came and within which they both dwelled, there could be no doubt that Grimaldi and Leno were extraordinarily alike in their comedy and in the quality of their stage presence. Of course Grimaldi was often a Harlequin and Leno often a Dame (although Grimaldi had sometimes dressed up as a female, most notably as Baroness Pompsini in *Harlequin and Cinderella*), but their characters and dispositions were much the same. They sprang from the same soil, and as Leno left the British Museum on that warm London evening he decided to walk down to Clare Market where Grimaldi had been born.

It was the same squalid, reckless, haunting confusion of shops, alleys, tenements and public houses which it had always been (swept away twenty years later, however, by the 'improvements' and the building of Kingsway); in the year of Grimaldi's death, Dickens had described the area in *The Pickwick Papers* as one of 'ill lighted and worse ventilated rooms' with vapours 'like those of a fungus-pit'. Leno entered Stanhope Street, and tried to imagine in which house Grimaldi had been born; but these were all poor lodgings and the great Clown could have emerged from any of them. 'Oh, Mr Leno, sir, good evening to you.'

'Good evening.' He turned to find a shabby-looking young man peering out from one of the porches.

'I don't believe you remember me, sir.'

'No. Forgive me, but I can't say that I do.'

The man, who could have been no more than twenty-two or twenty-three, had a wild and earnest look which alarmed Leno: he knew well enough the effects of heavy drinking upon the mind. 'I thought not, sir. I was one of the crowd in *Mother Goose* at the Lane three years ago, sir. I was the one who used to give you the hat and muff.'

'You gave them very well, as I recall.' Leno peered around into the gloom of this narrow court.

'Many of us theatrical folk live here, Mr Leno. You see how close it is to the Lane and to the smaller halls.' He stepped out from the porch. 'I was never a second late with that muff all the run, sir, if you remember.'

'Indeed I do. The muff was always on cue.'

'But I've had a lot of trouble since then, sir. Our profession can be a hard one.'

'Ah, yes, true enough.' The young man's jacket and shirt were threadbare, and he looked as if he had not eaten for a day or two.

'Yes, sir, I was touring with *Babes in the Wood* when I got badly bitten in Margate.'

'You must be wary of the landladies. Some of them are very careless with their teeth.'

'Oh no, sir. It was a real dog. It bit me through the wrist and ankle.'

Suddenly he felt such pity and sympathy for the young man

that he could have embraced him here, in the very court where Grimaldi had once lived. 'Wrist and ankle? What were you doing at the time? Scratching your leg?'

'Separating two dogs which were in the way of fighting. I was laid up three weeks in a hospital ward and, when I came out, my place was taken. I've been out of a shop ever since.'

Dan Leno took a sovereign from his pocket and gave it to the man. 'This is for the time lost on *Babes*. Think of it as coming from the profession.' The man seemed about to weep and so he added, very quickly, 'Did you know that the great Grimaldi was born around here?'

'Oh yes, sir. He came from the very lodgings I have now. I was about to tell you, because I guessed that was why you had come.'

'Could I intrude? Just for a moment?'

'You can come up and be welcome, sir. To have had Grimaldi and Leno under the same roof . . .' He followed the young man up two flights of cramped and dirty stairs. 'We live in no comfort, so you must excuse our circumstances.'

'Oh, don't mind me. I have known the life very well.' He was led into a small, low-ceilinged room, and at once he could see a pregnant woman lying quietly upon a mattress.

'My wife, sir, is almost due. Do excuse her if she doesn't get up. It's Mr Leno, Mary, come to visit us.' She turned her head, and tried to rise. Dan Leno went over to her quickly and touched her forehead; she was burning with fever, and Leno looked across at her husband in alarm. 'The doctor has given her some physic,' he said in a lower voice. 'He says that it's quite natural at her stage.' But, even as he spoke, he seemed about to weep again.

With that quickness of thought and perception for which he was remarkable upon the stage, Leno now decided to act. 'Would you be terribly offended,' he said, 'if I ask my own doctor to call? He is only around the corner, in a manner of speaking, and he has experience with childbirth.'

'Oh yes, sir. If you think he might be able to assist her.' Only now did Leno take in the rest of the room where, to his surprise, he saw some old playbills and song sheets plastered upon the walls. 'These are my special items,' the young man said. 'I could never part with them.' Here were pictures of Walter Laburnum, Brown The Tragedian (No Matter!) and the Great Mackney; even as the young woman sighed upon the mattress, Leno could see the song sheets for 'The Ticket of Leave Man' and 'Bacon And Greens'. 'And this is a little memento of Grimaldi himself.' He showed Leno a playbill in a corner of the room which announced in large black capitals that 'Mr Grimaldi's Farewell Benefit will be Performed on Friday, 27 June, 1828, with *A Music Melange* to be Succeeded by *The Adopted Child* and Concluded with *Harlequin Hoax.*' Leno went over and touched it with his finger: this must have been the occasion when Grimaldi announced that 'eight and forty years have passed over my head, and I am sinking fast'. But there, next to this bill, was one which astonished him. It was crudely printed, on paper which had already turned yellow, and it announced 'Still Champion of All Champions, Dan Leno, Vocal Comedian and the World's Champion Clog Dancer. One Week Only.'

'That was at the Coventry,' he said. 'Quite a little while ago.'

'I know, sir. I found it on the wall of a junk shop, if you'll pardon the expression, along the Old Kent Road. I snapped it up at once.'

So at least in this small room Joseph Grimaldi and Dan Leno had been formally united. He looked around again at the young woman suffering upon her narrow mattress, and saw above her the song sheet for 'She Never Complained, Except When We Were Wed'. 'I must leave you now,' he said. 'I can go at once to my doctor.' Quietly and gently he left another sovereign on a small deal table before following the young man out of the room. 'May I take your name, as well as your address,' he asked as they came out into the dark yard. 'He will need it.'

'Chaplin, sir. Harry Chaplin. Everyone knows us here.'

'A good old stage name.' He put his hand on the young man's shoulder for a moment. 'He will come to Mrs Chaplin presently, then. And once again, goodbye.' Leno left Clare Market and, on his way back to his house in Clerkenwell, he left an urgent message about Mrs Chaplin with his family doctor in Doughty Street; it could be said, in fact, that he had managed to save the unborn infant's life.

From that day in the Reading Room of the British Museum, Leno became obsessed with Grimaldi; he snatched up any material he could find, and had only recently come across De Quincey's essay on pantomime in which Grimaldi is described as 'the epitome of scream without speech'. He had read the essay until the end, as he sat in his chair in the drawing room, and only when he reached the last page did he extinguish his lamp and climb the stairs to his bed. That was why, on the following morning, the book on the side-table was turned to the next essay in this volume by De Quincey – it was the essay entitled 'On Murder Considered as One of the Fine Arts', just as Detective Inspector Kildare noticed when he came to question the funniest man on earth.

There were very good reasons for the policeman's visit although, naturally enough, he was also curious to meet the great Dan Leno. He was taken into the drawing room, which his wife had filled with wax fruit and wax flowers, ormolu clocks under glass and heavily embroidered cushions; Kildare had barely entered the room when he tripped on the edge of a thick rug. 'People often do that.' It was Leno's characteristic voice but when the police detective turned, half-expecting to be greeted by some outlandish creature caked in stage grease and make-up, he saw only a neat and dapper little man who put out his hand in welcome. 'Mrs Leno is a rug-fiend.'

It was a week after the murder of the Gerrard family in the Ratcliffe Highway, and Dan Leno had been expecting the visit; Mr Gerrard had once been his 'dresser' at the Canterbury and several other halls before entering the millinery business, and Leno had maintained a friendship with him ever since. There were other curious factors, however, which connected Leno to the murders committed by the Limehouse Golem. Jane Quig, the first victim whose body had been found on the stone steps at Limehouse Reach, had told a friend that she was 'off to see Leno' in his new pantomime and had boasted – falsely, as it turned out – that she was 'acquainted with 'im'. The next connection was more peculiar still; Alice Stanton, the prostitute murdered beside the white pyramid of St Anne's, Limehouse, was found to be wearing female riding gear with a small linen tag attached to the inside collar bearing the name of 'Mr Leno'. It occurred to the police detectives of 'H' Division that the Limehouse Golem might have been trying to kill Dan Leno himself, and was approaching him through these surrogates, but the possibility was soon dismissed as too fanciful. The true explanation was revealed, as we have seen, when they discovered that Alice Stanton had been in the habit of buying second-hand clothes from Gerrard himself, who in turn received them as 'cast-offs' from his old employer. So it was that Alice died in the costume of the female jockey from *Humpty Dumpty* who rode 'Ted, The Nag That Wouldn't Go'.

'This is a very interesting story, sir.' Kildare had already noticed the volume opened at the first page of 'On Murder Considered as One of the Fine Arts'.

Leno picked up the book, and glanced at it. 'I haven't come to that one as yet. Does it interest you particularly?' He gave a sharp look at Kildare and, for a moment, thought that there was something rather peculiar about him.

'It concerns the Marr murders, sir. By some coincidence they were committed in the same house as—'

'The Gerrards?' Leno looked at the first page of the essay in genuine horror. 'What a dreadful thing.' He turned the pages and read, quickly, that '. . . the final purpose of murder is precisely the same as that of tragedy'. 'It is like some Greek piece of business,' he said. 'Those Furies or whatever they were called.'

'Not Greece, sir, but London. We have our own furies here as well.' Kildare could hardly believe that this was the same man who could fill a theatre with laughter. 'Could you tell me now about your connection with the Gerrard family?' Leno recounted the details of his association with his erstwhile dresser, although all the time he was more concerned to question Kildare about the state of the police investigation.

'Tell me,' he said after he had completed his story. 'The newspapers say that there were no survivors, but I still have a faint hope that you might have found one of the little children . . .'

'Oh no, sir. They were all destroyed. Can I speak confidentially to you?'

'Of course.' Leno took the detective's arm, and led him over to a heavily curtained window.

'One member of the family did survive.'

'Who was that?'

'Mr Gerrard's sister, sir. She was sleeping in the attic storey at the time of the killings, but she was not found until the alarm was raised. She had taken laudanum for a toothache.'

'So she saw nothing?'

'Not as far as she is aware, but there is still a chance. She has been frightened half out of her wits, and at the moment makes precious little sense to me or to anyone else.' Kildare had paid this visit to Clerkenwell with no great determination to cross-question Leno or his family; he already knew that the comic had been performing on the stage of the Oxford at the time of the Gerrards' slaughter, and that he had been similarly engaged at the time of the other murders. All London was aware of the fact that Dan Leno worked the halls six nights a week. But Kildare had come to him as an observer rather than as an actor; he was shrewd enough to realise that Leno was the one man who would notice the smallest tone or detail in his encounters with other people. That was why he now changed the course of the conversation. 'Can you recall if Mr Gerrard ever seemed unaccountably nervous, Mr Leno?'

'No. Not in the slightest. He was busied over some new gowns when we last met, and we merely exchanged pleasant-ries.' He did not mention the fact that he had rehearsed his new singing and dancing number for the family – it seemed too bizarre a scene to recall now. 'Frank Gerrard had a lovely feeling for cloth.'

'Did he have any enemies?'

'Not in the theatre. Hall people have their jealousies and their rivalries, but it's all very mock-heroic. In any case most of them drink too much to remember if they bear any grudges.' He may have been referring here to his own reputation as something of an 'old sock' or 'blotting paper'; when Leno drank, he drank wildly and incessantly until he woke the fol-lowing morning without a care in the world. He knew that, in his drunkenness, he would enact many of his familiar stage characters – but he took them to such fantastic and elaborate lengths that even his closest friends could not keep up with him. When he woke up, in a strange chair or upon an unfamil-iar floor, he felt as much at peace as if he had performed an exorcism. 'No,' he went on. 'We never do the dirty. Besides,

Frank was a very good dresser.' He brushed a piece of thread from the shoulder of Kildare's coat, and the policeman opened his eyes very wide for a moment before recovering himself.

'There is something most peculiar I wanted to tell you, Mr Leno. It concerns that essay you were reading.'

'I haven't read it yet. I told you.'

'No, I believe you. I am not accusing you of anything whatsoever. But the odd thing is that the murderer must have studied it before he killed your friend. There are too many resemblances for it to be entirely natural.'

'So you think he may have been a literary man?'

'An educated man, certainly. But perhaps he was an actor playing a part.'

'With this terrible thing as his prompt-book?'

Kildare did not answer directly, but watched as Leno tossed the book onto the carpet. 'I once had the pleasure of seeing you in the spoof version of Maria Marten.'

'Oh yes. That *Red Barn* number was years ago.'

'But I can still recall the way the killer grabbed you around the throat, and almost throttled the life out of you. Didn't he then split you open with a razor?'

'It was a she. It was all very gory in those days.'

'But you see, this is my point. This murderer, this Limehouse Golem as they call him, seems to be acting as if he were in a blood tub off the Old Kent Road. Everything is very messy and very theatrical. It is a curious thing.'

Leno reflected for a few moments on this particular vision of the crimes. 'I was thinking the same myself only the other day,' he said. 'Much of it doesn't seem real at all.'

'Of course, the deaths were real enough.'

'Yes but, as you say, the atmosphere surrounding them, the newspaper paragraphs, the crowds of spectators – it's like being in some kind of penny gaff or theatre of variety. Do you know what I mean?' Both men remained silent. 'Can I see the woman who survived? Can I visit Miss Gerrard?'

'I'm not sure . . .'

'Let me talk to her, inspector. She knows me. She has seen me on the stage and, I suppose, trusts me. Perhaps I will be able to coax some details from her which your methods could not discover. People tell Dan Leno everything, you know.'

'Well, if you wish it. I need all the assistance I can muster.' So it was quickly settled and, on the following morning, Dan Leno was driven to a lodging house in Pentonville where Miss Gerrard had been secretly placed by the police; it was thought that she might at some stage be able to recognise the voice or tread of the Limehouse Golem, so it was considered necessary to protect her from the idle attentions of the newspaper reporters.

'Well, my dear Peggy,' Leno said as he was ushered into her room. 'This is a very bad business.'

'Very bad indeed, Mr Leno.'

'Dan.'

He watched her as she slowly moved her head from side to side, as if she did not like to stare at one spot for too long. She was generally a stout and well-made woman but, in the bleak light of the lodging-house window, she became almost ethereal. 'There was no noise coming from them, Dan. Nothing at all. Otherwise I would have come down. I would have stopped him.' It was clear to Leno that she was not to be diverted from her memories. 'It's the little children who should have been spared, Dan. He could have taken me. But not them. They were just like the babes in the wood.'

'Lost in the forest dark and drear, I see a figure coming near.' It was one of the first roles he had performed as an 'infant wonder' and, as he recited the verse, he experienced the horror of the Gerrard children for a moment. 'That's the beauty of the

pantomime, Peggy. It is believed only while it is being performed. In real life things are a bit harder, you know. And I
suppose that's what we try to do in pantomime. Soften the
hardness just a little.'

'You make them laugh, I know. But nothing can make me
laugh now.'

'No, I don't believe it could. At times like this, Peggy, I am
at a loss for words. Truly I am.'

'Never mind it, Dan.'

'But I do mind it. I wanted to comfort you by telling you
how I feel. It is all so absurd. So senseless.' He could find only
the most frail and timid words of comfort now, whereas on the
stage he could have delivered a great tirade of sorrow before
spoofing his own grief. 'It will be all right,' he said. 'Everything
will be all right.'

'I don't think so, Dan.'

'No, I don't think so either. But, you know, the badness will
pass in time.' He was feeling cramped and restless in this small
room, so now he began to stroll around the edge of the faded
brown carpet. 'And do you know what I'm going to do? I'm
going to set you up in a nice little clothes business a long way
away from here. Didn't the family come from Leeds?'

'From Manchester.'

'Well, then, what could be better than a business in
Manchester?'

'I could not—'

'You're his only relative now, Peggy. You owe it to him.'

'If you put it like that . . .'

'I do put it like that. But what I want you to do now is have
a little sleep. You're all knocked out, Peggy. Come this way. Is
that your retiring room over there?' Leno was always adept at
giving directions, and it was as if he were leading her through
a rehearsal. She got up and went towards the door, but then she

came back in again as if she were not at all sure what she was meant to be doing. 'Why do you think it happened, Dan?'

'I can't say. It's too – too deep.' This was a strange adjective to use of so brutal a crime, but he was at that moment reminded of the similarity between the Marr murders and the Gerrard murders. There was some element of ritual here which, despite his genuine horror, still interested him.

'There must be a reason for everything, Dan, don't you agree?' She was touching her neck with the fingers of her left hand. 'I can't say the word, but they talk of this – thing.'

'The Golem?' He dismissed the term, almost blowing it away as you would an iridescent bubble. 'That's just the easy answer. The funny thing is that people are less scared of a golem than they would be of a real person.'

'But people believe in it. It's all I have heard.'

'Oh, people will believe anything. I have learned that. And you know what I always say, don't you? Believing is seeing.' Once more he was restlessly pacing around the room. 'It is not inconceivable,' he said, 'that this murderer was known to your brother. Did you notice anyone in the vicinity? Before any of this happened?'

'I'm not sure. I've gone over and over it in my mind.'

'Go on. Go over it again.'

'I was leaning out of the attic window around twilight, just to get the air, when I thought I saw some kind of slim shadow. Do you understand me? I explained it to the police detective, but he told me they were looking for a large, broad-shouldered man.'

'A leonine type?'

'Something of the kind. But all I saw was a little waif.'

'Now let me see.' Leno's constructive intelligence about movement and gesture came into play at once, and he seemed to sidle into the corner of the room.

'It was something like that, Dan. Only the shoulders wriggled a little.'

'Like this?'

'That is closer.'

'Well, it's a very funny thing, Peggy. But, believe me or believe me not, I think you saw the shadow of a woman along the Ratcliffe Highway.'

Thirty-Five

There was a long silence after the verdict had been pronounced upon Elizabeth Cree. She realised then that silence would surround her for the rest of her life. It would surround her always. She might scream into it, but there would be no echo. She might plead with it, but she would hear no voices in reply. If there was such a thing as mercy or forgiveness, its tongue had been cut out. This was a silence filled with threat because, one day, it would swallow her up. But perhaps there was also a kind of happiness to be obtained there – to be joined, at last, in the communion of silence.

She had been found guilty of her husband's murder, and had been condemned to death by hanging in the yard of the prison where she was incarcerated. She had realised from the beginning that she would soon be looking at the judge's black cap, and she betrayed no particular feeling when he placed it upon his head; he looked, she thought, like Pantaloon in the pantomime. No, he was too florid and too fat. He was good for nothing except a Dame part. She was led from the court into an underground corridor, and taken from there in a horse-drawn van to Camberwell Prison. Even then she felt no need to sigh, or cry out, or pray. To what god, after all, could she pray? The one who knew the truth about her life and that of her husband? That night, in the condemned cell, she began to sing one of her old favourites, 'I'm a Little Too Young to Know'. She had sung it last after Uncle's funeral.

Thirty-Six

It was never the same with Dan and me after Uncle left us for the great pantomime in the sky. He was never actually rude to my face, but I knew that he was avoiding me; I suppose he was jealous of the fact that Uncle had left me £500, together with all the photographic equipment, but he never mentioned the subject. It occurred to me sometimes that he might know all about Uncle's dirty secret, and that he might suspect me of being involved in it, but there was nothing I could do about that little matter. So we tried to carry on in the same way but, somehow, my heart was no longer in it. I had a great success with one song, a tuneful ditty by the name of 'An Irish Maid's Lament for Home, or Where are the Potatoes Now?', but I was never really in the proper frame of mind. The death of Uncle must have affected me more than I realised, and I found myself turning to John Cree for company and consolation. Of course I already knew that he was a gentleman; I saw how he stood out among the other reporters, and Uncle had informed me long ago about his 'expectations'.

'Oh yes,' I had said at the time, very innocently. 'He has told me of the play he intends to write.'

'Not that, dear. The backsheesh. The bunce. Money. He'll be rolling in it one day. His father's as rich as Aladdin.' John

Cree had already been paying me particular attention, and I must say that Uncle's piece of news aroused my curiosity a little.

It so happened that, a month after the funeral, I was sitting in the green room of the Wilton with Diavolo, the one-legged gymnast, when he came in. 'Why,' I said, 'here is the *Era*. Have you seen Diavolo on the wire, Mr Cree?'

'I have not had that pleasure.'

'It is not to be missed. Yes, you may sit with us for a moment.' He drew up a chair and we gossiped, as hall folk generally do, until Diavolo decided to take a turn in the evening air; he was always very partial to saveloys, as I knew, and would soon be found wetting one with a glass of porter.

'Well, Lizzie,' John Cree said after he had left. 'You and I always seem to be thrown together.'

'Whenever did I give you permission to call me Lizzie?'

'It was in the second booth of the Blair Chop-House a week last Wednesday.'

'What a memory. You should go on the stage, Mr Cree.'

'John.'

'Be a dear then, John, and walk me to the door. It really feels very warm tonight.'

'Shall we follow Diavolo?'

'No. I know his habits. It would be indelicate.'

'May we take a stroll instead? It's a fine night for walking.'

So together we left the Wilton, and walked out into Wellclose Square. It was not in the best neighbourhood, situated by Shadwell, but for some reason I felt quite safe in his company. 'How is *Misery Junction* coming along?' I asked him.

'Oh, it goes on. I've almost completed the first act. But I can't quite decide what to do with my heroine.'

'Kill her.'

'Are you serious?'

'No, I am not being serious at all.' I tried to laugh. 'I think she should get married. The female lead always gets married in the end.'

'Is that so?' I said nothing, and we walked on towards the river. The houses were not so packed together now, and I could see the masts of the ships moored in the basin; for a moment it reminded me of Lambeth Marsh, when the boats were left on the bank by the fishermen. 'I was hoping,' he said at last, 'that you might play the part when I have completed it.'

'What is she called?'

'Katherine. Katherine Dove. At the moment she is very close to starvation and ruin, but I wonder whether I should rescue her in the next scene.'

'Oh, let her go down.'

'Why?'

'John, sometimes I think you really know very little about the theatre. People love to see degradation upon the stage.' I paused. 'Of course she can be saved in the last act. But not before she has suffered terribly.'

'Why, Lizzie, I had no idea you were a dramatist.'

'It is life. That is all. As stern and dark as life.' I took his arm, so that he could guide me across some broken cobbles, and I squeezed it to reassure him that I was not quite as serious as I must have sounded.

'I think,' he said, 'that you need someone to protect you against this life. If it is as dark as that, why, you need a prompter and manager.'

'Uncle was all that to me, and more.'

'Forgive me for saying so, Lizzie, but Uncle is dead.'

'There is always Dan.'

'Dan is too great an artist to sacrifice himself to you or anyone.'

'I was not talking about any sacrifice.'

'But that is what you need, Lizzie. You need someone to devote himself to you always.'

I gave one of my light comedy laughs. 'And where am I going to find such a creature?' We had come down by the riverside, and we could see the domes and spires and rooftops clustered in the distance. 'You must have a scene in *Misery Junction* painted like this,' I said in order to break the silence. 'It would make quite a strong effect.'

'London is always depicted in that way. I would like to show the interior of a furnished room, or a gin palace. That is where the genuine life is to be found.' He was still holding my arm, and now he put his hand over mine. 'Is that too much to hope for? Genuine life?'

'Oh, what is that? Do tell me.'

'I think you know, Lizzie.'

'Do I? Perhaps I should help you with your drama then, John. If my own life were somewhere within it—'

'That would be wonderful.'

Ever since the death of Uncle I had dreamed of leaving the halls and advancing upon the legitimate stage. With John Cree as my writer and patron, was there any reason why I could not become another Mrs Siddons or Fanny Kemble? We grew more intimate, after that night, and together we visited all the various old melodramatic haunts we loved – the diorama in Leicester Square and the artificial waterfall at Muswell Hill were my favourites, while he preferred the poor areas of the city. He said that they inspired him – well, as I have always said, there is no accounting for tastes.

There was already whispering about us in the green room, as you might expect, and one afternoon I put it to him that we could not be so much in one another's company without clarifying our position to the world. Apparently it is what he had expected, or hoped for, and on the last day of 1867 we became betrothed. I could not wait to be converted to his own religion – all the hall folk had a fondness for it – and our marriage followed the next spring with a simple ceremony at Our Lady of the Rocks in Covent Garden. Dan Leno led me to the altar, orphan as I was, while four sand-dancers held up my train; my old pals were there and Ridley, the skeleton comique, made a very nice speech at the wedding supper. I pressed Dan to say something but, curiously for him, he declined. I knew how to catch that monkey, though: I plied him with strong water and, after a few glasses, he came up trumps with a very gallant toast. 'I have known her as Lizzie of Lambeth Marsh for so long,' he said, 'that I shall never accustom myself to Mrs Cree. We met at the old Craven so many years ago that I feel now it is time she grew a beard. What hasn't she done on the halls? She has knocked about with the knockabouts, she has been the softest of soft shoes and the most simultaneous of dancers. She has been instrumental with the instrumentalists, turned with the double turns and been illusory with the illusionists. But now she has taken off her duds, picked up her props, and taken the brougham home for the last time . . .' He was a little unsteady on his feet now, so I patted his hand and thanked him. He raised his glass, put it to his lips, and then collapsed on the long table in a daze. It was a lovely occasion, and all the more moving because I was seeing most of the acts for the last time. It was the end of my second life.

Thirty-Seven

The Morning Advertiser *of the 3rd October, 1880, carried the following announcement on its front page:*

For the benefit of the public we are printing this illustration of a golem, taken from a woodcut in the possession of Mr Every, the Holborn bookseller extraordinaire. Please to note its size in relation to its victim, and its glaring orbs like those of a bull's-eye lantern. The legend beneath it in Gothic script informs us that the creature is made of red clay, but we beg to differ. The creature preying upon our citizens is made of some more solid material than clay, for how otherwise can it have wreaked such havoc on the bodies of the slain? We have discussed the matter with Dr Paley of the British Museum, who has made an especial study of the old folklore of Europe, and he confirms our suspicions. He sees no reason why it should not be made out of stone, or metal, or some other durable material. He adds (*horribile dictu!*) that it is also able to change its shape at will! He further informs us that the golem is always created within great cities and, by some awful instinct, is thoroughly acquainted with the streets and alleys of its birthplace.

This will come as no surprise to Mrs Jennifer Harding, the justly renowned poulterer of Middle Street, who claims to have seen the creature lapping blood in the shambles by Smithfield before making its way past St Bartholomew's Hospital. An itinerant match-seller, Anne Bentley, has been in a hysterical condition ever since Friday last, when she was apparently taken up by a pale creature with no eyes. She had been about to enter the Wapping workhouse, where her mother resides in the Foul Ward, when she was surprised by this monster and felt herself being carried off. She promptly fainted away and only recovered her senses in Charterhouse Square, where she was found lying with her clothes dishevelled. She claims that the Golem 'unpeeled' her and 'guzzled her' like a piece of fruit; she now believes that she is with child, and is fearful of giving birth to a monster. Any news of such an eventuality will of course be promptly reported in these pages. Meanwhile the unfortunate woman has been confined to Shadwell Asylum.

There have come frightful reports and observations of a similar nature from both sides of the river. Mr Riley of Southwark has written to inform us that a creature of ferocious strength was seen climbing along the rooftops of the Borough High Road at the beginning of last week – pray send us more intelligence when you can, Mr Riley. Mrs Buzzard who owns a chair-making establishment in Curtain Street was disturbed last Monday morning by a 'shadow' which, she tells us, followed her everywhere until she ran shrieking into Shoreditch High Street. She is now quite recovered, and has offered a free chair as a reward to anyone who can explain this mysterious occurrence to her satisfaction. Once again, in this incident as in so many others, the word 'golem' has been on everyone's lips. Let us say to those who profess to disbelieve these accounts, there are more things in heaven and earth, Horatio, etcetera, etcetera. In recent years we have discovered marvels in the most remote objects, from the solar system to the snowflake. Who is to say that there are not more marvels still?

Thirty-Eight

After our marriage John Cree and I took a little house in Bayswater near the old Hippodrome; here I began a life so different
from my old one on the halls that sometimes I had to pinch
myself to confirm that Lizzie was still there somewhere. But
there could be no more patter and no more songs – to the world
I was now Mrs Cree, and I was very careful never to mention
my past to the neighbours or the tradespeople. Of course there
was no reason why I should not eventually appear on the legitimate stage, and I persuaded my dear husband to continue work
on *Misery Junction* at times when he seemed uninspired. I would
never have allowed him to abandon it: the heroine appealed to
me very much, and I knew that I could find an element of wonderful pathos in the character. It was in one of my reveries on
the subject, in fact, that I hit upon the most charming idea –
ever since we had moved to Bayswater, I had felt the need for a
lady's maid. And where better to look for a competent servant
than at Misery Junction itself, where the hall folk would be
assembled? I knew most of them by reputation, and I felt
sure that I would be able to pick out some clean and serviceable
young woman who had tired of finding work in the halls.
She might have already played the part of a maidservant in
some low comedy or other, just as I had done, and so she would

need very little coaching with her general deportment. And, besides, what a fund of gossip we would share for the quiet hours!

I put on my bonnet at once, and, without saying a word to the dear dramatist upstairs, I left the house and hailed a cab on my own account. It seemed an age before we arrived at Misery Junction (or Poverty Corner, as Dan always used to call it) and I looked out of the window eagerly at the crowd of artistes: I recognised many of them, naturally, and it took quite an effort not to wave as I passed by. I stopped the cab around the corner of York Road, asked the driver to wait a few moments, and then walked quickly towards the sad ensemble. There was a contortionist there I had known from the Queen's in Popular; he greeted me with a very low bow, no doubt assuming that I was also out of a shop. I passed a terribly bad serio-comic from the Paragon, who professed not to recognise me, when quite by chance I noticed Aveline Mortimer leaning wearily against a wall. I admit that I smiled when I saw her: it had been Aveline, after all, who had counselled me to proclaim *Meesa Meschina* to the Hebrew crowd and almost brought about my own sudden death. She tried to perk up a little when I walked over to her, but I am glad to say that she looked desperately tired and defeated. 'Why,' she said, 'it's Lambeth Marsh Lizzie.'

'It is not. It is Mrs John Cree.'

'Nice work if you can get it.'

The idea occurred to me at once. 'How long have you been out of a shop, dear?'

'Only a week or so.'

I knew, from the state of her clothes, that she was lying. 'Would I be right in thinking, Aveline, that you are looking out for a nice little part?'

'What's it to you, Lizzie?'

'Only that I am willing to give you a position.'

She gazed at me in astonishment. 'You don't have a hall, Lizzie, do you?'

'Not as such. No. But I do need a full house.' She did not understand what I meant. 'I want to employ you, dear. As a maid.'

'A *maid*?'

'Just consider it for a moment. Thirty shillings a week plus full board. And every second weekend will be your own.' It was a very attractive offer, and she hesitated for a moment. 'I will not be a difficult mistress, Aveline, and any unpleasantness in the past has already been quite forgotten.'

'It is easy to say—'

I could see that she did not yet fully trust me, and suspected this was some elaborate revenge on my part. 'Think of all the fun we will have in talking over old times.' She hesitated still, and I whispered in her ear. 'Anything would be better than this degradation, would it not? Do you wish to end on the streets?'

'Will you make it two guineas?'

'Thirty-five shillings. I can give you no more.'

'Very well then, Lizzie. I am with you.'

'That's a good girl.' I took a shilling from my bag, and put it in her hand. 'I will have returned here in half an hour. Buy yourself some nice bacon and greens while you wait for me.' I was about to take the cab to Haste and Spenlow in Catherine Street, where I could purchase a neat little maid's uniform with starched cap and collar, but then I turned back. 'On second thoughts, Aveline, it is better that you accompany me. No doubt you know your own size, dear.' So we returned to the cab, where she sat quite pertly beside me.

'Will I have to cook?' she asked, as the driver whipped the horses.

'Of course, Aveline. I presume that is one of your many skills.'

'Yes. They taught me in the workhouse.' I must have looked surprised for a moment, because she became quite fierce. 'You

210

might as well know it now, so I can forever have my peace.' It was just like her to misquote from the wedding service.

'Were you in the Magdalen, dear?'

'No, I was not, thank you very much. I may have been poor, but I wasn't a whore. I was always a clean virgin.'

I did not believe this for an instant, but I decided to humour her: what was the point of an argument before I had even purchased a uniform? 'Did you know your parents, Aveline?'

'I knew my mother. She was on the parish for as long as I can remember.'

'That is very sad.' It is extraordinary, is it not, how some women can escape their backgrounds altogether while others remained trapped in them? Poor Aveline was still no better than her mother, while I was driving around in a hansom as if London was my oyster. 'Poverty must be a terrible thing.'

She was about to say something foul to me, I knew, but at this moment we drove up to Haste and Spenlow. Aveline jumped out very smartly into Catherine Street, and I waited only a second before tapping on the glass. 'Will you hand me out, Aveline? We are entering an establishment.' It was her first lesson in general deportment and with rather bad grace, I thought, she took my hand and guided me onto the cobbles. The shop was almost empty but, still, she would barely submit to being measured. Eventually, I found her a wonderful little costume, with a grey border, and I came back to the cab in high good humour. As soon as she was beside me again, I took the maid's cap out of its parcel and popped it on her head. 'There now. Don't you look a picture?'

'Of what?'

'Of young womanhood, Aveline. Womanhood in service. Now shall we try on the rest?'

'Where are we going? The Alhambra?' She was referring to the fact that, in the old days, we often changed our costumes in the brougham as we hurried from hall to hall. I suspect that is why she entered the spirit of the occasion and, by the time she had put on her black cotton collar, she looked every inch the lady's maid. 'A change of dress works wonders,' I said. 'A new woman is born.'

'I must look like a walk-on part.'

'Will you add madam to that sentence, please?'

'I must look like a walk-on part, madam.'

'Very good, Aveline. No. You are not walking on. You are one of the main characters. Now say after me, "Will that be all, sir?"'

'Would I be right in thinking that "sir" is the party from the *Era* you were sweet on?'

'I would not use those exact words, but you are correct. Mr Cree is my husband. Now say it!' I tapped her on the cheek with my glove.

'Will that be all, sir?'

'Yes, thank you, Aveline.' I had adopted my husband's deep voice for a moment, but now I returned to my own. 'What is it for dinner tonight?'

Aveline thought for a moment. 'Minced beef and potatoes?'

'Oh no. Be more select.'

'Fried fish?'

'Go higher, Aveline. This is Bayswater, not the Old Kent Road.'

'Oxtail soup. Then goose with all the trimmings.'

'Very good. That will be splendid. Now do you remember how we used to do the comedy curtsy?'

'How could I forget?'

'Show me then, dear.' So she got up from the seat and, narrow though the space was, she managed a short dip. 'Excellently done, Aveline. I will be giving you a notebook with some phrases in it, which you will learn by heart. Do you understand me?'

'I can learn a script, Lizzie. You know that well enough.'

I gave her a real slap this time. 'Mrs Cree!' She made no effort to fight back, and I realised that I had already gained the upper hand. 'Now act nice and demure. We have come into Bayswater.'

In fact she looked the very picture of neatness and propriety as we approached the house and, when she got out of the cab and held the door open for me, I could tell that she was already becoming accustomed to her new part. I suspect that, even then, she was beginning to enjoy it. Of course I could not have explained to her the true reason I had employed her – I believe that it did not really even occur to me until I had actually seen her loitering in the Waterloo Road like some creature of the night.

That reason concerned my husband. I had discovered, very soon after our marriage, that he was a man of ungovernable lust; he attempted to have intercourse with me on the night after the wedding, and it was only after much pleading on my part that he agreed to pleasure himself with his hand. I could not endure – I cannot endure – the thought of being entered by a man and I made it quite clear to him that anything of such a nature was quite out of the question. I could not allow him to touch me in that place, not after my mother had been there already. She had pinched me savagely, she had pricked me with her needle and once, though I was very young, I remember her taking a stick to it. Even though she was long dead, I could feel her hands there still. No one would ever touch it again.

So I would sleep in Mr Cree's bed, I would allow him to caress me with his hands or even with his tongue, but I would not permit that act. He seemed surprised and even dismayed by my decision, but he knew well enough that I was too accustomed to the world to be swayed by the so-called 'rights' of the husband – on the halls, as Dan used to say, we treat each other equal or not at all. A woman's voice was always heard, as much in the green room as on the stage. Fortunately my dear husband was too much of a gentleman to force himself upon me, and I appreciated his courtesy to the extent that I decided to repay him: it was then, while musing about the artistes crowded around Misery Junction, that the idea of lady's maid had occurred to me. If I could divert Mr Cree's attention to an adjacent and easy female, then his lust would be slaked and I would remain happily untouched. It was a great piece of luck that my eye should have fallen on Aveline Mortimer; I knew her to be of loose morals – she had once set herself up with a black-faced turn in Pimlico – and she could no doubt be persuaded to do the needful. 'Now then, Aveline,' I said, as we sat in the drawing room soon after our arrival. 'Do you think you will be quite happy with your new situation?'

'I hope so, Lizzie.'

'Mrs Cree.' Now that she was wearing her maid's uniform she had become more compliant and respectful; it is marvellous what a good costume can do. 'Then you must promise me this, Aveline. You must promise to obey me, and to do my bidding in every respect. Is that agreed?'

'Yes, Mrs Cree.'

She suspected that some game was at hand – I could tell from her serio-comic air – but I had not the slightest intention of forewarning her. I left Mr Cree and Aveline together on several occasions and, while I watched secretly from the wings, allowed nature to take its course. But I still pitied him, each time that I saw him put on his ulster and travel to the British Museum.

Thirty-Nine

John Cree often visited the Reading Room now because he was quite unable to continue work on his play. He was nervous and uneasy but his failure as a writer was not the sole reason for his distress – he was, in fact, most disturbed by his wife. He had first known her as a performer on the halls but, since their marriage, she had become a more unfamiliar and disquieting figure. He recognised very well what troubled him – she played the part of a wife perfectly, and yet in the very definition and completeness of her role there was an air of strangeness. There were times when Elizabeth Cree did not seem to be there at all, as someone else took over the part, but there were also occasions when she became 'wifely' with a fierceness and determination that were almost professional. This was the cause of his unease, and he often found himself wandering from the melodrama of *Misery Junction* to the unacknowledged drama of his domestic existence. So instead he read books concerned with the sufferings of the London poor, and passed his time beneath the great dome of the library.

A young man had developed the habit of sitting at the desk beside him – C3 – and for the last week John Cree had watched him write in a flowing hand across sheets of foolscap paper. He had long dark hair, and wore an astrakhan fur coat which he refused to give to Herbert, the cloakroom attendant, and which, against all propriety, he draped across his blue leather chair. He also seemed inordinately fond of his own compositions, because there were times when in the course of a particularly long sentence he glanced across at John Cree to make sure that he was being observed. He would often leave the Reading Room in order to take some air (John Cree had once glimpsed him walking among the pillars, smoking a Turkish cigarette), but he was always most careful to leave his papers visible.

Cree was not particularly interested in the young man's activities, however; he guessed, correctly, that he had recently come down from one of the great universities and was attempting to pursue a literary career in the capital. But the books which he ordered were of some interest – on one morning he had seen him read Longinus and Turner's *Liber Studiorum*. These were the marks of an authentic sensibility and he became more intrigued by the young man's work, laid so ostentatiously on the desk beside him. He even went so far as to take a page, after the author had left for his smoke among the pillars, and scan the contents inscribed in a beautiful hand: 'However we must not forget that the cultivated young man who penned these lines, and who was so susceptible to Wordsworthian influences, was also, as I said at the beginning of this memoir, one of the most subtle and secret poisoners of this or any age. How Thomas Griffiths Wainewright first became fascinated by this strange sin he does not tell us, and the diary in which he carefully noted the results of his terrible experiments and the methods that he adopted has unfortunately been lost to us. Even in later days, too, he was always reticent on the matter, and preferred to speak about "The Excursion" and the "Poems founded on the Affections". Murder may have been his occupation, but poetry was his delight.'

Forty

My husband was not advancing with his play. He spent so many fruitless hours in his study, sucking on his pipe and taking cups of coffee (from the hand of Aveline, naturally), that I became quite exasperated with him. I urged upon him the virtues of concentration and perseverance but he would sigh, get up from his chair and go to the window that looked out over the gardens. I even believe that, sometimes, he became quietly angry with me for reminding him of his duty. 'I try as much as I can!' he shouted at me one evening in the autumn of that year.

'Calm yourself, John Cree.'

'I do try.' He lowered his voice. 'But I seem to have lost my way. It's not like the days when we used to sit in the green room together—'

'That time is long gone. Don't ever wish it back. It is past.'

'But then, at least, I had a sense of the world which sustained me. When I visited the halls and worked for the *Era*—'

'It was not respectable.'

'At least I felt that I belonged to something. Now I am not so sure.'

'You belong to me.'

'Of course I do, Lizzie. But I cannot make a play out of our own lives.'

'I know. There is no dramatic interest. No sensation.' Even as I stared at him, and pitied his weakness, I formed my own resolution. I would finish *Misery Junction* for him. I knew more than enough about hall folk and, as for poverty and degradation, was there another writer in the country who had stitched sails in Lambeth Marsh? Had I not also flayed Uncle until the blood ran from his back, and walked through the streets of Limehouse in male duds? I had seen enough. So I would complete the play and then assume the role of its heroine upon the legitimate London stage. I knew the point my husband had reached in the drama, since I read it secretly at night, and had been eagerly expecting Catherine Dove to faint away from starvation in her Covent Garden garret. Then, at the last moment, she is found by her theatrical agent and taken to a private sanatorium near Windsor. But John could go no further. So I purchased a plentiful supply of pencils and paper from Stephenson's in Bow Street, and began work on his behalf. I must admit I have a certain talent for dramatic composition and, as a woman, found a natural affinity with Catherine Dove; with Aveline as my audience, I would rehearse scenes in the drawing room before committing them to paper and even found some of my greatest effects in improvisation. Already I had determined that Catherine Dove, the poor orphan girl, would be fully restored to health and would go on to triumph over her enemies. But still she had not suffered enough, and so I added one or two little moments of horror to my husband's version. There was one scene, for example, where in the depths of her distress she drinks gin until she collapses; she finds herself at dawn lying in a doorway off Long Acre, her dress torn and her hands caked with blood, with no knowledge of how she came to be there in such a condition. It was a most powerful idea and, I must admit, it was given to me by Aveline Mortimer: I half suspected that she had once been involved in something of the same nature, but I said nothing. So I improvised it, and recited it, and walked furiously up and down the drawing room until I had done it justice: 'Can this be me, who lies here? No, I am not here. It is someone in my place whom I do not know. [*Raises her hands to the sky.*] Oh, God in heaven, what might I have done? My sanguineous hands must bear witness to some terrible deed. Could I have killed an innocent child and recalled nothing of the crime? Could I commit murder and know nothing of it? [*Tries to rise but slumps down again.*] Then I would be lower than the beasts of the field who, though they show no remorse, are at least conscious of their deeds! I have some dark life which is hidden from me. I live in the cave of my own horror and am deprived of light! [*Faints away.*]' In my excitement I had knocked over one of the chairs and shattered a small vase on a side-table, but Aveline had cleaned up behind me. It was all very inspiring and, when the audience learn that the blood was shed in saving the life of a child from a drunken father, it would be very uplifting as well.

Within a month I had completed *Misery Junction* to my own satisfaction, with Catherine Dove's triumphant return to the stage; I had made a fair copy in my large, round hand and decided to send it at once by messenger to Mrs Latimer of the Bell Theatre in Limehouse. She specialised in strong melodramas, and I explained to her in an accompanying letter that *Misery Junction* was bold and very 'up-to-the-minute'. I had expected a proposal from her in the next post, but for an entire week I heard nothing at all – even though I had explained in my letter that several other managements were greatly interested. So I decided to visit the Bell myself, and hired a brougham for the purpose; I knew that it would make more of an impression if it was seen to be waiting for me in the street, and I stationed it just in front of the theatre while I marched through the famous stained-glass doors. Mrs Latimer – Gertie, to her intimates – was in her little office behind the bar, counting out the proceeds from the previous night's house. For a moment she did not recognise me in my wifely costume, but then she put back her head and laughed. She was what the comical element would call a 'fine-looking woman', and the fat quivered beneath her chin in a most distasteful manner. 'Why,' she said, 'it's Lambeth Marsh Lizzie. How are you, deary girl?'

'Mrs Cree now, if you don't mind.'

'Oh, I don't mind in the slightest. But it's not like you to stand on ceremony, Lizzie. Last time I saw you, you were the Older Brother.'

'Those times are gone, Mrs Latimer, and a new day has dawned. I have come here about the play.'

'I don't follow you, dear.'

'*Misery Junction.* It has been written by my husband, Mr Cree, and it was sent to you over a week ago. Why oh why have you not replied?'

'As the shop girl sighed? I see you haven't forgotten all your old songs, Lizzie.' She was not at all abashed. 'Now let me see. There was a drama by that name, or something of the sort—' She went over to a cupboard in the corner and, when she opened the door, I could see that it was filled with manuscripts and wads of paper. 'If it came last week,' she said, 'it will be on top. What did I tell you?' *Misery Junction* was the very first play she found, and she glanced through it before handing it to me. 'I gave it to Arthur, dear, and he declined it. He said that it lacked a really good plot. We need a plot, Lizzie, otherwise they get restless. Do you remember what happened with *The Phantom of Southwark*?'

'But that was a bit of nonsense. All that moaning and groaning.'

'It almost caused a riot, dear. I was the one who was groaning, I can assure you.'

I tried to explain to her the story of *Misery Junction*, and even went so far as to read out certain choice passages, but she was not to be swayed. 'It just won't do, Lizzie,' she told me. 'It's all gravy and no meat, dear. Do you know what I mean? There's nothing to chew on.'

I could have chewed on her, fat though she was. 'Is that your final word, Mrs Latimer?'

'I'm afraid so.' She settled down in her chair very comfortably, now that business was completed, and surveyed me. 'So tell me, Lizzie, have you quite given up the stage on your own account? You were ever such a good patterer. We all miss you.'

I was in no mood to be intimate with her, so I prepared to leave. 'What shall I say to my husband, Gertie Latimer, who has laboured night and day on this drama?'

'Better luck next time?'

I walked out of her office, passed the bar, and was about to make my way to the brougham outside the theatre when I was suddenly struck by a very interesting and curious idea. So I marched straight back to her, and laid *Misery Junction* on the table. 'What would it cost to hire your theatre? For one night only?'

She looked away from me, and I could tell that she was doing her calculations very rapidly. 'You mean something in the way of a benefit, dear?'

'Yes. And you will be the beneficiary. All I require is your stage. You will lose nothing by it.'

Still she hesitated. 'I do have a space between *The Empty Coffin* and *The Drunkard's Last Farewell* . . .'

'I need only that one night.'

'At this time of year, Lizzie, my takings can be considerable.'

'Thirty pounds.'

'And all the wet money?'

'Done.'

The money came from my own modest savings, which I kept in a purse concealed behind the mirror in my room; I returned with it a few hours later, and we shook hands on the spot. We agreed upon a night, in three weeks' time, and she promised me all the props and scenery I required. 'I have a very fine Covent Garden,' she said. 'Do you remember *The Costers*? It was used for the burlesque, but it will make a very good forlorn scene. And there is a lamp-post in the wings which you can lean against, dear. There may even be a dust-cart somewhere from *Oliver Twist*, although I have the strangest feeling that Arthur exchanged it for a flying carpet.' I thanked her for the use of the lamp-post, but in fact everything I needed was within my own self.

I already knew my part by heart, while Aveline had taken on the role of my wicked sister to great effect, and we needed only three walk-on males to complete the cast. They were easy enough to find; Aveline knew an unemployed prestidigitator who was an excellent study as the drunken husband, and I found two cross-talkers to play the parts of the theatrical agent and the heavy swell. They all came quietly to the house while my dear husband wasted his time in the British Museum – I wanted him to know nothing about my plans until I could reveal them to him 'on the night'. What a delightful surprise that would be! My only difficulty was the audience. Naturally I wanted to play to a full house, but how was I to obtain one without the benefit of bill posters or newspaper paragraphs? Then Aveline hit upon a solution – why not invite all the loiterers and dawdlers of Limehouse, as well as anyone else we could find who was unoccupied on the day? I was a little hesitant at first, because I had wanted to perform in front of a better class of person, but I saw the merit in her plan. It would not be a select house, but it would be a good one. We both knew the area well enough and, on the very morning before the performance, we distributed our own hand-written tickets with the promise of free entertainment. There were so many hawkers and street sellers and porters who wanted to be amused *gratis* and for nothing that we realised we had filled the theatre in less than an hour. 'Don't forget,' I said to each one of them. 'Tonight at six. Sharp, mind.'

I had asked Mr Cree to return home early from the Reading Room that day, on the pretext that I needed his assistance with an impudent plumber, and I was waiting for him at the door with such an expression of joy and affection that he stopped short on the steps. 'Whatever is the matter, Lizzie?'

'Nothing is the matter. Except that you and I are going on a journey.'

'Where?'

'Say nothing more. Just be pleased that you are travelling with one of the immortals of the stage.'

The cab was waiting for us at the corner of the street, the driver knowing our destination in advance, and we set off at a good trot. 'Lizzie. Dearest. Can you please tell me where we are going?'

'You must learn to call me Catherine tonight. Catherine Dove.' I was so bursting with anticipation that I could keep the secret from him no longer. 'Tonight, John, I will be your heroine. Tonight we are going to Misery Junction.' Still he had no conception of what I meant; he was about to speak, but I put my forefinger up to his mouth. 'It is what you always wanted. Tonight your play will live.'

'It is only half-written, Lizzie. Whatever are you talking about?'

'It is complete. Done.'

'I do not understand a single word you have told me since I came home. How can it possibly be complete?'

I might have become angry at his tone, but nothing could stop my enthusiasm now. 'I finished *Misery Junction* on your behalf, my love.'

'I beg your pardon?'

'I saw how you suffered with it, John. I knew you considered yourself a failure as a writer, because you could not finish it. So I set to work myself. Now it is done.'

He sat back in the cab, as pale as a sheet; he put his hands up to his head and clenched his fists. For a moment I thought he was about to strike me, but then he rubbed his eyes savagely. 'How could you do this?' he whispered.

'Do what, my love?'

'How could you ruin everything?'

'Ruin? What ruin? I have simply completed that which you began.'

'You have ruined *me,* Elizabeth. You have taken the one hope I had of fame and achievement. Do you know what that means?'

'But, John, you had abandoned it. You spend your days in the Reading Room of the British Museum.'

'Do you still understand nothing about me? Do you really think that little of me?'

'This conversation is becoming absurd.'

'Don't you see that I did not want to complete it yet? That I was not ready? That I wanted to keep it there as a perpetual centre for my life?'

'I am surprised at you, John.' I felt curiously composed, and even managed to look out of the window as we passed the Diorama in Houndsditch. 'You have told me more than once that you were never likely to finish it. I thought I was relieving you of a burden.'

'You don't understand, do you? As long as it was incomplete I could remain hopeful.' He had become quite calm, and I believed that I might still be able to rescue the situation. 'Don't you see that it was my life? I could hold out to myself the eventual promise of a literary reputation. And now what do you tell me? That you have finished it yourself.'

'I am astonished, John, at your selfishness.' I have found out that, with men, to attack them is to defeat them. 'Did you never consider my feelings in the matter? Did you never think that I might be tired of waiting? I was meant to be Catherine Dove. I have lived that play many times. It is as much mine as yours.'

He said nothing, but looked out of the window as we came up into Limehouse. 'I still cannot believe this,' he murmured to himself. Then he turned, and patted my hand. 'I will never be able to forgive you, Elizabeth.'

We had come up to the corner of Ship Street, and the cab had stopped to allow a baker's stall to be wheeled through; my husband opened the door, jumped out and, before I could say or do anything, began walking away towards the river. Ever since that day I have considered Limehouse an accursed and desolate spot. But what was I supposed to do? I had a hall waiting for me and I suspected that, whatever Mr Cree might say now, he would eventually realise that *Misery Junction* had created a new life for me upon the professional stage. So I hurried on to Limehouse Street, greeted Gertie Latimer at the door with a peck on the cheek, and went straight to the little dressing room where Aveline was waiting for me. 'Where is he?' was the first thing she said.

'Who, dear?'

'You know.'

'If you are referring to my husband, he sends his apologies. He cannot be with us tonight. Owing to an indisposition.'

'Oh lord!'

'It is of no consequence, Aveline. We will continue as planned. We will triumph.' Our three male walk-ons were in the other dressing room and, when I went next door to inspect them, I thought I could smell strong drink in the general atmosphere; but I chose to say nothing and, instead, took a small peep at the body of the hall. It was filling up rather nicely, although I could already distinguish a rowdy element in the pit. There were two or three loose females loitering at the back, and some porters were enjoying what Dan used to call 'illiterate operative character singing'. But I was accustomed to the habits of the crowd, and expected no trouble whatsoever.

'How is the house?' Aveline asked me when I came back. She had my first costume prepared, so I slipped out of my daily duds and began to change.

'Very good, I think. Ready for anything.'

'Do you remember how Uncle used to say, "A good time was had by hall"?'

'Don't think of Uncle now, Aveline. This is a different type of production altogether, and we must approach it in the proper spirit.'

'Talking of spirits, Lizzie, did you smell the breath on those boys next door?'

'I did. I will punish them later, but nothing can be done at this moment. Now be a good little maid and button me up.'

I was wearing a wonderful turquoise creation, symbolising Catherine Dove's high hopes on her first arrival in London; of course I had insisted that Aveline wear something much more drab, befitting her rank as my wicked spinster sister who spurns me in my hour of degradation and consigns me to a work-house. I was dressed soon enough and, as the minutes passed and the hall filled (I could hear the screams and shouts from the dressing room), was swept up in such a mood of anxiety and anticipation that I was close to fainting away. All thought of John Cree's ingratitude had left me, and I felt myself quite alone in facing my moment of glory. It was almost time. Gertie Latimer appeared with a 'restorative' and, between great gulps of porter, commented how full we were. But I was beyond caring. The curtain was about to rise and I summoned Aveline to walk behind me as we went onto the stage. 'Don't forget,' I whispered. 'Stay three paces from me, and do not attempt to address the audience. That is my task.' The curtain rose and Gertie's small orchestra whined its way into silence. I took a few steps forward, put my hand up to shield my eyes and looked dolefully around the hall. Catherine Dove had arrived. 'London is so large and strange and wild. Oh, Sarah dear, I do not know if I will be able to endure it.'

'Charlie, vot is it?' A fishmonger, or some such, had shouted from the gallery; I waited for the hubbub to die away.

'I don't know. But it's a miracle it can move.'

Another voice shouted from the gods. 'It's the two ugly sisters!'

There was general laughter, and I could have torn the heads off them; but I carried on, even louder than before. 'Will there be a bed here I can call my own, dear sister?'

'Yours and mine, if you're in luck!' It was another voice from the gallery, and the vile remark was followed by others of a similar nature. I recognised at once that it had been a mistake to invite an audience from the streets of a wretched area such as Limehouse; I had supposed that Londoners like myself would understand a tragedy, but I was quite wrong. Within a few minutes I realised that they considered *Misery Junction* to be some piece of light comedy; all my efforts at pathos and grandeur were wasted on them, and every line was greeted with hoots of laughter, shouting and applause. It was the most humiliating episode of my life, and my agony was compounded by the fact that our three male walk-ons played up to the gallery: they seized the mood, and began to indulge in the usual spoof and chaff. Even Aveline, I regret to say, allowed herself a little low buffoonery.

I could think of nothing after the final act. I rushed off the stage and fell, weeping, into a chair by the thunder-machine.

Gertie Latimer brought me over a glass of 'something strong' which, I am ashamed to say, I gobbled up. 'It's all one,' she said, trying to calm me. 'Tragedy and comedy is all one. Don't take it to heart.'

'I understand that perfectly,' I replied. 'I am a professional.' But it is hard to describe my horror and revulsion at the mob who had packed the pit and the gallery. They hardened my heart for ever – I can say that now – just as they finished my career upon the stage with ridicule and laughter. Yet something else happened to me in that terrible theatre, even as I reached the climax of the drama and was found moaning piteously by Long Acre. I reached out my arms to a passing stranger, played by Aveline in a white gown we had found in the wardrobe, and called out, 'Beneath these rags I am a woman like you. Take pity on yourself if not on me.' The hall found this irresistibly amusing but, amid the drunken cheers and laughter, I felt myself to be changed. It was as if I were alone in the theatre, like some hard and self-sufficient jewel which shines out even among ordure. But then that sensation faded, and I became so unsure and bewildered among the bedlam that I savagely struck my fists upon the wooden boards to awaken within me some sense of my own pain. I could see the faces of the fallen women all lit up by the gas, grinning and yawning, and at that moment they became the images of my own anxiety and bewilderment. I had surrendered myself to them – that was what had happened – and now I would never be returned. Something had left me – whether it was self-pride or ambition, I do not know – but something had gone from me for ever.

I could cry no more. Aveline and the males looked rather apprehensive when they came off the stage, but I could not bother myself with them. I took no calls, despite the clamour of the crowd. How could I? But, as Aveline and the others marched back upon the stage like a freak show, I quickly changed and left by a side-door. It did not matter what happened to me now, so I walked quite calmly through the filthiest lanes and byways of Limehouse without any certain sense of direction.

Forty-One

George Gissing came across the quotation from Charles Babbage just as he was about to finish his essay on the Analytical Engine for the *Pall Mall Review*. He had found it in one of Babbage's prefaces or 'Advertisements': 'The air itself is one vast library, on whose pages are for ever written all that man has ever said or woman whispered.' He repeated the line to himself as he walked through the damp and misty streets of London; it was late at night, and he had just dropped his article into the letter-box of John Morley's office in Spring Gardens. He did not want to return to his lodgings by way of Haymarket, in case he should see his wife in the vicinity, and instead walked eastwards towards the Strand and Catherine Street. But he walked too far, and found himself among the maze of streets by Clare Market; Gissing did not know this area of London, even though it was only a mile or so from his own lodgings, and he realised soon enough that he was thoroughly lost among the small courts and alleys. Some stray dogs were feeding off the scattered remnants of rubbish or excrement; he passed a hut or hovel but, when he glanced within, he saw that it was a rag shop illuminated by an old-fashioned rushlight. An old man, looking as rough and as ill-used as any of the rags around him, sat on a wooden box in the middle of the shop; he was smoking a clay pipe, and did not take it from his mouth as Gissing stood on the threshold. 'Could you direct me to the Strand?' The old man said nothing, but then Gissing felt a hand upon his leg. He backed away, startled, and saw two girls sitting upon the mud floor at his feet. They were naked, apart from some filthy undergarments, and to Gissing they seemed half-starved. 'Please help us, sir,' one of them said. 'We have so many mouths to feed, and nothing but a piece of yesterday's bread.' The rag-seller said nothing, but watched as he smoked his pipe. Gissing dug into his pocket, and found some coins which he put into the small girl's uplifted hand. 'For you and your sister,' he said. He was about to pat her on the cheek, but she made a movement as if to bite him and quickly he left the rag shop. He turned a corner and came across two men, in corduroy jackets and dirty neckerchiefs, banging upon a stove-pipe with some wooden clubs – he did not know what they were doing, but they looked as if they might have been doing it for ever. They stopped when they heard him, and gazed at him silently until he turned and walked away. He had to leave this place but, as he tried to make his way down one of the wider lanes, he heard someone whistle to him. A young man, wearing a long-sleeved waistcoat and a canvas cap, came out from the dark entrance of an oyster shop.

'What is it fer you're doing?'

'I am doing nothing. I am walking.'

'Walking, are you? Why in this spot?' There was menace in the young man's voice, but also something deeper and slyer. 'Are you looking for a chicken?'

'Chicken?'

'You seem like a man who would like a chicken.' He stroked the front of Gissing's trousers. 'A shilling will do for me. Do you see what I'm on about?'

Gissing pushed him away and began walking even more

quickly than before; then he started to run when he heard foot-steps coming up behind him, and he fled down another lane. But what was ahead of him? There was a vast form belching out light and heat; for one moment it might have been the Analytic Engine come to monstrous life among the poor, like some medieval spectre bathed in fire, but then he realised that he was standing in front of a manufactory. There was a sound of move-ment behind him still; he had no wish to linger here and, for want of any better escape, he walked towards the building. There was an extraordinary and almost overpowering smell of lead, or acid, or both mixed; he went over to an open door, which seemed to be the entrance to this place, and saw a line of women in dark gowns proceeding up a staircase towards a loft. Each one carried a large pot on her shoulder, and the smoke bellowed from these vessels towards the wooden roof; it wreathed through their dark gowns, and formed clouds around them, as they climbed upwards. On the floor of the manufac-tory there was another line of women, passing pots from hand to hand until they were pushed into a large, glowing oven. He had no notion of what they were doing but then, among the noise and the billowing smoke, he realised that they were all singing. They might have been proceeding up and down the staircase for eternity, as they slowly sang in unison. He could even make out the words now – it was that old melody from the halls, 'Why Don't They Have the Sea in London?'

He stayed a few minutes longer until he believed it was safe to venture out again into the night; he turned down another lane and, to his great relief, found himself in a street that led back down to the Strand. He had really heard tonight what 'man has ever said' and 'woman whispered' – and if the air indeed were one vast library, one great vessel in which all the noises of the city were preserved, then nothing need be lost. Not one voice, or laugh, or threat, or song, or footfall, but it reverberated through eternity. He remembered reading in *The Gentleman's Magazine* of an ancient myth which supposed that all lost things could be discovered on the other side of the moon. And perhaps there was such a place where perpetual, infinite, London would one day be found. But then perhaps he had found it already – perhaps it was in him, and in each of the people he had encountered that night. He returned to Hanway Street and, finding Nell asleep upon their narrow bed, kissed her gently on the forehead.

Forty-Two

It was just before dawn when I returned to Bayswater; I did not wish to wake my husband, but I aroused Aveline with a gentle knock upon the door of her attic room. She seemed very alarmed. 'Where were you? What has happened to you?'

'Whatever do you mean? Nothing has happened to me. Now be a good girl and prepare a fire for your master.'

'But you look so pale, and so—'

'Interesting? It is the morning air, Aveline. Most delightful.'

I left her and crept downstairs towards my husband's bedroom. I stood quietly for a few seconds, debating with myself whether I should wake him with an innocent kiss, but instead I whispered to him through the door. 'Nothing has happened,' I told him. 'Nothing has happened at all.'

Unfortunately he was sullen and truculent all that day but, when he saw how cheerful and patient I remained, he began to reconsider. I said nothing about the events of the night before, and from my general demeanour I managed to convey the impression that the whole episode was dead and forgotten. It was inconsequential. A few stern glances at Aveline made it quite clear that the subject was not to be raised, and indeed it was not; *Misery Junction* was never mentioned again in my presence and, after a few weeks, life in Bayswater appeared to resume its normal peaceful course.

I had hidden my anger so deep that there were times when even I could not find it. Yet it was always there, somewhere, just as I only had to look at my husband's face to recognise his failure and resentment. But why should I be blamed? Why should I be the one person in the house to be accused? To be made to feel guilty? What had I ever done, except to assist him with a play which was so wretched that it could not be performed without my savings and which even then had been hooted down by the Limehouse mob? Even Aveline looked at me in the strangest fashion, from time to time, as if I were somehow responsible for changing the atmosphere within the house. Well, it was not to be my burden or my fault. There were others weaker and more foolish than I. Did either of them really believe that I could be turned into their scapegoat?

'Will you take Mr Cree a hot beverage?' I asked Aveline one evening. My husband made a habit now of retiring early to his room, and reading; I never complained, since I was quite happy with my own company. 'And I think, Aveline dear, that you should bring him a cup of something every night. It will help him to sleep, don't you think?'

'If you say so.'

'I do say so. Hot cocoa can work miracles. Every night, mind.' I suspect that she understood my plan from the beginning, but she never objected to it. She had always admired Mr Cree from afar, as I knew, and she was certainly a creature of instinct. As for Mr Cree, well, as I have admitted, he was a man of ungovernable lust. It would take only a few weeks of cocoa.

Forty-Three

Aveline Mortimer was dusting the wax fruit when she heard John Cree enter the drawing room. So, in her old stage manner, she began to hum a tune that signified she was working very merrily.

'What is that song, Aveline?'

'Oh, sir, it is nothing. It is what is called a light air.'

'But you do not seem happy.'

'I am always happy, sir. That is how Mrs Cree prefers it.'

'You need not obey my wife in everything, you know.'

'Tell that to her.' She had sounded very sharp, but she carried on humming even more fiercely than before. She pretended to rearrange two of the wax pears and, glancing up, realised that Cree was looking out of the window.

'My wife tells me that you come from a poor family. Is that so, Aveline?'

'I was in the workhouse, sir, if that is what Mrs Cree meant. I have already told her I am not ashamed of it.'

'Nor should you be. There is no need for shame, when it is the hard fate of so many.'

'It may be mine again one day.'

'Oh, do not say that. Never say that.'

'Your wife does.' Aveline savoured the moment. 'She makes quite a drama of it sometimes. "Go back to the workhouse," she says, "go back where you belong."' Again she paused. 'Do you wonder why I am not always happy here?'

John Cree came over from the window, and placed his hand lightly upon her shoulder as she remained bent over the wax fruit. 'Mrs Cree is not always in command of herself, Aveline. She does not mean these things.'

'She is hard, sir, very hard. Just like she was on the stage.'

'I know it.' He withdrew his hand. He had not meant to admit so much, not even to himself, but he enjoyed sharing her anger and resentment. 'But I can stand against her, and protect you. I can be your guardian, Aveline, as well as your employer.'

'Can that really be so?' She was about to turn and look at him very fondly, when Elizabeth Cree entered the room. 'Yes, sir, if you wish it will be chicken tonight.'

'Does Mr Cree wish for chicken? Well, Aveline, I suppose you know how to prepare that dish.' She could have seen nothing, but there was no doubt about the coolness of her manner towards husband and maid. 'I am surprised at you, John. You know that white meat affects your digestive organs. You will be awake half the night.'

'It was a whim, Elizabeth. If you wish for something else—'

'No. Not at all. I doubt that my wishes are of any consequence in this household. And, Aveline, mind how you stuff it. Nothing too rich, or too salty. I am told that salt stirs the blood. Is that not so?'

She left the room as abruptly as she had entered, while John Cree and Aveline Mortimer looked at one another doubtfully. He sat down, trembling, and put his hand up to his head. 'Do you know, Aveline, what I wish for most in this world?'

'Chicken?'

'No. I wish that you and I might—'

'Go on, sir. Do.'

'Might help one another. Otherwise our life here would be—'

'Unendurable?'

'Yes. That is the word. Unendurable.' He looked towards the door, which his wife had slammed shut a few seconds before. 'Will you do something for me, Aveline?'

'Oh, gladly, sir.'

'Will you show me the workhouses?'

'What?' It was not at all what she had expected, and she could barely conceal her disappointment. 'Whatever do you mean?'

'My play has failed. I know it. My wife has made that very clear to me. But over the past weeks and months, Aveline, I have found a great theme. I wish to explore the lives of the poor.' He had become very animated, and she looked at him with horror. 'The spoils go to the victor. That is the lesson of our century. But do you know, Aveline, that now I think I would prefer to lie among the vanquished?'

'Don't tell me you want to move to the workhouse. Mrs Cree is not that much of a tartar.'

'I want to see them. I want to talk to the people there.'

She considered this the request of a man no longer wholly sane, but she knew that she could steer her own path with him and derive some benefit from the arrangement. So she agreed to accompany him, without the knowledge of Elizabeth Cree; she knew the places well enough, and she was acquainted with many of the people who inhabited them. They visited establishments from Clerkenwell to the Borough, and John Cree was exultant. He had never before seen such misery, and he could have picked up these rags of poverty and vice in order to lift them towards heaven. He could have taken the mass of foul lives, and held them above his head like some monstrance of grief before which all must kneel. He realised, too, that in Aveline Mortimer he had found a poor girl who might redeem him.

Forty-Four

I recognised all the signs – the sudden silences, the whisperings, the blushes, and, most important of all, the fact that he never looked at her during breakfast. I allowed a month to pass and then, at the beginning of December, I boldly stepped into his room without knocking upon the door: there they were upon the bed, as I had expected, lying with one another. 'Shame upon shame's head!' I cried out. He was quite distraught and jumped from the bed, while she simply looked at me and smiled. 'So this has come to pass!' In my excitement I echoed one of the phrases from *The Northolt Tragedy*. 'This is the fruit of my marriage!' I left the room and, banging the door behind me, began to weep as loudly as I could. Now I had him, tied with bonds stouter than cord. I would no longer be the guilty one. He would plead with me, praying for forgiveness, and at last I would be the master in my own house.

So it proved. He begged me to forget what I had witnessed, and to avoid what he described as a 'domestic tragedy'. He had only a second-rate imagination. I concurred reluctantly but gracefully, and from that day forward I had no trouble from him. I assume that he consorted with whores, because he never touched Aveline again, but that was of no account to me. He was, as Dan might have said, utterly squashed.

There was one consequence of the dreary fumbling with Aveline, however, which raised me even higher in the household. About three months later it became clear that she was with child. 'Aveline dear,' I asked her very sweetly as we stood together in the pantry. 'Am I correct in thinking that there is something kicking within your belly?'

She could not deny it, and stared at me in her usual defiant fashion. 'And who do you think put it there?'

'I would not like to say. It could be practically anyone.' I knew that she was about to hurl some obscenity at me, so I took her by the wrists and held on to her very tightly. 'I could turn you out of doors for ever, Aveline Mortimer, after what you have done. You would be on the streets without help or favour from the world. What would become of you then? No one cares for a pregnant woman. You would be back in the workhouse where you belong.'

'So what do you wish me to do?'

'What you must do, dear. You cannot have my husband's child. It is unthinkable. Unimaginable. The thing must be destroyed.' At that moment I heard Mr Cree entering the house and I conceived a master-stroke. I rushed into the hallway and, leading him into Aveline's presence, explained precisely what he had done. He was so dismayed and distraught that he leaned against the wall, weeping, and put his hands up to his face. 'This is no time for tears or lamentation, Mr Cree,' I said to him. 'It is time to act.'

'Act?'

'This child cannot be born. It is the offspring of a shameful coupling, and will carry a curse with it everywhere.' I believe that my mother had once said something of the same kind about my own unhappy origin, but I repeated it quite naturally. 'It is an abomination, and must be killed.' I am sure that Aveline had been party to some such arrangement in the past,

240

since she offered no resistance. He seemed about to object, but I stopped him with a motion of my hand. 'It is not for you to rule us now, Mr Cree. It is you who must bear the sin and the blame.'

'So what is to be done, then?'

'You need not concern yourself with female business. I have your agreement, and that is enough.' It was my plan to keep them both under me: if there were any sign of rebellion, I could threaten them with the details of their child's sad fate. Who would believe that I had played any part in it, when Aveline and Mr Cree could so easily have arranged everything together? I was not a child killer. I was the innocent, wronged wife. Over the next several days I gave Aveline a potion of my own manufacture; it encouraged cramps and spasms and would, I knew, expel the seed from her womb. She looked as sick as death but the thing was voided a week later. I put it in a tin chest, and flung it into the river by Limehouse that same winter's night. There were many such objects washed up by the tide, and no one would take notice of Aveline's rejected creature.

So it was done. At last I ruled the household, and need brook no interference from any other. By a stroke of good fortune Mr Cree's father died a few months after, just at the time we were visiting him in Lancashire, and with our greatly increased fortune I decided to move to a modern villa in New Cross. From that time forward, my dear husband always spent his days among the books of the British Museum. He said that he was composing a tract on the lives of the poor. It was a most disagreeable subject, but I thought it most unlikely that he would ever complete it.

Forty-Five

Inspector Kildare shared his house in Kensal Rise with another bachelor. George Flood was a civil engineer with the London Underground Railway Company, and he had a fine, enquiring mind which had in the past proved invaluable to his friend. Kildare gave him a quick peck on the cheek when he returned home after his interview with Dan Leno. 'Well, George, old fellow,' he said. 'We have a rum one.'

'The Golem, still?'

'The same. There is no solution to it. No solution at all.'

They settled down comfortably, facing each other in arm-chairs on opposite sides of their sea-coal fire. The grandfather clock ticked loudly in the corner. 'Would you like a nice gin and water, Eric?'

'No, thank you. I'll smoke a pipe, if it's all the same to you. It will help me cogitate.' He took it out, lit it, and looked con-templatively at his friend. 'You know, George, that I am not very keen on old-fashioned ways of thinking.'

'Why ever should you be?'

'But I have my doubts about this Golem matter. Do you think there might be such a thing?'

George looked into the fire, as the grandfather clock struck the half-hour. 'In my line of work, Eric, we use iron and rivets and pig-lead. We deal with material things.'

'I know it, George.'

'But there are times when we find that a certain piece of track, or a certain metal component, will *not* stay where it is put. It buckles, or it curves, or it goes out at an angle. Are you with me?'

'I am.'

'Do you know what we say then?'

'I would very much like to know, George.'

'We say that the material has a life of its own. We say that it is "contaminated". Let me get you that gin and water now. You look ever so tired.' He went over to the sideboard and came back with the drink, which he gave to Inspector Kildare after gently kissing the top of his head. Then he returned to his seat. 'We are learning things about materials all the time, you see. But has it ever occurred to you that, in the process, we are discovering new forms of life?'

'Like electricity, do you mean?'

'You have hit the nail on the head again, Eric. The ether. Electromagnetism. The whole lot.'

'That is not the same thing as the Golem, George.'

'I am not so sure of that as you are. We have created so many wonderful inventions in the last few years. We have seen so many changes. Do you think that the Golem might be one of them?'

Inspector Kildare got up from his armchair, and went over to his friend. 'You say some very curious things, George, when you're contemplating a problem.' He reached down and stroked his friend's mutton-chop whiskers.

'All I am saying, Eric, is that you must look for a material cause.'

Forty-Six

September 30, 1880: I have been confined to bed with a weakness in my stomach, while my dear wife ministers to me with her usual care. I had wanted to continue with a little business in Limehouse, but in these cases art must wait upon life.

October 2, 1880: My wife caught me reading an account of the funeral in the *Graphic:* the Gerrard family has been despatched to the little graveyard off Wellclose Square. I was satisfied, on their behalf, that they had been placed in their native soil. Of course I would have preferred to attend the ceremony, but my indisposition has prevented me. I did truly mourn their passing, since they had left the world without having the chance to acclaim my artistry – the flick of the knife, the pressure of the artery, the whispered confidence, are all, to quote Lord Tennyson, 'unknown to name and fame'. That is why I have come to detest this phrase, the 'Limehouse Golem'; it is no true title for an artist.

October 4, 1880: Mrs Cree came into my room this morning with an article of clothing and I admit that, for a moment, I lost my self-possession. It was the blood-stained scarf which I had kept after the Gerrard killings; it was dyed with the deepest red of the carotid artery, and I had wanted to preserve it as a memento. I had hidden it within the plaster head of William Shakespeare which rests on a plinth in the hall, and I had expected no one to find it. 'What is this?' she asked me.

'A nose bleed. I had nothing else to staunch it.'

She looked at me strangely. 'But why did you put it in the bust?'

'It is a head, not a bust. I came in when you were playing at the piano, and I did not want to concern you. So I placed it there. How did you find it?'

'Aveline has broken the head. She was dusting.'

'So Shakespeare is shattered?'

'Unfortunately, yes.'

We said no more on the subject. My wife left the scarf upon my desk, and I pretended to return to my newspaper.

October 5, 1880: Let me recall the chain of events today. I felt quite recovered from my indisposition, and so I came down for breakfast. Aveline told me that Mrs Cree was asleep still, and I finished my egg in peace. I was glancing over the front page of the *Chronicle,* where there was an interesting item on the police investigation, when I thought I heard a footfall in my study: it is just above the breakfast room and, as I looked up in the direction of the sound, I heard the unmistakable creaking of a floorboard. I left the table and mounted the stairs as quietly as I could; then I marched straight to my study and opened the door with a flourish, but there was no one within. So I walked down the passage and knocked on my wife's door. 'Who is it?' She did indeed sound as if she had been roused from sleep.

'Can I bring you anything, my dearest?'

'No. Nothing whatever.'

I returned to my study. I am meticulous by nature, and all my books and papers are arranged methodically: it took me only a few moments, therefore, to realise that my black bag had been moved slightly to the left of my chair. Naturally it was locked – it is the bag in which I keep all the tools of the trade – but it was plain to me that someone had been curious about its contents.

October 6, 1880: I do believe now that my wife suspects something. She had been asking me very casually about the night I had 'visited a friend in the City', which was the night of the Ratcliffe Highway ceremony, and I answered her casually in return. Nevertheless she observed me very closely and very strangely. I comfort myself with the reflection that she could not possibly imagine her mild and patient husband to be the killer of women and children, the Limehouse Golem itself. It would be too great a mystery to comprehend.

October 7, 1880: Today she asked me where I had purchased the shawl which I had given her some weeks ago. 'From somewhere in Holborn,' I replied easily enough. Then it occurred to me that, since I had bought it in Gerrard's shop, it might have his name or address marked somewhere upon it. I waited until she had left the house, in search of something 'fresh' for dinner as she put it, and I hurried up to her room. The scarf was draped over a small gilt chair in the corner: yes, there had been a tag attached to it. It had been ripped off.

October 8, 1880: But what if she does suspect? Is she likely to communicate with the police authorities? No, she cares too much for her station in life to hazard it. And if her suspicions were to be proved false, how would she ever be able to justify her actions to me? Who, in any case, would believe her? A respectable and prosperous man such as myself – a scholar, a gentleman, a householder – could hardly be capable of such monstrous bloodshed. The Limehouse Golem living in a villa in New Cross? She would be treated with derision, and I knew her pride to be such that she would not willingly undergo the ordeal. No. I am safe.

October 9, 1880: Something else has happened. I had brought to her attention a little item in the *South London Observer,* about a pickpocket who had been apprehended in the neighbourhood, when she looked wildly at me and began muttering about punishment. I think she intends something.

Forty-Seven

The Roman Catholic chaplain attached to Camberwell Prison had been asked to visit Elizabeth Cree in the condemned cell.

FATHER LANE: There is no sin that cannot be forgiven, Elizabeth. Our Saviour died for our sins.

ELIZABETH CREE: You sound like my mother. She was a very religious woman.

FATHER LANE: She was a Catholic like yourself?

ELIZABETH CREE: No, nothing of the kind. She worshipped in a little tin chapel off Lambeth High Road. She was a daughter of Bethesda, or some such thing.

FATHER LANE: But who guided you, then, to the Church?

ELIZABETH CREE: It was my husband's wish. I took a course of instruction before our marriage, and was then converted.

FATHER LANE: Did your mother object?

ELIZABETH CREE: Good God no! She was long dead. But you see, even before I met my husband, I knew a great deal about the Roman ceremonies. Many of the hall folk were Catholics – my old friend Dan Leno used to say that it was in the blood. He saw a connection between Rome and the pantomime, as I did after a time. Sometimes he took me to mass at Our Lady of Suffering off the New Cut. It was such fun.

FATHER LANE: Did you understand the meaning of it?

ELIZABETH CREE: I understood everything. It all seemed so natural to me. The costumes. The stage. The bells. The clouds of incense. I had seen it all in *Ali Baba*. Of course, in church, the artistes are more devout.

FATHER LANE: Elizabeth, you understand that I have come to hear your confession and to absolve you of your sins?

ELIZABETH CREE: So I shall be pure before I hang?

FATHER LANE: I cannot administer communion to you until you freely confess.

ELIZABETH CREE: Could you prompt me then, father? I am afraid that, for the first time in my life, I have forgotten the lines.

FATHER LANE: Bless me, Father, for I have sinned. It is—

ELIZABETH CREE: Many years since my last confession? I was not thinking of those lines, father. I was thinking of my speech in *Ali Baba*, when I turn upon the forty thieves and strike them down with my wand.

FATHER LANE: Perhaps you are disturbed still?

ELIZABETH CREE: I am not disturbed in the slightest. I am excited, perhaps. You see, I am to be hanged in two days.

FATHER LANE: That is all the more reason to make your confession. If you die in a state of mortal sin, then there can be no hope.

ELIZABETH CREE: And I will fry eternally? I am surprised at you, father, for such childish notions. I cannot think of hell as some fish-shop. Punishment for earthly things is upon the earth.

FATHER LANE: Do not talk so, Mrs Cree. I beg you to think of your immortal soul.

ELIZABETH CREE: A sole may be fried, too. But I have had enough of this. You are talking like my mother. And, if there is a hell, she is surely there.

FATHER LANE: So you have nothing to confess to me?

ELIZABETH CREE: Shall I tell you that I poisoned my husband? But what if there were greater and darker crimes than that? Perhaps I know of sins, bloody and terrible sins, that far exceed anything committed against my husband. What if other deaths cried to heaven? I can tell you this, Father Lane. I have no need to beg pardon or absolution from you. I am the scourge of God.

Forty-Eight

Three weeks had passed since the murder of the Gerrard family in Ratcliffe Highway, and the identity of the Limehouse Golem had still not been discovered. Dan Leno had already been discounted as a most improbable suspect, and the investigation of the police detectives turned into a series of profitless and haphazard speculations. A seaman was arrested because he had blood upon his clothing, and an itinerant cage-maker found himself in the cells of Limehouse Division simply because he had been seen in the vicinity of the last crime.

There had been more sinister consequences, however. After the burial of the Gerrard family in the cemetery by Wellclose Square, a mob ransacked the house of a Jewish tea merchant in Shadwell since his misanthropic habits led the more credulous inhabitants of the East End to the conclusion that he was also a golem; in Limehouse itself a group of prostitutes savagely beat a German on the grounds that he looked 'as if he might do a mischief'. There were also foot patrols of 'interested citizens' who spent the night drinking in the various public houses along their route before careering down the streets in search of any Jew or foreigner.

Other activities were of a more benevolent nature. There were questions in the House of Commons once more on the conditions of the East End poor, and parties of respectable ladies were to be seen wandering through the less salubrious areas of Limehouse and Whitechapel in search of deserving cases. Charles Dickens and certain 'problem novelists' had described the horrors of urban poverty before, but these accounts were characteristically sentimentalised or sensationalised to take account of the public taste for Gothic effects. Newspaper reports were not necessarily more accurate, of course, since they tended to follow the same patterns of melodramatic narrative. But the pressure of parliamentary questions, and the lengthy expositions which appeared in the intellectual quarterlies, encouraged a more sober analysis of urban conditions in the late nineteenth century. It was no coincidence, for example, that a programme of slum clearance began in the area of Shadwell only a year after the crimes of the Limehouse Golem were first revealed.

But the Golem itself had vanished. After the killings in the Ratcliffe Highway, there were to be no more deaths. Some newspapers speculated that the murderer had committed suicide, and the Thames was watched by eager rivermen for weeks, while others suggested that he had merely switched his attentions to other cities and might even now be in the industrial areas of the Midlands or the North. Inspector Kildare's own private theory, which he put to George Flood before supper one evening, was that he had fled the country on a steamship and was probably somewhere in America. Only the *Echo* surmised that the killer had himself been killed – perhaps by a wife or mistress who had found evidence of his crimes.

But the most bizarre speculations came from those people who really believed in the legend of the Golem: they insisted that this man-made creature, this automation, had simply disappeared at the end of his career of death. The fact that the last killings had taken place in the same house where the Marr murders had been enacted, almost seventy years before, only confirmed their belief that a secret ritual had been performed and that the clothes shop in the Ratcliffe Highway had once been some temple to a strange god. The Limehouse Golem had faded away within the blood and limbs of its victims, and would undoubtedly re-emerge in the same spot after a period of years.

There was some discussion of these matters at the monthly meeting of the Occult Society in Coptic Street, only a few yards from the Reading Room of the British Museum. In fact the secretary of the society spent most of his time among the books of the library and, for the benefit of the other members, he had already transcribed certain old texts on the subject of the golem and its mythic history. For him, as for many others, the Reading Room was the true spiritual centre of London where many secrets might finally be revealed. Indeed, if he had known it, he could have solved the riddle of the Limehouse Golem beneath the great dome – if not precisely in the manner he might have expected. All the participants in the mystery, willing or unwilling, had come to this place – Karl Marx, George Gissing, Dan Leno and, of course, John Cree himself.

In fact there had been one other significant visitor; Elizabeth Cree had forged two letters of recommendation and, on the added strength of her husband's long use of the library, had been admitted as a lady reader in the spring of 1880. She had sat at the special row of seats reserved for her sex, and had called for the collected works of Thomas De Quincey as well as Daniel Defoe's *History of the Devil*. While she waited for these books to be delivered to her, she contemplated the shabby clothes and awkward manners of those who, in George Gissing's words, lived 'in the valley of the shadow of books'. She pitied them for it, even as she despised her husband for sinking so low. She did not know that Dan Leno had encountered Joseph Grimaldi here, and had thereby found his inheritance; that Karl Marx had studied here for many years, and out of his books had created a giant system; that here George Gissing had been led towards the mysteries of Charles Babbage's analytical machinery; that here her husband had dreamed of future fame. Elizabeth Cree had finished De Quincey's essay on the Ratcliffe Highway killings before ordering other books which would have some effect upon the lives of the characters in this history; she asked for certain volumes on contemporary surgical techniques.

Forty-Nine

'For these and all the sins of my life I am heartily sorry, and humbly beg God's pardon and absolution from you.'

'But you have told me nothing, Elizabeth.'

'Well, father, that's just my way. I have to finish the lines, once I have rehearsed them.' It was the night before her execution, but Elizabeth Cree now did the strangest thing. She took the purple stole, which Father Lane had put over his surplice and cassock in order to hear her confession, and began dancing with it in the condemned cell. 'Did you ever see that wonderful drama, *The London Phantom*? It is a real shocker of the old school.'

'No. I don't think so.'

'I don't believe you have, father, because I am composing it at the moment.' Still she danced around him with the stole in her hand. 'It has ever such an interesting story. It is all about a woman who poisons her husband. What do you think of it so far, at least?'

'I cannot judge you, Elizabeth.'

'You are not a dramatic critic, I suppose. But would you like to see such a play?'

'I only want to hear your confession and absolve you.'

'No.' She stopped in front of him, and slowly put the stole

around her own neck. 'I am here to absolve *you*. I forgot to tell you the rest of the story. I gave my play its title. *I* am the London phantom.' Father Lane was still kneeling on the stone floor of the cell, and could sense the cold rising within his body. She bent down and began whispering in his ear. 'The husband is not poisoned until the third act, when he threatens to reveal my little secret to the world. No one in the audience had managed to guess it, you see, and so it comes as rather a surprise to them. Do you want to know what it is?' The priest was sweating, despite the cold, and she dried his forehead with the end of the stole. 'Well, I cannot tell you. It would ruin the whole drama.' He wanted to call out to the warders on the other side of the door, and fly from this place. But he forced himself to remain still and to listen to her; this would be her last conversation upon the earth. 'There is a bit of a game *en travesti*. Do you understand me? That is when the female serio puts on her male clothes and fools them all. Then some of the flash girls have a shocking bit of bad luck. They want to know what is in my little black bag, and I show them. I had no trouble with that part, father. When my mother made me, she made me strong. I'm a natural for the blood tubs, I always have been.'

'I cannot follow you, Mrs Cree.'

'First there was my dear mother. Then came Doris, who saw me. There was Uncle, who soiled me. Oh, I have forgotten Little Victor, who touched me. The Jew was a Christ killer, you see, as my mother used to say. And the whores of Limehouse were the dirtiest of their kind. Do you know that they mocked me when I tried to redeem them upon the stage?'

'*In nomine patris, et filii, et spiritu sancti . . .*'

She put her forefinger upon his head; he stopped his prayer and, appalled, looked up at her. 'You see, father, my late husband was a dramatic writer. But he was never a success, I'm afraid. That is why he tried to steal my plot. He wanted to change the denouement, and expose my little adventures to the world. So then I managed the funniest bit of business. Do you remember how Harlequin always blames Pantaloon? Well, I made up a diary and laid the guilt upon him. I had finished a play for him once, you see, so I knew all the lingo. I kept a diary in his name, which will one day damn him before the world. Why should I bear any blame, when I know that I am pure still? Is it true, father, that the Lord giveth and the Lord taketh away?'

'It is.'

'Well, I saved him half the job. I took away. Wasn't it a neat piece of business, too? When his diary is found, I will be exonerated even for his death. The world will believe I destroyed a monster.'

'What are you confessing, Mrs Cree?'

'He threatened me. He wanted to prevent me.'

'But these others you mentioned. Who are they?'

'He suspected me. He watched me. He followed me.' Now she took off the stole and draped it around the priest's shoulders. 'Surely you have heard of the famous Limehouse Golem?'

Fifty

After the body of Elizabeth Cree had been taken from the yard of Camberwell Prison, it was transported to the police mortuary in Limehouse where her brain was removed for surgical analysis. Charles Babbage himself had first proposed that this organ might act like an analytic engine, and that in aberrant types of personality certain observable and detachable parts might be the clue to unsocial behaviour. Since Elizabeth Cree was a female murderer of vicious disposition, it was naturally believed that her cerebellum would be worthy of further study; but no abnormality was discovered. No doubt a longer examination would have been performed if the authorities had known that she had savagely killed women and children. Her head had been removed from her body, but the rest of the corpse was consigned to the mortuary yard in Limehouse and covered with quicklime to encourage speedy decomposition – her final home was just twenty yards from the spot where the first of the Ratcliffe Highway murderers, Marr, had been buried in 1813. These are the words with which Thomas De Quincey ended his study of that ferocious killer: '. . . in obedience to the law as it then stood, he was buried in the centre of a quadrivium, or conflux of four roads (in this case four streets), with a stake driven through his heart.' And so it was that Elizabeth Cree now entered her own house of lime.

Fifty-One

The authoritative version of *Misery Junction* was to be performed at last; the murder of John Cree by his obviously deranged wife had provided too good an opportunity for the playhouses to miss. Gertrude Latimer still had the script which Elizabeth Cree had sent to her at the Bell in Limehouse; she had read the reports of the trial with mounting excitement and, when it became clear that Lizzie was to be hanged (and therefore could claim no rights of ownership after her condemned body was lifted from the gallows), she took out the play and asked her husband, Arthur, to enliven the plot with some topical references. The name of the actress, Catherine Dove, was changed to Elizabeth Cree – and she was *not* to be saved. She was to destroy her husband with poison, and then be condemned to death for her crime. A week before Elizabeth Cree's execution, the management of the Bell announced the newest and most up-to-the-minute shocker, *The Crees of Misery Junction*. It was billed as the true story of their lives, and was to be performed on the evening after Elizabeth Cree's execution. The advertisements declared that it had largely been written by the Crees themselves, and Gertie Latimer even decided to add some passages allegedly written by Lizzie in the condemned cell.

'ELIZABETH CREE: I understand that I have committed a great sin, which cries to the very heavens for vengeance. But have I not suffered more than any woman? He beat me mercilessly, even when I begged for mercy, and when I was too weak to cry out he laughed at my misery. I was a frail and defenceless woman and, when I saw nothing ahead of me but suffering and an early grave, I grew desperate as only a desperately wronged woman can.'

There was much more to this effect, composed by Gertie and Arthur Latimer, which purportedly recorded the true history of the Crees. An additional touch of authenticity was afforded by the players themselves: the part of Elizabeth Cree was taken by Aveline Mortimer, who was headlined on the bills as 'The Woman Who Was There'. In fact Aveline found the role to be a particularly pleasing one; she took great satisfaction in playing her hard mistress and knocked around Eleanor Marx, who had taken the part of the maid, with something like abandon.

Of course the announcement of the play had created much public comment and controversy – with *The Times* leading the way, suggesting that a 'sensation' should not be made out of a 'tragedy' – and the audience of the first night was more distinguished and varied than for most Limehouse 'blood tub' extravaganzas. Karl Marx was in the pit, despite his failing health; his daughter, against his wishes, had decided to begin a career on the popular stage after the failure of Oscar Wilde's *Vera*. How could he miss her first professional performance as the maid of Elizabeth Cree? He had brought with him for company Richard Garnett, the Superintendent of the Reading Room in the British Museum. Two rows behind them sat George Gissing, who was in the process of composing another essay for the *Pall Mall Review*, entitled 'Real Drama and Real Life'. Nell had insisted on accompanying him, since she had conceived a strange fascination for the case of Elizabeth Cree, but now she sat beside him with an expression of startled preoccupation that Gissing had never noticed before. The truth was that she had caught sight of Inspector Kildare, whom she had last seen leaving their lodgings in Hanway Street just before her husband was taken away; the memory of that extraordinary and terrifying episode had never left her, despite her immersion in strong drink, and for some unaccountable reason she connected it with the horror about to be performed upon the stage. Kildare had not noticed her; he had come to the theatre with George Flood, and they looked exactly like two professional gentlemen who had left their wives at home. In fact Kildare was here out of professional curiosity – Inspector Curry, a colleague from 'C' Division, had investigated the case against Elizabeth Cree. But of course he also wished to relax after his unsuccessful search for the Limehouse Golem. Other, more professional, critics were also present; the theatre reviewers for the *Post* and the *Morning Advertiser* had entered the Bell for the first time in their careers, and were already scribbling down sentences of amused scorn and patronising dismissal. But there was one critic who had a more keen comprehension of the melodrama: Oscar Wilde had been asked by the editor of the *Chronicle* to furnish an essay on the character of first-night audiences, and he had decided to begin with the theatrical sensation of the hour.

The real sensation, however, was to be seen when the curtain finally rose in front of the loud and excited audience. Gertie Latimer had hit upon a masterstroke of theatrical spectacle: she had decided to begin with the execution of Elizabeth Cree in the yard of Camberwell Prison and, after a most realistic hanging, to dramatise her strange history. The audience gasped at the sight of a scaffold and a noose, as Gertie had anticipated, and at once she pushed the procession onto the stage: the governor of the prison, the sheriff and the chaplain were all played by seasoned professionals of the 'school of gore', while Aveline Mortimer in her role as Elizabeth Cree brought up the rear. Her hands were tied behind her back with leathern thongs (last used by Gertie for the black-face drama, *The Revolt of The Caribee Slaves*) and she wore a simple convict dress; her face was one of inexhaustible suffering, but when she looked mournfully towards the audience she was able to suggest sad patience and resignation also. She moved towards the scaffold, and the murmuring of the audience ceased; she mounted the first step, and the chaplain began to sob quietly. She mounted the second step, and the sheriff turned his face away just for a moment. She mounted the third step, and became very still. All was silence in the Bell Theatre.

It was at this point that Gertie Latimer introduced one of her more daring innovations. She had read the accounts of the hanging in the evening newspapers and, at the last moment, had decided to include the very details of the real execution. So Aveline Mortimer refused with a proud gesture the offer of a hood, and lifted her pale neck for the noose. It was now that she gazed down at the audience and uttered her immortal words, 'Here we are again!' This was the cue for Gertie Latimer's other masterstroke. She had always admired the use of the elevating platform and trapdoor, which she had seen employed very effectively in *The Last Testament* at Drury Lane; at great expense she had installed one of these engines for *The Crees of Misery Junction,* and now began to superintend that moment when the condemned woman's body would land upon the trapdoor before being quickly lowered beneath the stage by the descending platform. It would indeed look as if she had been hanged by the neck until she was dead.

All this time Dan Leno had been watching from the wings. He had agreed with Gertie Latimer that he would perform a spoof after-piece, when *The Crees of Misery Junction* was finally over; he was to play the role of Madame Gruyère, the famous French murderess, and to sing a ditty extolling the virtues of Gallic poison. He had already dressed for the part (sometimes he could hardly wait to remove his conventional clothes) and had begun to mince and to wiggle in the approved French fashion; he was preparing himself, he would insist, but those who surreptitiously watched 'the funniest man on earth' noticed that he was whispering words to himself as if he were addressing someone else. 'You silly old bitch,' he was saying. 'What do you mean by making fun of Lizzie? You dirty old bitch.'

Aveline Mortimer waited patiently as the hangman tightened the noose around her throat, and at this moment Karl Marx turned and whispered fiercely to Richard Garnett. This play was a disgrace, since it had converted matters of social purpose into a cheap melodrama! Truly the playhouse was the opium of the people! And yet he could no longer keep his eyes from the stage as Elizabeth Cree began to fall. He remembered that, many years before, he had written to a friend about his own death, and had said: 'When it is all over, we shall hold hands and begin again from the beginning.' The critics from the *Post* and *Morning Advertiser* were also transfixed but, even as they marvelled at the scene, they knew that they would eventually dismiss it as 'pantomimic' and 'unreal'. George Gissing glanced across at the face of the man from the *Post*, whom he knew slightly, and was to write later in 'Real Drama and Real Life': 'It is not that human beings cannot bear too much reality, it is that human beings cannot bear too much artifice.' But then, as he watched the pale neck of Aveline Mortimer, he remembered his sensation of wonder and horror when he had scrutinised the corpse of Alice Stanton in the morgue of Limehouse Police Station. 'Fate', he had told his wife the next day, 'is always too strong for us.' Inspector Kildare noticed with some displeasure that the details of the execution were not entirely accurate, but even he could not shake off the sense of terror and enchantment which filled the whole theatre. It was a scene which Oscar Wilde remembered when, in 'The Truth of Masks', he wrote that 'Truth is independent of facts always, inventing or selecting them at pleasure. The true dramatist shows us life under the conditions of art, not art in the form of life.'

But what was this? The condemned woman was really falling through the trapdoor and Dan Leno, with his instinctive knowledge of stage techniques, knew that something had gone terribly wrong. He realised at once that the rope had not loosened, that the elevated platform had fallen without a brake being placed upon it, and that the neck of Aveline Mortimer must surely be broken as she dangled beneath the stage. Some of the audience had gasped, while others had screamed – not because they had any notion of the catastrophe played out before them, but because the whole scene had been mounted so impressively and so realistically. Dan Leno rushed beneath the stage, where the call-boy and the prompter were already cutting down Aveline Mortimer's body in an effort to revive her. Gertie Latimer, optimistic to the end, had brought a bottle of brandy to administer to her; but Dan Leno brushed her aside, and knelt over the dead woman. Nothing could be done for her now, however, and at this moment the stage chaplain clambered down the rope which hung from the scaffold; he was already gone with drink, but he attempted to give absolution to the dead actress while the others stood around in an attitude of simple worship.

Leno allowed them to remain in position for a minute, but then he took Gertie's arm and held it very tightly. 'Put the priest into a heavy swell costume,' he said, 'and help me up onto the stage.' She was too dazed to do anything but comply, and within a few moments she had hoisted Dan Leno in the dress of Madame Gruyère back through the trapdoor and into the gaslight. He held onto the fatal rope as he clambered up and, in mock homage to that great melodrama *The Hunchback of Notre Dame,* he pulled on it three times when he was within sight of the audience. They understood the allusion at once, and laughed in relief after the scene of terror before – here was the hanged woman revived, and ready to start the fun. Here was Elizabeth Cree in another guise, just as she had been before when she played the 'Older Brother' or 'Little Victor's Daughter', and it was a source of joy and exhilaration that the great Dan Leno should impersonate her.

The audience filed out into the dark night after the performance was over, the young and the old, the rich and the poor, the famous and the infamous, the charitable and the mean, all back into the cold mist and smoke of the teeming streets. They left the theatre in Limehouse and went their separate ways, to Lambeth or to Brixton, to Bayswater or to Whitechapel, to Hoxton or to Clerkenwell, all of them returning to the uproar of the eternal city. And even as they travelled homeward, many of them remembered that wonderful moment when Dan Leno had risen from the trapdoor and appeared in front of them. 'Ladies and gentlemen,' he had announced in his best mammoth comique manner, 'here we are *again*!'